Last Date

A Travis Bowie Thriller

To the lovely Sharon

I was stunned. Had I heard right? My mouth was flapping open in an undignified way, sort of like a catfish gasping on the bank.

"What?" I asked stupidly, as if I had gone hard of hearing.

"My feelings have changed, and I don't think it's fair to either one of us to continue on as if they hadn't."

We were sitting in Vincenzo's, a cozy little Italian place set just off the soulless West Esplanade Avenue in Metairie, a neat, clean and mostly unremarkable throughway in Jefferson Parish outside New Orleans. Up until a few seconds before, I had been contentedly munching on the pencil-thin crisp bread sticks, dipping them into the herb butter and enjoying her company and my own for a change. Now half a breadstick nestled half-chewed in my mouth and I felt like I had been metamorphosed into a termite trying to eat wood, while the other half of the breadstick sat in my left hand like a broken conductor's baton.

"So this is about being fair?" I asked, after managing to swallow the bread stick half and nearly choking. I reached for the sparkling water with its festive lemon wedge, my ex-drunk's drink, and took a gulp. That sure went flat in a hurry.

She flapped her hands a little, brushing away annoyances, which apparently now included me, and took a breath, gathering steam for a speech she had evidently planned. She looked stunning this evening, all the more so for being in the process of becoming surprisingly and suddenly unattainable. Her auburn hair hung almost to her shoulders and curved impeccably this way and that, not too busy but not without art. Her hazel eyes were pitiless, thank God.

"You know what I mean." In the background, some Sinatra favorite was playing, not the soundtrack I would have picked for this moment.

"I do? Up until a couple minutes ago, I thought we were two people in love having dinner and a wonderful evening, so I don't think I know very much at all." My tie felt tight, the lemon water tasted bitter, maybe pesticide residue.

"Travis," she continued, an adult talking to a small child, "we are much too different, you and I. You are a loner and I like to be together more, just hang around the apartment, cuddle on the sofa and watch TV. I know you don't like to watch the programs I watch, they bore you. And you're smarter than me, better educated."

I observed the swirls of orange and green in her long dress, which I knew without seeing from the other side of the table swept down to her pretty ankles and her feet in the cute orange and tan sandals, and gathered the energy for this brutal but necessary rite of blood-letting, knowing the inevitable futility of it. She was already gone,

"Did I ever try to act superior? Did I…?"

"Sometimes," she answered, and I was shocked to hear it.

"When? How?" I held up my hands in an attitude I found undignified, a penitent pleading for mercy.

"The comments about where I grew up, in Westwego, when you grew up in New Orleans." Her hands were in her lap, probably to avoid me trying to capture them.

"Really? That's it? I have been making Westwego jokes forever with guys. It's a joke."

I should have known that wasn't it. When a woman starts to catalog your faults, you can be pretty sure it's going to be a comprehensive list. The waiter hovered like a drone, but I asked him to give us a few minutes. It was beginning to look a lot like dinner tonight wasn't going to be here. How miserable would that be? Kind of like Socrates having dinner before a drink.

"And you wearing your late wife's wedding ring on a chain, even when when we're intimate, it's just degrading."

"You do remember she's dead, right?"

Her eyes flashed the total justice of her cause, like some jihadi suicide bomber or some other fanatic, "Now you're just being sarcastic."

"Me?"

"This was probably a bad idea," she said, but I could tell she meant I was being immature. She probably had a point. She had a good bit more experience than I had. She was married and divorced twice, I had been married for thirty-three years until Mae died. She had dated other men, I was limited to one romantic interlude with Susan Hadley in north Louisiana while being shot at and half-blown up. I was as close to being a middle-aged virgin as a guy with children and grandchildren can be.

"Andrea, what part of this could have possibly seemed like a good idea? All dressed up and both of us trapped with each other in a nice restaurant with no place to go from here." I was already dreading the drive back across the River with nothing to say. Everything important had evidently been said.

"I felt I owed you an explanation, Travis. You've been very kind to me."

I slapped the table, lightly, but she started anyway, perhaps flashing back to husband number one who used to slap her around. I never did learn why she left number two, maybe she was just fickle and just dumped him over trivia too.

"Kind is what I am to animals and old people. I love you."

She sat there silently, but it spoke fully to me, so I gently pressed, reaching for her hand, "So when you told me you loved me, it wasn't true?"

Then the tears came, hers I mean, but in a very ladylike way, just welling up in her eyes, which she dabbed with her linen napkin, "It was true, Travis, but I'm not getting any younger, and I hope to find a forever-type man. I may not find him, and if not, so be it, but you're not it."

"So this is some sort of bookkeeping decision, debits and credits?" Okay, it was a bitter comment. She shrugged in response, and we sat there awkwardly for a few moments.

I was almost grateful for the gunshot which shattered the coziness of the little restaurant. It gave me something to do to recover my pride or to at least put me out of my misery. The hostess went down first, backing away from the hole in her chest until she stopped at a wall and slid down to a sitting position, her legs folded beneath her.

The shooter was a greasy white guy about thirty with heavily tattooed arms emerging from the shoulders of his sleeveless tee shirt.. It was greasy and so were his jeans. He would never have been let in the back door of the restaurant, much less allowed to dine. His second shot caught a matronly diner in her wine glass and then her throat.

I was already reaching for the Beretta PX4 by the second shot. As I drew, I simultaneously reached over with my left hand and grabbed a fistful of Andrea's dress and dragged her to the floor. Curiously, although the gunfire was deafening, I could still hear threads ripping in her dress.

Another shot, another victim, a waiter who bravely threw a water pitcher at the shooter, hitting him in the head. The pitcher opened a cut on his head, but he shrugged it off like the Terminator and he proceeded through the dining room, selecting victims as he came.

I swept the candle off the table onto the floor and braced an elbow on top. I found the glow of the front sight and positioned it on the blurry target in front of me, heading my way. I took a breath, let it out a little. I pulled the trigger, and then did it again, and again, until the shooter dropped to his knees. I could see his hand lose its grip as he lost blood pressure and his pistol's trigger guard twirl around on his finger harmlessly. I shot him in the forehead anyway. I was already in a bad mood.

I was sitting in the Sheriff's Office, I mean his personal office, in a chair designed to be comfortable, but I wasn't sitting easily. I looked around surreptitiously to take in the bare floors and walls, the floor stripped of its carpet in preparation for new treatments, then back to an eye to eye with The Man himself. I was coming up in the world, I guess. The last time I had gotten myself in this much trouble I had ended up facing three Deputy Chiefs. This time I had managed to get the attention of Himself, and was having to explain my actions of the past two weeks in order to save my job, my rank, my career, three things which I could be quite ambivalent about on most days, but which loomed importantly at the moment.

I was presenting a sanitized version to the Sheriff, sitting across from me in a new throne-like leather executive chair, while his Comptroller Fred Capacolla, a bloodless consigliere who always had an expression on his face which seemed to betray his resentment at being short, and who always reduced everything, events, people, situations, into a spreadsheet of dollars and cents, stood with his back to the window with a partial view outside of the fiefdom which he helped the Sheriff rule. The Sheriff's counsel, Andy Landry, slouched like another bookend behind the Sheriff, propping up another section of windowsill, and ran his hand lightly over his silver and black hair lest one strand be out of place.

I had committed the full story to writing and kept it in a safe place. This is it.

"Go on, Travis," the Sheriff urged.

The fact that he addressed me by my given name brought no comfort. It promised no safe haven from a decision which would be made from legalistic, public relations, and political considerations, not to mention being run through the algorithm of the Comptroller's brain.

The Sheriff himself, sitting composed, with his slightly too-long dark hair brushed back and his handsome middle-aged face giving nothing away, would make his decision after considering the council of the two suits behind him.

I continued. Some of what I said is in my private file which follows, some of it not, to protect some people who don't need any more aggravation, like myself.

II

I helped Andrea to her feet and sat her in her chair after kicking the shooter's pistol away and touching his eyeball with the hot barrel of my own and getting no reaction. Some of the restaurant patrons were trampling each other on their way to the exit while others had drawn their smartphones and were busily posting to FACEBOOK, INSTAGRAM and YOUTUBE. There was glassware and other dining ware crashing here and there.

"Did anyone call 911?" I yelled through the ringing in my ears and the clatter of the stampede, but no one answered. I finally holstered. Then I drew my own phone and managed to punch in 911. I noticed my hands were trembling a little, which was not surprising considering the adrenaline which was flooding my system. Between Andrea blowing up my life and the shooter cutting a bloody swath through the restaurant, I had been on a fight or flight high for what was probably an eternal couple of minutes.

"911, what is your emergency?"

"Lieutenant Bowie," and I gave the operator my radio number, "Active shooter incident at Vincenzo's Restaurant," I added the address, "Three victims down, perp down, Code 4 for now, send supervisor with units, send Homicide, send EMS in case one of the customers has a heart attack or something. I don't think the victims need medical, but I'll check. I'll be the middle-aged white guy in black shirt and gray suit holding my ID up out front. Don't shoot me."

"Sending units now, sir," the operator said, and I knew none of these people had called it in. And citizens wonder why cops quietly hate everyone.

I checked the waiter first, because I honored his fight to defend himself with a water pitcher against a pistol. He was sprawled on the floor with blood bubbling out of his mouth, and his eyes tight with pain. That was encouraging. I called 911 back to tell them there was one victim breathing and to step it up.

"Hang on, son, medical is on the way." He tracked me with his eyes and he blinked. I squeezed his hand and he squeezed back. Good. The blood from his abdominal wound had soaked his white shirt red and was pooling on the floor beneath him. I hoped the worst things in his future included surgery and a catheter. He couldn't have been more than twenty.

The shooter had no pulse, which was not surprising considering the facts of an entry hole in his forehead and a crater in the back of his head. I spent no more time with him. I could faintly hear sirens beyond the sound system which continued to play festive Italian music and Sinatra standards. The young hostess, a woman of no more than twenty or so, had not moved from her sitting position. She wouldn't either. The matronly lady had slid down in her chair and her stylish pink silk blouse was awash with blood and red wine and sprinkled with glass, When she had been shot in her throat, her mouth had moved as if she were trying to clear her throat of the insult, and I flashed to the scene in THE GODFATHER where Michael Corleone shoots Captain McCluskey in the throat. Life as parody of art as parody of life. Her husband was holding her hand. I patted him on his shoulder and looked over at Andrea. She looked shocky, so I grabbed a wine bottle which had somehow managed to stay upright from another table and poured her a full glass. She took it.

"Drink it. It'll help," I said, and she took a gulp.

I then went to the front of the restaurant and stepped outside as the first unit arrived. My hands were held high and empty except for my wallet open with the picture ID and badge visible.

"What we got, Lou?"

"Some asshole came in shooting up the place, hit three, he's calm now, 10-7, two others too, but there's a kid in there needs EMS quick."

I knew the deputy, but had to glance at his name tag, C. Coker, from when he had worked the jail, had taught him as a new hire, and he had worked his way to the street. He nodded, "Let me clear the place and Code 4 it and we'll get them here right quick. Stay here for me, Lou?" I nodded back, even though I thought I should be backing him. He entered the restaurant, and a minute later other units and the ambulance came screaming into the little parking lot.

The EMTs jumped out of their ride and pulled a gurney out the back, it legs dropping and locking as they pulled. Their bags were piled on top of it. They were in a hurry, since they had been advised one was still alive. I held the door for them.

Crime scene arrived. Detectives arrived, Shoot Team and Homicide arrived. The District Commander arrived, wearing jeans and a golf shirt, evidently called from his home. News crews arrived. I didn't see Andrea for awhile. I wondered how this affected us, if at all. Two deputies cordoned off the parking lot, which was only about sixty feet wide with a row of parking places on each side and room for two cars to pass each other entering and exiting. They strung the yellow crime scene tape generously around trees and posts and vehicles in the lot. Some of the people inside were in for a long wait to get out.

The two EMTs, a short blonde with the look of a Crossfit athlete about her, and the tall black man with skin so dark his skin reflected the flashing blues and reds like a mirror, came bursting out the door, the girl hip-bumping it open. They had an IV started on the kid and an oxygen mask on his face. They loaded him and prepared to get out of there. As they backed up, the beeping alarm as they drove in reverse keeping a beat like a heart monitor, two deputies stepped up on the rear bumper and stretched the crime scene tape high over their heads so the high box of the ambulance could clear it.

Then they jumped clear and guided the vehicle, known forever as a C.O., from the time long before these officers had even been born, when the ambulance service had been run by the Coroner's Office, back into the street. Traditions, and jargon, are held tight to in the fraternity. It sometimes helps keep you safe when no one from outside knows what the hell you're talking about. The electronic sirens maxed out immediately and they were gone. I sent a quick Buddhist blessing along with the kid.

The next several hours were busy, mostly for everyone else. There were statements to be taken, evidence to be collected, including my own weapon. I was glad I had decided to carry my duty weapon that evening instead of my Kimber. I had no emotional attachment to it, although now that it had been used to strike down a murdering piece of shit I would probably treasure it, but I didn't like the idea of my Kimber, with its similar history, sitting lonely in the Property and Evidence vault until they got around to returning it. After the investigation, after the department review, after the District Attorney's Office blessed it. I was glad the shooter had been white, so maybe Al Sharpton wouldn't show up to make my life miserable. I had enough on my mind already, like why Andrea didn't love me anymore.

I knew that I would be last, because I was a principal to the event and because I was on the JOB, and that I would have to wait until they were damned good and ready to talk to me. I took a seat in a unit, the front passenger seat, not a perp seat, and thought about Andrea. Maybe she would think I was her hero, and the thought was ridiculous to me. I'm not really that inclined to optimism.

The coroner's investigator, a beautiful blonde with enormous blue eyes whose personal number officers were always trying to get while standing over bodies, arrived, pronounced the obvious, and the Coroner's Office ghouls started removing bodies one by one into separate vans which showed up. They were bagged and on their way to the attractive post-modern Forensic Center building on the West bank in Harvey. Two more C.O.'s arrived to treat patrons for shock and minor injuries, and to be on hand in case someone had a heart attack.

At one point, I badged my way back inside to check on Andrea, the deputy on the door logging me in, although that seemed superfluous. She had been moved to the other dining room along with the other witnesses. It was separated from the scene of bodies and medical litter and broken glassware by a portable folding screen set up by Crime Scene along with a decorative screen belonging to the restaurant. She was sitting with another woman and a man, both young and looking relieved and tired.

"How are you holding up?" I asked her. I took her hand, but after a barely polite few seconds, she withdrew it to keep her other hand company in her lap. Her dress had not been damaged too badly by me pulling her down to the floor, but I could see a couple of loose threads.

"It was horrible, those poor people." She stared right through me for a moment, and then dropped her gaze.

"Yes," I agreed, "it really was. Do you need anything?"

"I just want to go home."

"As soon as they finish with our statements, I'll get you home."

"No, just me, I want to go."

I started to walk away when the young man stopped me with a hand on my arm, "I just want to say, thank you. If you hadn't been here, ..." His voice trailed off without voicing the unthinkable. I nodded bitterly and went back outside to the parking lot.

"Lieutenant! Lieutenant Bowie!" It was a reporter, a tall thin woman wearing jeans and tee shirt. She was probably print or digital, since she wasn't of the blow-dried variety. She was yelling at me from the other side of the tape. Department policy was that you didn't speak to the media. The Public Information Officer did that, or the Sheriff, so I ignored her. I would have anyway. I slumped back into the seat in the unit and closed my eyes. Yes, those poor people, of course, but what about poor me? What makes a woman turn on a dime like that? I didn't have a clue.

The Sheriff looked at me and said, "It was really good work that you did that night." I thought I detected a subtle emphasis on THAT night, and maybe an implied BUT... No mention of what went after.

III

It was a long night. At one point, the Sheriff came over to speak with me. I stood up out of the unit I was sitting in. He reached first to shake hands, a good sign.

"Travis, how are you doing?" It was the right question to ask an officer after he has been involved in a critical incident. Contrary to the notions held dear by anti-police demonstrators, about half of officers involved in a shooting leave the force within five years voluntarily. No one goes around hoping to find someone to shoot. The Sheriff was being correct, but not smiling. He didn't want a photo published showing us smiling and laughing.

"All things considered, Sheriff, I'd have rather just had dinner."

He nodded non-committally, "It looks like a lot of people were lucky you decided to have dinner here this evening." He wasn't going to put himself out on a limb until the investigation was complete. It looked like a good shoot, but he didn't want to be caught wrong-footed if something turned up wrong. The Sheriff would back you if you were right, and cut you adrift in a heartbeat if you weren't. Loyalty was a one-way path, and it ran from the bottom to top, not the other direction.

"Well, take some days and see the psych. We'll take care of the leave administratively."

"Yes, sir," I said, but he was already walking away. He turned, remembering something else, "and the lady you were with, she asked for a ride since you're going to be tied up a while longer. I had a unit take her home after her statement."

"Oh, good idea, thanks," I managed to say. He gave me a longer look and then walked away again. I had missed Andrea when she left, and she hadn't said a thing.

They let me drive myself to the Bureau, since I wasn't a suspect. They did read me my rights, though, just in case I blurted out some crime I had committed while being interviewed. The detective who took my statement was Sal Baker, not the best investigator in my opinion, but then, there didn't seem to be much to investigate. I was encouraged that the interview was in Sal's office, not the Fish Bowl, with the one-way mirror for observers to spy on the process.

When we were done, we both stood and shook hands. Sal smiled, "It was a righteous shoot, Travis. No worries."

"Any idea who the shooter was? Why he did it?"

Sal shook his head, "No ID. No connection we've found with anyone in the restaurant, customer or worker. We have to figure out who he is first, go from there."

"Okay, thanks."

When I emerged from the office into the corridor, my daughter Amity and my son-in-law Steve were waiting. She was in uniform for her day watch, Steve still in uniform from his night watch which had just ended. Amity threw her arms around me in a rare display of emotion, and I felt the reassuring clink and creak of her duty gear. Ever since her mother had died, she tended to worry about me. Steve also grabbed me in an awkward man-hug, something unprecedented and not particularly welcome, but I guess obligatory. We separated as soon as we could.

"Are you all right?" From Amity, it was less a question than a demand.

"What could be better, I got in a shootout, didn't get dinged, killed somebody, and I'm not under arrest?" I even managed a smile.

"Don't be an idiot," she ordered, but I caught Steve in a smirk.

I shrugged in response, and she asked, "Where's Andrea?"

"She went home."

"Way to stand by her man in a time of need."

"Well, actually, she dumped me right before the shooting started."

"Bitch."

"Be nice."

"Fuck a bunch of nice. So I ask again, are you all right?"

"I don't know about all right, but pretty right. I'm kind of tired, though."

Steve asked, "Do you feel better about being alone or being with someone to talk it out? I'm off now."

"You have the baby to take care of, and I just want a nap." He seemed relieved as he nodded, and I know I was. Sharing is overrated, I think. It is true, though, that police officers often don't do well after a critical incident, contrary to media portrayals of cops as trigger-happy gunslingers. I've never heard a cop say they are looking forward to shooting someone. I had already been there though, and had weathered it okay. I guess I wasn't the sensitive sort.

I drove home. Sunday morning's sun was just peeking over the buildings and trees. I was beat. The adrenaline dump had faded hours before, and now, with nothing to eat except for bread sticks and herb butter, I felt hung over, the way I used to after a long night of drinking.

Kiddo greeted me at the door, her big black Labrador head nuzzling me and sniffing me all over, no doubt gleaning the residual aromas of marinara, garlic, adrenaline, fear and blood, like a furry Crime Scene tech. She looked at me as if to ask, "What have you gotten yourself into this time?" She was ever empathetic, though. She would never dump me, especially at dinner.

If I had had a couch, I would have lain down on it, but I had thrown it out years ago because the cats and Kiddo had made such a mess of it shedding hair all over it. Instead, I went to the kitchen, got the vodka bottle out of the lower cabinet, walked back and placed it on the dining room table. Then I took a chair and stared at it for awhile. Whenever I had a crisis, I took it out and remembered the time I would have opened the bottle and drunk it. It had never been opened, the seal still intact. After awhile, I went to sit in bed and hopefully fall asleep.

I drifted off sitting slumped against the back pillow. I dreamed some weird things I didn't remember, and finally woke up in the first quarter of the Saints/Atlanta game I had preset to come on. The score was tied at nothing. As I watched without much interest, being more obsessed with Andrea dumping me, and oh, yeah, the shootout, I replayed the loop of the event in my head. Over and over.

Bang! That was the first I had registered the shooter's presence in the restaurant. His greasy look and his position near the hostess station indicated that he had just entered. I look up. The shooter proceeds to his left into our dining room. He looks around and takes a step. He sees the woman with her husband at his right, shoots her. He scans the room. The waiter throws his water pitcher at him, hits him in the head, he shoots the boy without even looking at him very hard. Takes another step. He stares in my direction, even before I have begun to draw my pistol. He's looking at me. I steady up and fire repeatedly. He goes down.

Replay from the beginning. Bang! Wait. Before he steps into the dining room on our side of the restaurant, he pauses. He looks to his right, into the other dining room. Then he steps to his left. His gaze is fixed. He's looking right at me. After shooting the woman and the boy, he steps past tables to his right and left, swinging his pistol back online in my direction. I draw and pull Andrea to the floor and shoot.

Do I know this guy? Have our paths crossed before that he would target me? And if so, how would he know to find me there?

I closed my eyes again and remembered the scene again. Bang! Shooter takes a full couple of seconds to check out the other dining room, and only then steps inside ours. He misses seeing the waiter who is standing five feet from him. Reason: he is looking at our table, focused in on me. No, wait. I pull Andrea to the floor. His weapon is up. The he looks down at Andrea. He doesn't even register me pulling my own weapon. He is after her. I shoot, he falls, still looking at Andrea, until I put a bullet in his head.

I replayed the scene a few more times and it came out the same. All the facts of the different versions stayed the same. My conclusion is that the shooter was never after me. He was there to shoot Andrea. Because she was a woman? There were other women who were available to him. Because she was a woman of a certain age, like the other woman whom he had shot? Again, there were others closer to him than we were. Okay, let's say I'm not wrong, and Andrea was the target. Why? She was a secretary/receptionist in a department of an oil industry testing company. What was so exotic about that, that would make her a target for assassination? It made no sense. There were plenty of people who were high-profile enough to draw attention-seeking crazies. If the shooting was random, then it made a certain sense. Could shooting the other poor woman have been to make it look random?

I was getting off in the weeds now. Should I tell Homicide my thoughts? Would they just think I was trying to create a sweater out of a thread? Detectives were a pampered class within the department, and generally considered their judgment superior to everyone else's, especially that of a lowly jail cop like myself. Maybe I should just wait until they asked me some more questions if they had any, since this investigation was looking like finding a horse tied to a tree, and the closure would be quick. If they did have any more follow-up questions, I could volunteer my memories, and if it turned out I was right, they could take credit for discovering a connection, as they always did.

I fell back asleep for a little while, the game at Saints 10, Atlanta 7 at the half. I had missed all three scores during my little contemplation exercise. I usually follow every play of a Saints game, since I had a tiny superstition that if I didn't pay close attention, the Saints would lose. Maybe I was right. When I woke up again, the Saints had lost by three while I hadn't been paying attention.

IV

I decided to take a ride to Andrea's. I opened the door for Kiddo and she jumped up in her seat. That was probably another reason Andrea had dumped me. She was indifferent to dogs and hated cats. Two strikes against me for a long-term relationship. I always cleaned the car and sprayed air freshener before we went out, but it probably still smelled like dog to her.

At her apartment complex, I texted her so she would open the gate and let me in, if she let me in. No reply. I called. No answer. I left Kiddo in the truck, which was still new and smelled new to me, my other truck having been blown up in north Louisiana during another misadventure.

As I climbed over the gate, Andrea's across-the-breezeway neighbor, an older wrinkled black man wearing his Saints game-day jersey, stepped out his door with a garbage bag in his hand. He watched me climb over without displaying any alarm. I smiled at him as he headed past me, presumably on his way to the dumpster.

I knocked on Andrea's door. As the neighbor shut the gate leaving it ajar so he could get back in, he said, "She's not here. Don't you know it's Sunday, casino day with her mom?"

Of course. I felt stupid. "Oh, right. I forgot." I walked back to the gate and pulled it open.

"She told me you wouldn't be coming around no more," the neighbor said, with a little suspicion in his voice. What was she doing, warning against some anticipated stalking by me? And here I am, caught climbing over her gate. I was embarrassed, but I was annoyed too. Just how much of a loser did she think I was? She hadn't said anything about that last night, just that we were on different tracks, heading to different destinations. That wasn't what she said, actually. She wasn't prone to speaking in metaphors as I was, but that's the meaning I got.

"I had something to ask her," I said, and felt as lame as it sounded.

Both of us standing outside the gate now, he said, "I'll be sure to tell her you dropped by." Of that, I had no doubt. And the next thing would probably be a restraining order. I left, wishing I could borrow Kiddo's tail so I could hang it between my legs.

I wasn't sure what to do. I figured maybe I would ride around until Andrea's neighbor forgot about me and then come back to wait for her to come home so I could warn her. While I was driving away, I got a call. Caller ID told me it was unknown, but I recognized the number as one of the rollover group belonging to the jail.

"This is Bowie," I answered.

"L.T., Sergeant Miller, sorry to bother you. I know you're on admin, but guess who's back and asking for you."

"Not much of a guess, Anthony. Got to be Eddie, right?"

"You got it. He's asking for you, driving everyone crazy. Says it's urgent."

"It's always urgent to an inmate, and more so with Eddie."

"Yep."

"Well, I'm on the shelf for a few days, so I don't know if I can even come in. I'm not suspended, so I guess maybe I can. Can you tell Eddie I'll be there when I can? Maybe that will satisfy him for a little while."

"Okay, L.T., thanks, and oh, good work last night. Saw it on the notifications. Lucky you were there, and a jail officer a hero for a change. Nice."

"Thanks, Anthony."

"Okay, take care. You all right? Need anything?"

"Still processing, but okay. Look, I'll come in and see Eddie. Tell him, okay?"

"Will do. Thanks again." We disconnected.

V

I figured I might as well go see Eddie. I was trying to keep my mind off myself after the shock Andrea had delivered the night before. I wasn't indifferent to the gravity of the shooting, or the victims, but I'm as self-absorbed as most, and the Andrea thing loomed larger. Eddie was a regular at the jail. If they gave frequent flier miles for incarcerations, Eddie could have gotten a free trip to Australia. He was a career criminal, but not a very successful one. He was a life-long screw-up, with a twenty-six page rap sheet for non-violent crimes ranging from theft to burglary. He was a drunk and he stole, often shoplifting alcohol. He was also intelligent. He had helped us many times with cases, both criminal and civil.

After he had helped us one time by wearing a wire for Homicide when he had befriended an inmate who was charged with murder and then testified in a hearing for us, avoiding a trial when the inmate pled, I had explained to an Assistant District Attorney that while Eddie was not a model citizen, he was a model inmate, and had helped us with other cases through the years. And Eddie had dodged another long prison term as a career criminal eligible for multiple billing at sentencing. Now he was back.

I parked my new black Ford pickup on the street in front of the jail and entered the main lobby. I was not in uniform, so I asked Deputy Anson at the desk to call Sergeant Miller. While I waited, the deputy asked me about the incident.

"Were you scared, Lieutenant?" Her big brown eyes regarded me from her seat behind the counter. I thought about it for a few seconds and tried to remember. I really couldn't remember being afraid, maybe because it had happened so fast, or maybe because I was still locked onto what Andrea had dumped on me. I did remember the adrenaline dump and my heart thumping, so I guess I was afraid.

"Oh, yeah, Barbara." I smiled, and her light mocha face grinned at me.

"Maybe one day I can get to the Academy and be able to help in a situation, like you did."

"Hang in there, Barbara." It was an old story. People got hired for the jail, and had to work years in the mind-numbing environment before they got the opportunity to go the Academy and become fully certified, to carry a gun and arrest people. Then they were eligible for transfer to Patrol and make a career path. The Sheriff's Office was a gun culture. If you didn't carry a gun, you were a lesser mortal, and got less respect. There were fully certified officers in the jail, but they were a minority, which included me and my investigators.

Sergeant Miller, an earnest twenty-something with spiky blond hair, entered the lobby and we shook hands. "Thanks for coming, Lou. He seems agitated this time."

"He ought to be. He's running out of road. It wouldn't take much for him to get billed for twenty to life as a multiple. There's only so many times we can pull a rabbit out of a hat."

Anthony nodded and led the way to an empty office we used for interviews when we wanted to minimize inmates' exposure to prying eyes. It wasn't perfect. Inmates watch everything, and any inmate movement was noted. On top of that, correctional officers were notorious blabbermouths, and inmates picked up what they were discussing among themselves. We waited for an officer to fetch Eddie.

While we waited, both of us sat in two of the three office chairs, with me behind the desk and Anthony to the side. When the knock on the door came, Anthony got it. Eddie was in his familiar orange jumpsuit, escorted by a young black female officer whose name I could not place. I realized I had never seen Eddie in civilian clothes, ever. He was cuffed to the rear as policy dictated. It had taken a year or so and a number of officer suspensions for me to get the message across that it was dangerous to cuff inmates in front.

26

Sergeant Miller looked over at me and I nodded. He was in charge, I was unofficial at best with my administrative situation.

"You can unhook him, Miss Jones." She unlocked the handcuffs and stowed them in her pouch.

"You want me to wait, Sergeant?" Anthony nodded and shut the door, leaving her to wait in the corridor.

Eddie took his usual seat in front of the desk. We had done this many times before. He looked, well, scared. I reached over and shook hands. His hand was clammy and made me wish for some hand sanitizer. His face was drawn and he had lost weight. I wondered if the HIV had gone active. He had neglected to take the meds when he was on the street and it had to catch up with him sooner or later.

"So what's the emergency, Eddie?" I asked.

"I heard about the shooting, You okay, Lieutenant?"

Inwardly I rolled my eyes. I doubted my name had been put on the news, which inmates watch religiously in case it mentions them and their case or one of their low-life friends or relatives, or hopefully hear one of the witnesses against them got hit by a bus. He had probably picked it up hearing the jail officers gossiping.

"I hope that's not why you've been demanding to see me."

"No, no, Lieutenant, that's not why." He waved his hands around. With any other inmate, I would have told him to keep his hands down, but Eddie and I had a long history, which is how officers get attacked, but I didn't think that was going to happen.

"Okay," I prompted by drawing out the word.

"I need PC," he said.

I looked at Anthony. He looked at me. This was different. In the past, Eddie had always volunteered to be put where he could be of use to us, and to help himself by having us, and the DA, owe him something. He might still be of some help on the protective custody pod, but he had never needed it before.

"Because?" I bent my fingers toward myself in a gimme gesture.

27

"I can't tell you everything right now, Lieutenant, but I have enemies." He knew very well that he had just uttered the magic words which obligated us legally to protect him. The other magic words which activated special procedures were, "I'm going to kill myself." Inmates regularly used that one when they didn't get their way, sometimes for something as minor as having a piece of cake on their tray they thought was too small. A few days of suicide watch usually convinced most inmates that wasn't the optimal way to express their grievances.

Sergeant Miller took his little notebook out of his shirt pocket and prepared to write down names so he could give them to Classification.

"Enemies? Who?" I asked.

"I don't know, Lieutenant." It was one of Eddie's quirks that annoyed me, saying Lieutenant in every sentence.

"Come on, Eddie, that's a new guy move, just saying you got enemies but not giving up names, usually because they're just scared and there aren't any enemies. You know better than that, and you were never afraid before. What's going on?" I was losing patience, and I didn't have much to begin with. This had been the weekend from hell.

"I don't know who it is in here, Lieutenant, but there's some guys on the street who are turning over everything to find me, and they ain't playing."

"What did you get yourself mixed up in this time? Did you do something beyond your usual nickel and dime shit?"

He nodded several times like a bobblehead, "Yes, sir, Lieutenant, me and some guys I know, but I can't tell you about it right now. I got to work some things out first, Lieutenant." I noticed his blue eyes had faded to look like washed-out denim. He was definitely sick.

"Let me guess a little bit here. You're feeling heat on the street, so you get yourself arrested so we can keep you safe in here. And," I pointed a finger at him, "you're still working whatever scam you got cooking. So you want us to enable you to commit a crime. Not good, Eddie. Friends do favors for each other, but they don't use each other like that."

"Yeah, yes, sir, Lieutenant. I got myself arrested so those guys wouldn't find me, but they might have friends in here too." He was sweating, his hair, also faded to a graying blond, was sticking out all over. "And, Lieutenant, you owe me."

I drew back in my chair as if slapped, "Now that's just bad fucking manners, Eddie. And I think, if you're keeping score, we're pretty even." My patience was gone now. I was pissed.

"I'm sorry, Lieutenant, I'm sorry. Shouldna' said that, but I'm scared. I'll tell you everything soon as I can."

I stood, and I stared at him until he dropped his gaze. "Sergeant, can you put him in AdSeg and have Classification take care of the paperwork tomorrow when they come in?"

"Sure, Lou," Anthony said.

"Aw, come on, Lieutenant," Eddie stood suddenly, "AdSeg? I was thinking one of the PC pods. The jail had several Special Housing Units, for flamboyant homosexuals likely to be victimized or to cause fights among inmates vying for their favors, for child molesters and rapists, for crazies. AdSeg was the second-most restrictive, second only to Disciplinary, where the inmates were locked down twenty-three hours a day, with only an hour to walk around, use the phone, take a shower. It was still protective custody, though, and he had asked for PC. It was my little revenge.

"We've got to keep you safe from unknown enemies, Eddie. How do we know one of the inmates on a PC pod won't shank you or hang you or beat you to death with soap in a sock?" I gave him a nasty smile. He closed his eyes. He knew he had made a mistake.

"Get back to us when you want to talk," I said, and Anthony and I left the office, leaving Eddie to be handcuffed again and, at Sergeant Miller's instruction, escorted to AdSeg.

As Anthony and I reversed our course back to the lobby, heavy steel doors clanging shut behind us as the operator opened them for us, I thought about what Eddie was up to. I was still on Administrative Leave, but I would pass on to one of my investigators to monitor Eddie's phone calls, see if we could unravel this rope.

VI

I checked my watch as I got back to my truck. It was almost six in the evening. I decided to go see if Andrea had made it home from her excursion with her mother. Her car was parked in the line of parking spaces outside her gate.

I tried the gate, but it was locked. My heart did a quick heavy thump as I texted her, "I'm here. Please come open the gate." I waited, two minutes, three, but there was no reply. I called her. She didn't pick up, but she did emerge from her apartment. She was wearing jeans and a lightweight red sweater. She was barefoot, showing off her always-perfect pedicure with burgundy nail polish.

She walked to the gate and stood behind the black steel bars, hands on hips. From each other's perspective, I guess we could have looked like we were in separate cages. She didn't look happy.

"Edsel told me he caught you climbing over my gate."

"He saw me, but I don't know about catching me. I wasn't hiding. I needed to talk to you." I had my hands clasped in front of me in what I hoped was a posture that was non-threatening, but not needy.

She had removed her hands from her hips and was now hugging herself in what looked like a distancing, self-protective mode. She shook her head slowly.

"I think we said everything we needed to say last night, Travis."

"Well," I said, frustrated, "I remember we were rudely interrupted before I could ask why we never even had a conversation about this before you dropped this on me. You went home without even saying anything to me. Are you going to let me in or are we just going to stand here talking through the gate?"

She seemed a little bit in shock, as anyone would be after the horror of the night before, and she stared off into the distance beyond my shoulder, "It was horrible, just horrible. I was so scared."

"Yes, it was," I said gently, and reached through the bars to grasp her hand snugged up under her breast. She let me take it, but didn't respond. I always liked her hands. They were pretty and well-kept for a woman of her age, her nails immaculate.

"And you," she darted a glance at me, then looked away again, "I didn't know you could be so, so violent."

"It was the time for it."

She nodded, then shook her head, "But it showed me I was right. We're so different. I'm not like that." She reclaimed her hand and resumed hugging herself with both arms.

"Okay, I get it, sort of, but that's not why I had to see you. Are you going to let me in or not?"

"No," she shook her head firmly. She started to turn away, so I said what I had to, "It wasn't random. You were the target."

Now she was angry, "That's ridiculous. I'm just a secretary. I don't have people who want to hurt me. You're just saying that to make me feel grateful to you. I mean, I am grateful, but me, that's just, desperate," she said with a look that told me I was pathetic. Any respect she might have had was fading fast.

"Really, Andrea, you have to listen. You didn't see the guy when he was shooting. I did, and he kept looking over right at you. He could have shot any number of other people, but he was heading for you. Not me, you."

She waved her hand as if shooing a bug, me I guess, and shook her head vigorously. She stepped back, said, "I feel we need to make a clean break here, Travis. Please don't come back." Then she turned and walked away.

I was left understanding how Cassandra must have felt when she warned the Trojans and was ignored until she went mad. I was feeling a little crazy myself, but I still had to convince the department psychiatrist I wasn't. I couldn't make that appointment until tomorrow.

I drove home, not knowing what to do next. Kiddo was waiting for me at the front window. I let her out in the front yard where she watered the grass and then spun around a few times and did her other duty. I scooped up after her and upended the small spade into an empty dogwood bag in the garbage can. Then I went inside and washed my hands.

The vodka bottle was still on the table, so I sat and looked at it awhile. I closed my eyes next and tried to just be still, or tried not to try to be still. When I finished the meditation, I felt as if I had been far away. Kiddo was resting with her big black head on her forepaws, watching me. She studied me the way people read books. I think she understood me more than anyone in the world.

"Am I wrong, girl? Did I just imagine this whole thing? I mean, she's right, she's a secretary, why *would* anyone want to hurt her, kill her? It makes no sense." Then I replayed the memory of the last night once again, and it came out the same.

I finally ate something. I did an egg over easy on a piece of toast. When you live alone, you tend to eat a lot of eggs. They're quick, they're easy. Kiddo got one too as a garnish for her dog food.

I was having trouble keeping still, or focusing on anything, probably an after-effect of the shootout. I wasn't shaking nervous, but I was restless. Kiddo and I took a walk. In South Louisiana, in areas which had once been swamp and lowland forest, the neighborhoods are drained by a vast system of canals. Rainwater from the neighborhoods runs into catch-basins and then through underground culverts to canals, where the excess water is then pumped out by large pumping stations. The canal banks on either side, with wide servitudes, run for miles. Kiddo and I would walk and she could run free without concern for traffic or other people. The canal bank system makes for a kind of linear park environment, where ducks, egrets and herons, pelicans, hawks, raccoons and snakes, and yes, alligators, flourish. By the time we got back, it was dark, and cooling off.

After a shower, I sat in bed, propped up against my back pillow, and fell asleep watching the Sunday night game and trying not to feel sorry for myself.

VII

It was Monday when I awoke, early Monday, more Sunday night really, My first thought was of Andrea. Great. I knew I wouldn't be getting back to sleep, and what was I going to do caught between night and morning? Obsess, of course.

Why did I care that Andrea had dumped me? Was she the lost love I had been looking for? Was I even really looking? Had she just happened, and then un-happened? Was it pride that I wasn't the answer to her question? Was it that I had to acknowledge that I wasn't as self-sufficient as I styled myself? Was I more lonely than I liked to admit? Had the death of Mae, my wife, after years of illness and decline, been more a loss than the relief that I had tried to convince myself it was? Was it the loss of her touch, the release and fulfillment of her body? And so it went until I got up, changed, and drove to Andrea's.

I had no intention of talking to her. I just wondered, if someone was trying to harm her, even if she didn't want my help, what was my duty? I parked across the side street from her apartment complex, in the line of spaces used by the patrons of the lesbian biker bar and the laundromat next door. I backed in so I could watch her gate. What if she came out, no one tried to hurt her, and she saw me sitting there like a stalker? Hurt her? I had convinced myself someone was trying to kill her. If so, why? It made no sense. It made more sense that I was just wrong.

The hours of the night crawled by. I couldn't sleep before, but now I caught myself nodding from time to time when my head dropped.

I had half-argued myself into leaving when I saw the white van cruise slowly down the dead-end street, It didn't stop at the bar or the laundromat, but backed and turned until it was stopped on my side of the street at the curb. Its lights were off, even as it had rolled onto the street. Smash and grabbers getting ready to harvest the line of vehicles parked at the complex? Maybe. Maybe not, but there didn't seem to be any legitimate reason for it to be there. I could be wrong about it. Maybe it was someone waiting to pick up someone to drive to work, but why park all the way down there away from the gate, and why no lights?

As I slumped lower in my seat, a figure exited the passenger side of the van. His face was obscured by the hoodie. I couldn't tell if he was black, white or something else. He, I was guessing it was a he, crossed over to the line of parking spaces alongside the apartment building and walked on the sidewalk. He didn't stop until he got to Andrea's little red Ford Focus. He tried the passenger side door, and then the driver's door. Locked. I considered what he might have in mind. Steal it? Disable it to make her more vulnerable to an attack. Waiting in the backseat of the compact and grabbing her was no sure thing, and killing her as she got in and then getting out with a body in the way was not either. I waited. I needed to grab this guy, not shoot him, so I could hold him up like a dead rat to Andrea and say, "See?"

I could have called the police, I guess, I mean besides me, and I could have kicked myself later that I didn't. Does any of us ever grow up? I've thought not over the years, and have provided plenty of evidence. I think like children we're always either showing off or running away, or maybe it's me.

When the hooded figure used the slim jim to pop the lock and leaned into the car, I opened my door and stepped out. I just pushed the door to, but didn't shut it all the way. I heard the hood latch on the Focus click. I started to circle around to my left, away from the waiting van, to catch him blind. Then the van's horn bleated twice. The driver had seen me and warned his partner. The guy leaning into the car jumped out like he'd found a snake and began to run for the van.

I was closer to my truck than to him, and he had a head start. At fifty-six, I don't run as fast as I used to, and I was sure he was younger, so I opted for my truck to block their escape. I started the engine and drove toward the van and the guy running for it. I floored it, and I got a glimpse of the face inside the sweatshirt hood. He was young, thirty-ish, with a blond goatee and mustache. And his eyes were like cue balls as they saw my truck bearing down on him.

We zigged and zagged, and then he stumbled and fell. I felt my tires on the right side double-thump as they rolled over some parts of him. I was past the van when I stopped, and in my rear-view saw the guy in the hoodie staggering to his feet, limping with one leg and dragging the other as he made it back to the van. It was speeding back up the side street and onto Lafayette Street before I could get turned around. Shit, shit, shit.

I pulled back into my parking place and looked at my watch. Almost seven. Andrea would be leaving for work soon. Text her, call her, wait? I waited. I just knew this wasn't going to go well. If I had caught the guy, maybe, but this just looked like stalking.

When she emerged from behind her gate, I thought she looked lovely in her tan slacks and blouse with swirls of yellow and blue on the black background. She wore black heels. She noticed her hood was loose right away, and then she noticed me walking slowly toward her. I saw disdain, then I saw fear. Losing her hurt me, but her fear stabbed my heart. She started to back toward her gate and fumbled in her purse, for her phone I guessed.

"Andrea, wait," I stopped twenty feet from her, "someone broke into your car. He popped your hood, probably to pull something loose. I stopped him."

She shook her head to clear it, of me, my story, "Listen, Travis, you need to leave me alone, I'm warning you."

"I'm not making it up, listen to me. You're in danger. Look at your hood. I didn't make that up."

37

"You cops carry those slim thingies, you opened the door."

"I have enough trouble with keys. I don't have a lock-out kit, don't even know how to use one. Please believe me."

The fear seemed to have faded a little, and the anger was back, "You're si..., you need help, Travis, now stay away or I'm calling somebody." She pushed her hood shut emphatically and edged back to her car door when she saw I wasn't getting any closer, got in, started up, backed out, and drove away as quickly as she could, just glancing once at me as she passed me standing in the street.

It was clear to me now that I was not going to be the one to keep Andrea from getting killed. I was going to have to pass this on to Detective Baker and hope he could figure things out before this stubborn woman got herself killed.

"And why didn't you report this incident to Detective Baker, instead of continuing to play policeman when you were on Administrative Leave?" The Sheriff asked the question, and the two bookends bobbled their heads.

I thought the phrase "play policeman" was an unfortunate one. I mean, I had always been told we might not be on duty, but we were always on The Job. Was that a reference to my being in Corrections instead of Patrol or the Bureau?

I had to tread carefully here, as much of what happened next was not in my report, and it had caused me to hold back.

I shrugged and answered, "Things kind of took on a life of their own, Sir."

VIII

It was almost eight o'clock. I knew it was too early to catch Sal Baker in the office. Detectives. Lords of the department, usually strolled in at uncertain times, after "working" breakfasts at one of the eateries which gave police discounts. The investigation of my shootout wasn't a whodunnit, more of a whydunnit, and the suspect was well in hand, or at the Coroner's Office, so there wasn't the urgency to solve it, but the PR pressure to explain why good, affluent people at an East bank restaurant had been terrorized still was.

I drove back home to get Kiddo and go the supermarket close to the house. By the time I got home, there was a secretary in Homicide, so I left a message for Sal. Kiddo jumped into the truck and took her usual seat.

As I got out, I left my phone wedged in a corner of the dashboard against the windshield, as usual. I went inside, bought some flowers for the vase next to Mae's funerary urn. I liked to keep them fresh. I knew I was just delaying the call I needed to make to the psychiatrist. I had never seen, as in *seen,* a psychiatrist. I didn't mind seeing him. I just didn't want to make the call. I typically procrastinate with phone calls, because I didn't like talking on the phone.

After checking out, I walked back to my truck. I didn't see Kiddo sitting in her usual spot behind the steering wheel, looking out over it. When I got to the truck, I saw the door was slightly ajar. Had I failed to shut it properly? I opened the door and looked around inside. Kiddo was gone. I started to panic. If she got out and got hit by a car, I would never forgive myself. My heart was pounding a lot more than it had been during the shootout, or when Andrea had dropped her load.

I looked around the parking lot. I climbed into the truck bed to give myself a higher view. I didn't see her anywhere. I called out.

"Kiddo, hey girl!" I shouted it over and over, but no big Labrador showed. I wanted to cry.

Finally, I remembered the phone. I always left it in the truck with the motion sensor app on to catch photos of her so I could see how she spent her time when I left her there. I checked the video clips. There were several, but the last three were the important ones. The most recent showed a shot of the door being pushed shut, and a shot partially blocked by the door and window frame, of a figure, his arm extended toward the door. The one before that showed Kiddo sitting behind the steering wheel and then jumping out of the vehicle with a rope leash around her neck. The one before that gave me a glimpse of a man through the driver's window. He was white, maybe forty, with a shaved head and tattoos on the arms and hands he was holding a tool in and slipping into the window seal. As I watched him work, I could also see a gray pickup truck behind him, pulled up parallel with mine. The part of his truck I could see was part of the passenger door and part of the truck bed. I couldn't tell what make or model it was. After popping the lock, the man opened the door and leaned in. He was holding a leash which extended toward the camera. There was even audio.

"Come on, dog," he cooed. I could hear his false sincerity, but Kiddo couldn't, I guess. There was movement and then that clip ended.

I was frantic, scared, enraged. I was hyperventilating and felt light-headed. I leaned down with my head between my knees and took some breaths. I didn't feel better, but I felt more functional. Then I ran back to the store.

I found one of the managers standing by in front of the checkout area, watching the retail action in case she were needed by one of the cashiers.

"Someone just stole my dog out of my truck in the parking lot. I need to see your video." I was still holding the bouquet of yellow roses and had to look ridiculous.

"Sir," she said, "that video is not for just anyone to see, it's for security."

I pulled my ID wallet from my back pocket and let her see it, "Well, you have a security matter, as in the theft of my dog. You don't want to tell me No."

She opened her mouth as if to say something, but then waved at me to follow her. She led me to a security office where there was a monitor with the video from about twenty cameras playing in real time. I leaned toward the monitor and saw my black pickup parked.

"That one," I pointed, "can you go back fifteen minutes and play it?"

She didn't seem too happy about it, but I didn't care, as long as she just did it. She enlarged the screen and used the mouse to back up the timeline to fifteen minutes before. We watched at slightly faster speed. I saw my truck parked with empty spaces on either side. Then a champagne colored Nissan parked in the space next to the truck on the passenger side. A black woman in yoga pants and a red T-top got out and walked toward the store. A few minutes later, seconds on fast forward, there was the gray pickup. It stopped in front of my truck. Kiddo had probably caught his attention as he was driving by. Then he proceeded up the lane out of sight, but then reappeared in the frame coming back on the next lane. The gray pickup pulled in and stopped next to my vehicle.

"Stop it there. Please." She did. I identified the truck as a Dodge Ram. It was older, and the driver's door had a dent in it. When I asked her to resume, I could see the man with the shaved head get out. He was carrying a slim jim in his right hand, but holding it close to his body so that it wasn't obvious. In his left, he held a rope which he took from around his neck. He was big, but more so horizontally than vertically. He stood lower than the six feet or so of his truck's height, by several inches. He was maybe five eight, but weighed probably two sixty, a lot of it around his middle.

The horror show continued. I had to watch, fascinated and enraged, as the guy slipped his tool between the window and the seal and expertly popped the lock. He'd done this before. It was hard to see what he did with his vehicle partly obscuring the action, but not a minute after getting out of his truck, I could see him lead Kiddo to the back of his truck and get her to jump up. There was no tailgate that he had to lower. I saw him fiddling with a chain around Kiddo's neck. He walked quickly to his driver's door, tossing the slim-jim inside and looking around the parking lot to see if there was any trouble for him. No doubt if I had showed up and confronted him, he would have said he had found her wandering around and put her in his truck for safekeeping, I wouldn't have believed him, but I wouldn't have had evidence other than this video we were watching, and my secret cell phone video. The manager, a woman about fifty, with bleached blond hair, seemed upset as well.

"Can you follow him out of the parking lot? I need to see which direction he goes." As the gray Dodge pulled away toward the highway out of frame, I strained to see a license plate, but the video resolution wasn't good enough. The manager switched back to a view of all the cameras, and in one of the small screens we could see the Dodge turn left at the end of the aisle and drive toward the exit with the traffic light. The manager maximized the camera showing that view. He was in the left turn lane to go toward Plaquemines Parish. That was good in a way, since there were only two ways in and out of the parish, if you didn't count the two ferries which connected the west bank to the east. I could only hope this traffic light had LPR cameras. The truck turned left and disappeared from view.

"What's your name, ma'am?" I decided to try a little charm.

"Sharon, but sir, the store isn't responsible for lost or stolen items,"

"No, that guy is, but I need to find that guy. That dog is all I have after my wife died."

"Oh, I'm so sorry."

"Would you burn me a disc of what we just watched, Sharon? Please. I would be grateful."

She hesitated, but then I said, "Don't worry, I'm not going to use it in court or anything." She nodded and went to work. When I left the store, I had the disc.

I sat in my truck and made two calls. The first was to Lieutenant David Vinet, who was in charge of the surveillance cameras which were all over the parish, mounted on traffic lights, utility poles and some places no one outside of his unit were supposed to know about. I hoped he was in. He was. He might have been a detective, but he was known for being the first one in the office and the last one out.

"Lieutenant Vinet," he answered.

"Dave, Travis."

"Trav', how are you? I heard about the excitement the other night. It's a good thing you were there."

"Yeah, thanks, Dave, I need a favor, really quick."

"Name it, brother."

"Someone stole my dog out of my truck at Rouse's on Belle Chasse Highway, about a half-hour ago. He went through the light at the exit. Please tell me you have cameras there."

"Let me check, hold on." I could hear a couple of keystrokes in the background, and then all I could hear was his breathing as presumably he moused through a menu.

"Yeah, we have cameras there, since it's right at the edge of the parish, and if someone takes off in that direction, we can bottle him up."

"Oh, man, that's great. Can you check at 0847 for a gray Dodge pickup turning toward Belle Chasse?"

"You got an item number?"

"Not yet, Dave. I want to track him as quick as I can, and then call in Plaquemines Sheriff. Please. This is my friend." I didn't like the sound of myself begging, but I lived with it.

"Well," he drew the syllable out, "Make sure you get that item."

"I will," I said, and probably meant it at the time, at least partly.

"Let me call you back."

"Thanks, Dave."

My next call was to Sonora Richard. In south Louisiana, that's *Ree-shard.* I had told her on more than one occasion that she worked harder and smarter than any white man I knew. I knew she'd be at her desk, working files and listening to inmate phones with a headset on her sometimes elaborate, but regulation, hairdo.

"Deputy Richard," she answered.

"Hi, Sonora, Travis.

"Hi, Trav, did you get my text?"

"I did. Thanks for reaching out. Hey, I'm on the shelf until cleared by the shrink. Look, can you monitor Eddie's phone calls? You know he's back, right?"

"Yeah, I know." Of course she did. She knew just about everything that went on among inmates and officers in the jail.

"He's asking for PC, but they probably already called you about it. That's unusual for him. He's got some kind of scam working and got himself arrested so he can be safe in jail, but he's scared of something happening to him inside the walls."

"You got it. What's wrong? You sound funny."

If I had known what was going to happen down the line, I wouldn't have left such a trail behind me, but I answered, "Someone stole my dog. I'm trying to track them."

"Oh, No, Kiddo?"

"Yeah, I've got to go, thanks." I hung up quickly because my emotions threatened to intrude. The truth was, as worried as I was about Andrea, I was more concerned about Kiddo, and Andrea would have to wait. Maybe she was right, that I was more in love with my dog than with her. All I knew was that Kiddo would be grateful for me going after her, whereas Andrea wasn't at all.

While I was waiting for Dave Vinet to call back, my phone rang. I answered, "Hello," not recognizing the number and nothing coming up on caller ID.

"Lieutenant Bowie?"

"Yes."

"Doctor Windsor. I'm calling about your interview."

"Oh, yes, sir. I was going to call you." That came out lame.

"Did you have the number?"

"No, I didn't. I was going to call to get it." Even more lame.

"No problem. Sometimes officers delay calling after an incident, so I just call them to get things started. Can you come in this morning? I have an hour free."

There was no way I was going to sit in this doctor's office while I had leads to pursue with Kiddo, so I said, "I can't right now, Doctor. I'm kind of tied up right now." An awkward pause intruded while we listened to each other's background noises.

"This isn't optional, Lieutenant. You need to come sooner rather than later."

"I'm not trying to avoid you, Doc, really," and I berated myself for saying that, because I had been trained too, and I knew that when someone said *really* they usually meant *not really.* He would pick that up right away, being a psychiatrist and all.

"You're on leave now, Lieutenant, so you can make the time. I don't wish to be unpleasant, but...,"

I interrupted him, "How about tomorrow morning, Doctor. I really do have personal business to take care of this morning."

"This is about as personal as it gets, but I don't want us to start off in an antagonistic posture. You have personal things to attend to this morning. All right. Two-thirty this afternoon." It wasn't a request. If I didn't accept, his next call would be to the

Sheriff, and I would be indefinitely suspended. I only knew of a couple of officers who had ever come back from an indefinite suspension without being fired. I didn't have the Sheriff's cell number; he did.

"Yes, sir."

"Goodbye, Lieutenant." I just punched the END button. Could anything else go wrong?

IX

I did the automotive equivalent of twiddling my thumbs, nervously driving around south of the parish line into Plaquemines, hoping to see the gray Dodge truck with Kiddo and the guy who had taken her. Of course, I didn't.

I was trying to be polite and not call Dave Vinet back, but I couldn't. He answered with a tone that was friendly, but said, yes, you are being a pest, "Hey, Travis, hold on, got something for you." A moment later, "Okay, the camera was able to pull a plate off a gray Dodge at the light heading south in the time frame you gave me. It's expired, two years, but the last known is, ready to copy?"

I told him I was, and he gave me the plate number and last registered address.

I thanked him and said goodbye, but he said, "Don't forget to call me back with the item number you get from Plaquemines if you recover your dog, and the sixty two C (auto burglary) item from us."

"No problem, Dave, thanks for your help." At the time, I still meant it. Okay, time for some investigation, something I was comfortable with.

The address for Anson Danson, the last registered owner of the gray Dodge, was down the parish. It was a lane of trailers, mobile homes, which I was surprised my phone GPS found. The limestone drive off the blacktop street led to the trailer, a nicely kept dwelling with flowers planted alongside to obscure the underside of the trailer. Parked to the side was a fairly new blue Chevy sedan with a current handicapped plate. I knew this wasn't going to be as easy as I had hoped.

I knocked on the storm door and waited. I was raising my hand to knock again when the door opened and an old man appeared. He squinted at me, "Yes?"

I lowered my hand to my side and gave him a smile, which some people said struggled for sincerity, "Hello, Sir, I'm trying to find the owner of a gray Dodge pickup truck, one that's registered at this address." I was trying to play this by ear, not wanting to identify myself as police if the shitbird was his son or something.

The old man, who must have been in his eighties, with more hair sprouting from his ears than the top of his head, said, "Sold it. Three years ago. Wait a minute, you saying that son of a bitch didn't change the title like he said?"

"That's what it looks like, Sir." I decided to go official, at least in his eyes, since I was actually out of my jurisdiction. I showed him my ID.

"I should have known," the old man, who was Anson Danson, shook his head.

"Do you remember the name of the man you sold your truck to, Mister Danson?" Please, please, please, I prayed.

"Let me think a minute, "he said, and he took his full sixty seconds while I heard a clock ticking in my head, and maybe even the FINAL JEOPARDY theme music. I still had the appointment at two thirty with Doctor Windsor, and my watch reminded me it was a little after eleven.

"His name's Clyde, Clyde something, can't recollect his last name, but they call him 'Booger', I remember that, 'cause I thought that's a disgusting name for any kind of man."

It was something, not enough, but something, so I prodded him, "Do you know where he lives? Or where he works?"

Mister Danson thought some more, taking his time. It was clear he wasn't on any schedule, at least not one that matched mine. Finally, he said, "No."

"Okay, Mister Danson, thank you, you've been a big help," I said, without feeling all that confident, "you've been a great help."

I backed down the steps and started to walk away, figuring how I was going to get somebody to run the databases for Clyde no last name AKA "Booger", when Mister Danson stepped out on the small porch attached to the mobile home.

"Deputy," he called out. I didn't correct him.

"When you catch up with him, you make sure you tell him to get that title changed." He shook his cane for emphasis.

"Well, Sir I have to find him first."

"Well, look at The Clove Hitch. I seen my old truck parked there when I go to the doctor's lots of times."

I shrugged, "The Clove Hitch?"

"It's a bar," he gestured north with his cane, one of those with the little feet at the end, but all the feet were pointing north too, "don't you know that, being a policeman?"

"I'm from Jefferson Parish, Sir. How far?"

"Maybe five miles, on your right."

I waved at him, but I wanted to kiss his furry ears.

X

The Clove Hitch might have once been a fisherman's bar, but the quality of its clientele seemed to have declined. There were still a few mounted fish on the walls, but photos of fierce dogs, a Confederate flag, and a poster of some kind of cross-like symbol which was suggestive of a swastika without actually being one, adorned the walls. There were three white guys, two fat and one skinny, wearing black T-shirts with the arms cut off, clustered around the pool table at the back. Their leather jackets were draped on barstools. They must have belonged to the Harleys parked outside.

I was glad to be white. I was pretty sure anyone other than white would have been unwelcome. I ordered a draft at the bar. The bartender brought it without a smile. It wasn't that kind of place.

I didn't smile either. He wouldn't have appreciated it anyway. He was scrawny, with buzz-cut hair all one length, which was to say zero, with fading and murky tattoos on his only arm, the right one. The tattoos were either very old, or he had lost a lot of weight so that as his body shrank, the tattoos melted into themselves.

"Clyde around?" I asked. The bartender looked at me like I was speaking another language. I had affected a woodsy accent reminiscent of my kin in North Louisiana. It wasn't the local accent, which I hoped he would notice, and not think I was local, like a cop.

"Booger," I prompted.

The bartender looked around the bar, then turned to me, "You see him around?"

I shrugged, "Wouldn't know him if I did. I was, uh, referred."

"Referred, huh?" It was a slow day, so I guess he decided to play along for the moment. He leaned his one and only arm on the bar.

"Yep. Referred. Looking for a dog." I took a sip of my beer, and ten years of sobriety went out the window. It was just a little sip, though. I knew Mae would forgive me.

"And," he lit up, reaching for a pack on the bar, shaking it until a cigarette appeared, snagging it with his lips, then tossing the pack back down and firing up the lighter from his shirt pocket, "who might that be who referred you?"

I picked a name out of the smoke he blew mostly away from me, "Black Mike, up in Washington Parish."

"Who?" He squinted at me.

"His skin's not black, just his heart," I said. The bartender laughed. I thought that was progress.

"What kind of a name is Black Mike for a white man?"

"What kind of a name is Booger?" I shrugged again. He laughed again. Two guys bonding in a bar.

"What kind of dog you looking for, working or training?" I almost threw up. This guy had stolen my dog to use to train fighting dogs, meaning to be attacked, savaged, killed. I took another small sip of my beer to calm myself.

"Well, you need one, you need the other. Am I wrong?"

"You got ID?" He seemed a little more relaxed.

I reached into my front pocket, not for my wallet, and peeled a hundred out of the inside of the fold. I placed it on the bar and slid it toward him. He looked at it for a few seconds. He picked it up.

"Okay, I guess you and Booger can work out your own arrangement." He gave me directions.

"I'm not going to have to come back for more directions, am I?" I even smiled, but he knew it was a threat. He didn't know me well enough to know if I could cause him trouble. He swiveled his head back and then back again in the universal No sign.

"Thanks. Maybe you can hit Booger up for another referral fee." He nodded as I got off the barstool. I took my plastic cup with me.

Outside, where no one could see, I poured the rest of the beer on the ground. I wasn't going to count this as a slip in my sobriety. I drove to the highway and turned south again.

"Hold on, girl. I'm coming."

XI

My hands were shaking as I checked my watch. I wondered if it was from rage or fear. Eleven forty-five. I pulled up Google Earth on my phone and punched in Bostich Road. I half-expected it not to come up, some road in the middle of nowhere, but bless Google's little corporate heart, there it was. It branched off Perez Lane about twenty miles south. I drove fast.

There was no way Booger wasn't going to notice my truck driving past his place, especially since I just knew that as soon as I left the Clove Hitch, the bartender had called him to set out the fine china for company coming. I just hoped the bartender hadn't seen my truck to give Booger the description.

I studied the Google Earth photos. According to the bartender, Booger lived in the third blue house on Bostich Road where he kept dogs. I didn't know if that meant there were three blue houses, or if it was the third house painted blue. The satellite photos showed several acres of cleared land behind the third house, bordered by a stand of trees of some kind to the east and screened from the next property by another, narrower, line of trees. The road dead-ended at what looked like open pasture, or maybe marsh.

I parked across Highway 23 behind an old roadside fruit stand which was closed, even though it was citrus harvest season and the active stands would have been open. I ran across the highway between big rigs, jumped the barbed wire fence and ran into the trees. The weather had been dry, but there were low places where cypress thrived and they were muddy. By the time I made it through the trees to the open area behind what should be Booger's place, if the bartender hadn't sent me off on a skyhook hunt, and if he had, I was going back and pull off his other arm. It was twelve ten by my watch.

It was the right place. There were small, dog-sized huts in two areas, one dog neighborhood better than the other. In one, there were pit bulls, five I could count, chained in a fenced area with individual fiberglass doghouses, or kennels that looked like igloos, as they're marketed nowadays, with another, smaller fenced area. I concluded the smaller area was where the fighting dogs practiced on the bait dogs. The other area held three dogs of decidedly non-fighting pedigree. I saw a poodle, its white fur matted with dirt, another some kind of terrier/hound mix, and Kiddo. They were chained each next to a sheet metal lean-to.

I picked my way along the thin line of trees which separated the property from the one north of it, so that I could conceal myself if someone appeared out the back of the house. I could see past the blue house to the road, and there was Booger, out on the road, looking for his visitor. Don't worry, Booger, I thought. I'm coming. That was the first time I admitted that retribution was part of the mission. If I had considered it earlier, I wouldn't have left such an easy trail to follow.

I don't know whether Kiddo caught my scent or if she saw me. All I could smell was dogshit and fear, mine, the dogs', who knew. She started to whimper and then howl mournfully, something I had never witnessed. It was if she were mourning her loss of innocence and her discovery of evil. She had never been mistreated in her life. I ran.

I slid to a muddy stop behind Kiddo's lean-to, trying to be small and invisible. Kiddo tried to get to me, but her chain was too short to reach. "Shh, girl," I whispered. The other forlorn dogs joined in. In the enclosure, the pit bulls regarded us as prey, their brown eyes flat. Pit bulls don't waste a lot of energy barking, I'd found. If they were going to attack, they just did. They scared me.

Booger came out the back door. I could see him at an angle from behind the sheet metal. He was carrying what looked like a CB radio antenna, about six feet long. He took a vicious swipe at the poodle, and it yelped as it scooted to the length of its chain trying to get away. Then Booger walked toward our position.

"Shut up, you goddamn dogs. You'll be quiet soon enough, or be crying for ya' momma." He turned sideways to me to address Kiddo, said, "You started up all this racket, bitch?" He raised his arm to flog her, and my phone rang. Stupid, stupid, stupid. I leapt up, stepped to him, and punched him in the right kidney before he could turn, then the left one. His back arched toward me as he dropped the antenna. I reached around to his chin with both hands and pulled him back toward the ground. His head struck the dirt with a sound like dropping a cantaloupe on the floor. I stomped him in the face. He twitched and moaned.

I kept an eye on the house in case someone else came out. What was I going to do if someone did? While I watched the house for the next couple of minutes to see if someone else came out, during which Booger moaned and gurgled in his throat, I thought about what to do next. He didn't look good. He was very pale with shock. I searched his pockets. A ring of keys held not only his truck keys, but padlock keys as well.

Kiddo and the other dogs were secured with chains padlocked around their necks tightly. I worked through the keys until I found the one that fit the lock on the chain around her neck. She was dirty and there was blood on her muzzle. She had never been struck in her life.

I dragged Booger to the pit bull enclosure. The gate wasn't locked. I then dragged him inside, almost within range of one of the dogs. I grabbed his belt and rolled him closer without getting myself where the dog could reach me. I was hoping that when he was found, he wouldn't remember what had happened, or that whoever found him would conclude his dog had attacked him. I closed the gate and left him.

I found some rope leashes like the one used to abduct Kiddo behind the house. I freed the other two dogs and leashed them. I looked at the ground around and scuffed out anything that looked like my boot tracks. I wiped Booger's keys on my shirt to smudge any prints and then threw them over the fence next to him. Then we all ran for the woods. I stole a glance at my watch. It was one fifteen. An hour and fifteen minutes to make my appointment and keep my job, if I weren't arrested for second-degree battery or attempted murder in the meantime.

XII

We were all muddy by the time we made it through the woods to the highway. The poodle had been fighting the leash all through the woods, and I had had to carry him most of the way. I carried him as we crossed the highway too.

I drove to PAWS, the no-kill shelter for Plaquemines Parish. I left Kiddo in the truck and walked in with the two other dogs. A lady with close-cropped black hair with gray streaks, wearing a safari shirt and cargo shorts, who, if she wasn't a lesbian, was missing an opportunity, was in the lobby.

"Hi," I said, trying for sincerity again, "do you work here?"

"Yes, sir, I do. How can I help you?" She smiled at the two forlorn dogs, and at me too.

"I found these babies wandering on the highway, and I was afraid they'd get hit, so I brought them here. They look a little the worse for wear, but I'd bet they're someone's pets."

"Oh, thank you. Some people wouldn't take the time. But, if you found them on the highway, why are you all so muddy?"

"I had to chase them around a field to convince them they needed to come with me."

"Silly things," she laughed. "Could I get your name and address for our records?"

"I'd be glad to, but I have a doctor's appointment in Harvey in," I looked at my watch, "thirty minutes, and I've got to make it. Can I call you back with the information?"

"Sure, that would be fine. Thank you again."

I waved at her, patted the forlorn, now rescued, pups on their flanks, and left. I found a pay phone at a convenience store I passed on Woodland Highway. I didn't see any cameras mounted outside the store. I called nine one one and spoke through my handkerchief. I told them a man had been hurt. I hadn't liked the way Booger looked.

By the time I had dropped the dogs at the shelter, gone to a do-it-yourself car wash and pressure washed the mud off Kiddo and my boots and my pants, and driven to Doctor Windsor's office, parked and made my way up the stairs to the waiting room, it was two forty-five. I was late. Too bad. Doctor Windsor would probably make a note about passive aggression. The aggression which had made me late was certainly not passive, but I had no intention of telling the doctor that.

I caught my reflection in the glass of a framed print hanging on the wall, tried to see what the psychiatrist would see: a middle-aged man, thin, a little over average height, thinning black and gray hair cropped short to obscure the incipient baldness, a little disheveled in damp cargo pants and long-sleeve tee, black and black as usual, like my mood. You never get a second chance to make a first impression.

I smiled at the receptionist when she slid open the little frosted window. She was a woman in her forties with short brown hair and brown eyes made larger by her oversized glasses with pink plastic frames. She didn't smile back, just asked, "Name?"

"Yes," I answered. Now that was passive aggression.

She looked up from her appointment book with her pen poised over it like the sword of Damocles and bestowed a look that told me that what they were doing in the office was very serious, and that she took it and herself very seriously. She opened her mouth to speak, but I interrupted her.

"Oh, my name, Travis Bowie. I have an appointment." I smiled again, but I wasn't even trying for sincerity. When I smile at people and they don't respond in kind, I usually get childish.

She looked down at her book again, "For two thirty."

"Yes," I stared at her until she dropped her eyes. I didn't care if she wondered if I was some psychotic liable to shoot her and everyone else.

"It's two forty-five," she tried to cover herself with her officious bitchiness, but kept studying her book.

I took an obvious look at my watch, "So it is. Would you like me to reschedule? Fine with me."

"No," she reached for a clipboard and handed it through the little sliding window which separated the waiting room from the inner sanctum where miracles were performed, "fill this out."

I took it and asked, "Shouldn't common office courtesy be, 'Could you please take a seat and fill out this useless questionnaire, Lieutenant Bowie,' followed by a smile?"

She slid the frosted window shut. I took a seat. The paperwork had to do with the confidentiality of doctor/patient communications as mandated by the HIPAA law, which I didn't believe for a second. Doctor Windsor would report to the department's insurance division any findings he made. Then there were all the biographical questions: height, weight, address, phone number, all the things they liked to collect and didn't need. Then the medical questions: medications, had I ever thought of killing myself, did I eat regularly, was I angry, and on and on. I answered more or less truthfully, with a bias toward making it appear that a visit to a psychiatrist was completely unnecessary in my case.

When I was finished, I tapped on the little frosted window. I could see the receptionist's shadow behind it. She let me wait a minute in revenge, but finally slid the panel open. I noted the severe scrub uniform she was wearing, no decorations on it. I always wondered why medical office people who had nothing to do with procedures which might get their clothes messy with body fluids and such affected scrubs. Some sort of status thing, I guessed, but in my case, I think she might have been hoping to assist with an emergency lobotomy. She took the clipboard back and started to close the window again, but then decided to leave it open.

"Could you take a seat, please?"

I smiled at her, "Sure." That's all I ask, a little civility. She probably left the window open to make sure I didn't steal something, like an out of date magazine.

I took a seat where I could watch the doors. Call it curiosity, call it watchfulness, call it paranoia, call it habit, but I had been glad to be able to see what was coming on Saturday night, at least the shooter part. The Andrea thing I wouldn't have seen coming no matter where I sat. And I figured a lot of people might want to kill their psychiatrist, in which case I didn't want to be collateral damage. The receptionist was on her own.

I nodded to the only other victim in the room, a thirty-something black man with close-cropped hair whom I recognized from the jail. He was an officer who had started hearing voices and imagining that after he left work, he ended up in some mythical town where dead people stalked the streets. He had been referred for counseling, or treatment. I for one was glad he didn't carry a gun, at least officially. If I knew about his problem, it proved my point about the leakiness of confidentiality. It was I who had been awakened in the middle of the night by a nervous supervisor who wanted advice on what to do with the officer who was wandering away from his duty station. I had advised that two officers, including a supervisor and at least one gun-carrying officer, take him to the nearest hospital emergency room and have him evaluated. I pretended not to recognize him, but he spoke.

"Hi, Lieutenant. I heard about your shootout. I've been having the same problem." He nodded slowly.

"Hi, Deputy Peters. I guess that's why we're both here." I smiled sickly at him. He nodded again, and I hoped we weren't going to have a conversation.

I took my phone off my belt to discourage further contact, and also because I remembered my phone ringing back at Booger's place just before everything got interesting, but in all my haste had forgotten it until now. There was another call too which I had missed after muting the sound after the Booger incident, when it no longer

60

mattered. I checked the numbers, but I didn't recognize either one of them. I routinely ignore phone calls from numbers I don't know, so I checked for voicemail. I stepped out into the corridor to listen to it. There was a message from what sounded like an hysterical old woman. She was berating me for something that had happened to Andrea. My heart jumped, with guilt, with dread. The other call was from Sal Baker.

I called the first number back. It was Ms. Esther, Andrea's mother. As soon as I identified myself, she started crying and screamed at me, "Travis, you did this. You police. She told me y'all broke up, and now she's in jail."

"Whoa, Ms. Esther, slow down, what are you talking about? I don't know anything about this."

"Yes, you did. You made up something about her and got her arrested to get even with her. How could you do that to her?"

"Ms. Esther, listen. I don't know about this, I swear. When did this happen?"

"This morning, while she was at work, in front of all the people she has worked with for twenty years."

"Why?"

"They say she stole something. They got her in New Orleans jail."

"Why New Orleans? She works in Jefferson Parish." This made no sense.

"I don't know, I just don't know," and she started sobbing again.

"Let me see what I can find out, Ms. Esther. I'll call you back."

She hung up on me. I returned to the waiting room, and waited some more. The chaos of the last couple days was threatening to overwhelm me. I could feel myself getting light-headed as I started to hyperventilate. I closed my eyes and did some deep breathing. I dabbled now and then with Buddhism and yoga practices, including meditation. I needed to calm down or the shrink wasn't going to sign off on my return to full duty. Or wait a minute. Maybe I should come clean with him, at least a little bit, and stay away until I could sort out the mess that was becoming my life. I even threw some silent mantras in with the deep breathing. Maybe I was a mess, but I didn't need to faint on the floor. The last thing I wanted was for the receptionist to come give me mouth-to-mouth. Assuming she would.

Deputy Peters was gone. He probably had my appointment, and I was being punished for being late. The bureaucracy strikes back. I took the time to get the number for the Orleans Parish Prison and called. I identified myself to a Deputy Williams who could have taught the receptionist some manners and asked my questions.

"Sure, Lieutenant., I can check that for you, but you know that information's online, right?

"I do, thanks, but I'm not near a computer right now."

"Hold on, please." The clicking of keystrokes followed in the background. While I waited, Ms. Personality slid the window open, frowned at me, and pointed to the NO CELL PHONE USAGE sign. I guessed the radio waves interfered with the psychiatric magic, so I stepped back into the hallway.

"Lieutenant?"

"Yes, ma'am."

"Okay, she's been booked into the Federal Wing on charges of criminal mishandling of hazardous material." I shook my head at the insanity of it.

"Thank you, Deputy, you've been very helpful. You take care."

"You too, sir."

I stood there with the phone in my hand, staring at it as some Amazon Basin lost tribesman might if he found it. Hazardous material? About the most hazardous thing Andrea handled were the large amounts of sugar she used for her candy creations which everyone was always demanding of her.

I recovered enough to return Sal's call. Since Andrea was in jail, I didn't share my theory of Andrea being the intended target of the shooting. For one thing, I figured he would assume, like most policemen, including myself, that if you were in jail, you probably belonged there, and secondly, I needed more information. I just asked him about an update on the shooter, which, if he had, he didn't share.

The receptionist's window slid open and then shut again, she seemed to be having trouble making up her mind. I guess she was confirming that I had come back from the corridor.

It was three forty when Deputy Peters came back through the waiting room and passed into the corridor without even glancing my way. The man creeped me out. Five minutes later, the receptionist opened the door to the consultation area and beckoned me through. She led me to an office with comfortable furniture and left me there. I didn't know whether to take a seat on the couch or in one of the stuffed chairs which were angled toward each other in front of the desk. Maybe it was a test, but I guessed I wasn't supposed to take the seat behind the desk. I chose one of the chairs in front and breathed some more.

Doctor Windsor wasn't what I expected. He was about five eight, two hundred pounds of what looked like muscle over a sturdy skeleton. His nose had been broken at least once, and he had a strong grip. No Freudian beard, clean-shaven, wearing a blue Oxford button-down shirt with a tie that had stripes of LSU purple and gold. Khakis and loafers, no tassels. His blond hair was a little long, but not so much that you'd think it was eccentric. The hair whorl which belonged at the back of his head was instead in front. It looked like he'd been scalped and then had it reattached backwards. I found it distracting.

"Lieutenant, good to meet you," he smiled as I stood and we shook hands.

"Well, Doctor, it was necessary to meet you." He gave me a half-grin and gestured for me to sit. He took the other chair so there was no barrier between us.

He opened a leather portfolio and unclipped a pen inside. It wasn't a Mont Blanc or a Waterman, just a regular one like you got at Wal-Mart.

"Do you mind if I call you Travis?"

"Sure, Doc, what's your given name?"

He remained expressionless, but asked, "Does that mean you don't want me to call you Travis?"

I was equally expressionless when I asked, "Does that mean you don't want me to call you by your first name?"

He laughed, "I don't mind at all. It's Andrew."

"Fine, I'm Travis."

"Are you angry, Travis? Is that how you're handling the incident Saturday evening?"

"Why would you ask that?"

Being a trained professional, he picked up that I was answering his questions with questions. He lowered his pen and stared at me, asked, "Are we going to dance like this for the next hour, or are you going to answer my questions?"

"I'm going to answer your questions, but I don't like this convention of answering my questions with a question. If I ask you a question, I want an answer, not just another question, okay?"

He leaned forward, laughed, said, "Fair enough. So tell me how you're dealing with this, or anything else."

"To start with, I'm sorry to tell you that your receptionist is a nasty woman, and she needs anger management or treatment for her Asperger's."

He actually stood up and walked around laughing, and burst out, "Wow, Travis, you're kind of forceful, aren't you?"

"It's probably not on the list of the first ten words I would use to describe myself."

"Would others describe you using that word?" He sat back down and was studying me like the subject I was.

I thought about a bit and nodded, "Probably."

He made a note, "I see that you take some medications. Why is that?"

"I take escitalopram because I'm depressed, probably my whole life. That's probably also why I tried to drink myself to death for about twenty-five years. I take celebrex because I have arthritis here, there and everywhere. It's mild, but it's there. I take Temazepam because I don't sleep well."

He made some more notes, "How long have you had trouble sleeping?"

"Since I stopped passing out from drinking every night, since my wife got sick, since she died, since the woman I started seeing told me she doesn't love me after all, since some asshole came into a nice restaurant with nice people and started killing them until he made me kill him." I stopped before I blurted out the story of Kiddo and Booger, but I was really angry about that too.

"So you are angry?"

"Mad as hell, Andrew."

"How is the sleep medication working?"

"Not very well at all."

"Do you ever think about taking the whole bottle?"

"No." I would shoot myself like a good cop, but I didn't tell him that either.

"Any flashbacks?"

"Of course. Does that make me crazy?"

"No, not at all. You're depressed, but you have good reason to be. You suffer from insomnia, probably because you're depressed. You understand what's happened to you, and why. You're not crazy. Do you ever cry?"

I looked at him eye to eye for a few seconds, took a breath, and answered, "No."

"Maybe you should."

"I'm not sure I know how. When my dog got killed by a car a few years ago, I was hysterical. A week after my wife died, and I went to tell her about something that happened during a Saints game, and she wasn't there, I bawled so bad it upset my dog. Not since then. I don't want to upset my dog again."

More notes, his pen gliding noiselessly, and he asked, "Are you closer to your dog than to people?"

"Yes."

"Do you think that's because it's safer for you?"

"Do you?"

He didn't answer, just moved on, "You were involved in some violence in North Louisiana a year ago, right? You were a hero."

"I was involved, yes."

"How do you feel about violence, Travis?"

"It exists."

"How do you feel about your involvement with it?"

"Sometimes it's necessary, and I seem to be pretty good at it."

"Does it make you proud? Or ashamed?"

"Neither. Necessary. I believe there's good violence, and bad violence."

"Can you give me an example?"

"Well, Saturday night was an example, the reason I'm here. Some evil son of bitch starts killing people, that's bad violence, and I used violence to stop him, that's good violence."

"So you believe in good and evil?"

"Sure."

"Are you religious?"

"I never know if that means you do or don't believe in God, or you do or don't believe in church."

"Do you believe in God?"

"I don't know."

"Would you hesitate to use violence again after the other night?"

I already knew the answer to that one, thanks to Booger. "No," I said.

"Okay, Travis, I'm going to change your meds. I think you've built up a tolerance to the ones you've been taking for a long time. I want to see you again, and I want you to stay on administrative leave. Not light duty, just leave. I want to see you again in a week. That work for you?"

"Why wouldn't I return to full duty like other guys when they've been in an OIS (officer-involved shooting)?"

He leaned forward in his chair as if sharing a confidence in a crowded room, said, "I did some checking on you before you came. Your chief has nothing but great things to say about you, but I get the impression you're kind of a workaholic. Am I right?"

I nodded, and shrugged.

He continued, "I don't want you repressing your experience by diving back into work just yet."

"So I should go to the beach and get in touch with my feelings?"

He laughed and said, "Something like that."

I nodded. As I got up, I noticed I was sweating. He noticed it too. I think he noticed the cuffs of my pants and boots were wet too. We shook hands again and I left.

"You didn't tell Bucky Windsor about the incident with your dog," the Sheriff said. It wasn't a question, so I didn't respond. Bucky? Really? So much for confidentiality.

"Well?" That was a question.

"It didn't come up, Sir." I fought the urge to fidget.

"You held back, as you did at every stage of this affair. Try, Lieutenant, not to hold back now."

"Yes, Sir."

XIII

I left Doctor Windsor's office confused and conflicted. I thought I probably did need a shrink, but not one who was going to report back to the Insurance Division. Maybe I needed a priest. Maybe I needed a nice cruise.

I checked my phone for messages when I turned the sound back on. Sal Baker had called again. I called him.

"Baker,"

"Sal, Travis. Did you figure out who the dirtbag was?"

"No ID, but prints come back to Janathan Kruger, that's JAN, not JON, rap sheet out of Tangipahoa Parish for batteries, assaults, burglary, no previous mass shootings."

"Not surprising. Something like that tends to be a one and done."

"Yeah, exactly," he laughed.

"Okay, thanks, Sal."

For some reason perhaps explainable by someone other than myself, I still did not tell Sal about Andrea being the target of the shooting. For one thing, it was entirely possible I was just wrong about that. For another, I wanted to know why a woman who in her fifties, a secretary who had never been arrested, was sitting in Federal detention. There are lots of coincidences in the world, contrary to what conspiracy buffs believe, but I found myself leaning toward connectedness. It just made more sense than coincidence. Decisions take us down roads we would never travel if we had chosen differently. Finally, I wanted to help Andrea. I was a fool. I didn't mind. That was what loving her had taught me. It was okay to be a fool sometimes.

There were two other calls on my phone from numbers I didn't know. Recorded messages from the Orleans Parish lockup instructing me to accept the collect call by agreeing to pay ten dollars for ten minutes. I would have if the calls had come in when the phone was on, but I had had it on vibrate only in the doctor's office, something I should have thought of back at Booger's.

I saved myself the ten dollars for the call by just driving over the new bridge, with the ostensibly peppy, but actually clunky, name Crescent City Connection. Some ten year-old had won the naming contest. I don't know what she won. I finally found a parking place in the area of Tulane and South White and walked to the jail. I found a public entrance and badged the deputy at the counter. She looked at the ID, compared my photo on the facing flap of the ID wallet with my face, decided she wasn't impressed, and asked, "Yes?"

"You have a prisoner by the name of Andrea Barrois?"

"Spell it." I did, slowly. Orleans Parish Sheriff's Office people were famously surly, and I wondered if this one had been the most congenial they could have found to be put on the public desk. Maybe she was, although the officer I'd spoken to earlier had been nice enough. As I waited, I studied the deputy. Forty or so, ebony skin, crisp starched greens, orange hair, inmate orange. I thought it should have been incarcerated.

"Yeah, she's here. Federal wing."

"I need to see her." I tried a smile, but it had no effect.

"I'll get someone to escort you. Lock up your weapon. No knives either."

Duh, I thought. I drew my Kimber and placed it in one of the lockers, along with my karambits and spare mags. I turned the key, removed it and put it in my pocket.

I waited several minutes until a sergeant exited an elevator. He had his hair skinned on the sides and a half-inch on top. His green fatigue uniform was starched and pressed too. He didn't smile, but his body language was polite. Police aren't the smiliest people. I was used to it.

"Lieutenant, could I see your ID again, please?"

"Sure," I handed it to him. He seemed satisfied with it and handed it back. He was a big man, mocha brown, with green eyes. I checked his name tag, Broussard. I wondered if he came from bayou country, where light-skinned blacks with green eyes were not uncommon. I considered how the reputation of OPP officers as lazy, brutal and corrupt contrasted with their always immaculate starched uniforms. I also thought about how my own jail's officers' uniforms were often sloppy, perhaps in protest at having been made to change from the standard departmental midnight blue to a lighter blue to further segregate them in a kind of cultural *apartheid* from the *real* police.

"Come with me, Sir." He noted my empty holster with satisfaction. I tagged along through corridors and into an elevator which took us up. At each door or gate that opened, both being jail police, we paused to let the other go first out of habit. Since it was his jail, he won, and walked slightly to the side and behind me, as a good escort officer should. It makes me crazy to see officers, whether jail officers or arresting officers, escort a prisoner while walking in front. In another corridor which looked like the other one on the lower floor, we waited for gates to open and then close again with the decisive clank of jail. Finally, we came to an interview room with three chairs and a scratched wooden table bolted to the floor.

"I'll have the inmate brought to you, Sir," he said, and then locked me in. It's something you get used to. Doors are supposed to be locked. I was used to it. I lived a third of my life in a jail.

Another thing about jail you get used to is waiting. It takes time to move people. A deputy who was free would have to be found and dispatched to the housing area, check Andrea out with the deputy on duty there, then escort her to the interview room, waiting along the way for someone to open one gate after another. I waited and thought about the bad feeling I was getting about the past couple of days. A lot had happened. I was starting to think a lot more was going to.

70

When Andrea arrived, escorted by a female deputy who was short and round, she was handcuffed behind her back. The deputy carried a large brass jail key she used to unlock the door. She gestured Andrea inside the room.

"Can you take the cuffs off?"

The deputy gave me a look, but unhooked Andrea and stowed the cuffs in her pouch. Then she locked us in, stepped back to the wall across from the room, and watched us through the window.

Andrea didn't look as sure of things as she had before. I wasn't gloating. Orange was not her color. I don't know whose it is unless you're a carrot. It gave her face a yellowish cast. If she stayed there very long, that would change. White people in jail tend to get very pale in a kind of ecru shade, black people tended to get gray, and I didn't mean their hair.

She darted a glance at me and then looked down. I could tell she was terrified. My heart broke.

"I can't give you a hug. The deputy will know it's personal and report it."

She shrugged, "It's okay, I don't want a hug anyway." My heart slammed. I did want a hug. Her hands and other parts had administered a lot of healing after Mae had died. It had been less Mae's death than her dying and her life of the past several years which had closed me off, walled me in. I was grateful to Andrea for waking me up, as I had been when Susan Hadley in North Louisiana had started the process a little more than a year before. The truth was, this healing was a lot more painful than not healing, like debriding dead flesh from a burn.

"Well," I said, then, "Tell me what happened." I leaned back to give her space.

She sat as tightly wound as an E string an octave too high, and kept her hands in her lap, maybe to hide them from the cuffs. More than the table separated us. She took a breath. There was that look of confusion common even to career criminals once they were behind the walls.

"I don't know what happened. How could this happen? All the isotopes are gone." Tears ran down the sides of her nose in sad little distributaries.

"Isotopes?"

"Isotopes for the X ray cameras, the ones the techs use out in the field. They're kept in the vault."

"How many people have access?" I asked, still with that bad feeling.

"Five of us. The president of the company, the General Office manager, Sally, she's out with surgery, my boss Larry, and me. But my name is on all the sign-out sheets, and they're all gone, the isotopes."

I learned more than I ever knew about gamma emitters and X-ray cameras than I'd ever wanted to know in the next half-hour. She told me that the switch which controlled the camera on the door and interior of the vault had been turned off at the server. That told me that perhaps someone who was not authorized to enter the vault might have gotten the combination and entered.

"Why isn't Larry in jail too? Or the executives? Why just you?"

"Because it's just my name on the logs, and Larry's been on vacation in Costa Rica."

"Isn't your name supposed to be on the logs?"

"Yes, but…"

"Did the Feds mention any other evidence against you?"

"Just my fingerprints."

"Again, is there any reason your prints would not be on the vault?"

"No, but nobody else's are."

I nodded, partly to myself. A piece of the riddle fell into place. It made more sense of my theory that Andrea had been targeted at Vincenzo's. If she had been killed, and then the theft of the isotopes was discovered, she would have been the perfect suspect, and the trail would die there along with her, at least according to the theory of the plan. If there were such a plan.

"How often do you issue the isotopes?"

"It depends, whenever they're needed."

"How was the disappearance discovered?"

"I found it and reported it. Grant, the manager, called the FBI and the ATF."

Oops. Andrea not getting killed on Saturday or kidnapped that morning messed up the timetable. What that meant I had no idea. It did make me wonder why today of all days my dog was taken. I know coincidences happen, there's chaos loose in the world, but I was suspicious.

"When do you go to court? For your hearing?"

"The FBI agent told me tomorrow morning. I'm going to tell them I'm not guilty of anything."

"That's the only thing you are going to be able to say, Andrea. It's a magistrate hearing. He, or she, will take your plea, but only if it's not guilty. A magistrate can't take a felony plea of guilty, and believe me, this is one big felony. They'll set bail."

"How am I supposed to afford a lawyer? How am I going to get money for bail?" She wrung her hands in her lap, as she stared off in the distance at a nightmare future. She continued, "My Mom is on Social Security. She can't help me. My sister spends all her money."

"Let's leave them out of it for the moment, but call your mother. I'll be in court tomorrow."

"Why would you? We broke up."

"Not exactly. You broke up. I was just standing in front of the train. You did call me, I'm glad you did." My voice sounded to me like it was coming out of a well.

I stood. She started to stand as well, but I motioned for her to stay seated.

"Better to wait for the officer to tell you to get up. You're not free anymore, Andrea. Don't discuss the case with anyone, and I mean anyone. You have no friends here. Be polite, don't get into arguments, don't argue with the officers, even if they're rude to you."

Now she was sobbing. She had held it together for as long as she could, but she had run out of resources. I wanted so badly to hold her and tell her it was going to be all right, but I could not touch her, and I had no idea whether it was going to be all right at all.

"And don't cry. Really, don't let them see you're vulnerable, Andrea. I'll do everything I can."

"Thank you, Travis. You've always been so kind to me. But…"

"Yeah, I get it. It wasn't enough." I knocked on the door. The officer watching through the glass window in the door unlocked, let me out, locked Andrea in, and led me back through the maze of corridors to the sunlight. I didn't feel free at all.

XIV

When I was back in *that world,* as inmates call free air, I checked my phone messages. There was one from Sonora, just saying call her. I did.

"Travis," she launched without a hello, as she usually did, not wasting any time or breath, "Eddie got shanked in PC. He's at the hospital."

"How bad?" I guess he did have enemies.

"Not too bad. Guy used a toothbrush he had all sharpened up. Stuck him a few times in the hands and arms, one in the chest. Not too deep. But when he got to the hospital, they found tumors hanging out his ass. It don't look good."

"Who did it?"

"We charged this white guy, just came in on burglary, said he was scared, we put him on Admin. He's got a short rap sheet, little stuff, but he has Nazi ink and a Confederate flag. That by itself would have put him on Admin. He wasn't going to do well in General Pop."

"You think maybe he jumped Eddie just to make sure he stayed out of GP?"

"Don't know. He's not talking. Denied it, but the black inmates ratted him out. Even gave statements. Hey, they like Eddie, like everybody else, and they don't like skinheads." It was a mystery how Eddie could navigate the jail environment. He worked for us as a snitch, but it never seemed to stick to him with the other inmates.

"Okay, I'll go see him, see if he's more in a mood to tell us what's going on."

"You gonna' get yourself in trouble. You're on leave, remember?"

"We'll see. I mean, I'm going to get in trouble for doing the job?"

"You know, with some folks, rules are more important."

"Okay, Sonora, thank you."

I wasn't even a mile from University Hospital, which was where we took inmates for treatment beyond the capacity of the jail medical staff to handle ever since Hurricane Katrina had destroyed Charity Hospital, Huey Long's legacy monument, or one of them, which had towered over the city as the largest hospital in the state. It still towered, but as a gutted hulk like something out of a Gothic novel. I decided to pay Eddie a visit.

I was still driving my personal vehicle, since I was on administrative leave, instead of my marked unit, so when I parked in a NO PARKING spot, I tossed a placard with the Sheriff's Office shield onto the dashboard, and walked inside. I badged the clerk at the Information Desk and nodded to the hospital police officer. Hospital police were useless and invisible when shit hit the fan between our inmates and our officers. They didn't like us, partly because we weren't from New Orleans. We were from another parish. Louisiana is very tribal, down to which side of the River you live on, which neighborhood, which family, which school you graduated from or dropped out of. The clerk gave me the room number and I took an elevator.

Eddie looked smaller in the bed, as people tend to. His face was gray against the white of the bed sheets. Deputy Cline was seated in a corner chair where he could watch Eddie and the door, and still play Angry Birds or whatever on his phone. I stood in the doorway and motioned him to the corridor.

He was in his early twenties, putting in his time at the jail and awaiting his chance to go to the road. He already had the totems, the spiky highlighted blond hair, the swollen arms which came from lots of bench presses and curls, but had nothing whatsoever to do with handling people when they needed to be handled, but looked impressive, which might be enough in most situations.

"What's up, Lou?"

"Hey, Bennie, how you doing? Look, I need to talk to Eddie a minute. Has he said anything?"

Bennie shrugged, said, "He's been pretty quiet. I heard the doctor talking to him about the tumor hanging out his ass like a bunch of grapes. Didn't sound like it was much of a future they were discussing."

I nodded, "Look, call me if he says anything about some score he's been working or people he was with, okay?" He nodded along with me as I continued, "He got arrested to be safe from whatever he stirred up out on the street, and he was afraid it would follow him inside, and I guess it did. You need to be careful and keep an eye out. I don't know if they might try to reach him here, but it's a whole lot easier for them here with just one officer."

Bennie had a gleam in his eye at the prospect of action. Of course he did. He was, what, twenty-three years old, and in his mind, not five seven but ten feet tall and bulletproof. I just hoped he didn't have to test his illusions on his own just yet. He said, "Sure, no problem, Lou." I patted him on his barbed-wire-ringed biceps and entered the room.

"Hi, Lieutenant," Eddie said weakly, "Thanks for coming to see me."

"What the fuck, Eddie? You stirred up some yellow jackets this time, looks like. Want to tell me something?" I stood at the foot of the bed so he wouldn't have to turn his head to see me. One shackle was hooked to the bed rail and the chain led to the other one, on Eddie's ankle.

"They're gonna' do surgery on me, Lieutenant, cut this thing offa' me. Look here," he flipped his sheet over to expose his nether region, with his penis, testicles, and a growth hanging from his rectal area like a fist of shriveled brown grapes."

"Jesus, Eddie, don't show me that, you're going to make me puke or pass out. The hell is that, anyway? And cover yourself up."

He flipped the sheet back over him and said, "I'm going to sue somebody. They shoulda' caught this before it got this bad."

"Did you tell anybody about it the last fifty eleven times you were in jail? Did you take your HIV meds when you were on the street?"

"They shoulda' found it, Lieutenant."

"Okay, you're going to get rich from suing the jail, the hospital, the Sheriff's Office. And hey, you're going to be rich from whatever career con plan you got going, if you don't get a toothbrush stuck in your eye."

"I need money to get away, Lieutenant, get paid treatment, like in Houston, you know, the cancer clinic there."

"You're going to need a whole lot of cash for that, Eddie."

"I know, Lieutenant, that's what I'm saying." He held both arms out to his sides as if he were being crucified on his own brilliance.

"Let me indulge in some Eddie-think here. You make your play, get paid, then give us your friends to get a deal, get out, get treatment, get a settlement for medical malpractice and live happily ever after?"

He looked insulted, "No, Lieutenant, not my friends. I give you the real bad guys."

"Oh, my mistake. So you're not going to give me anything."

"Not yet, Lieutenant. I need to work this."

"I'm not going to help you commit a crime, Eddie, and I'm not going to be grateful if you do it anyway."

"Oh, you're going to be grateful, Lieutenant. Really." He had tucked his arms back around himself as if he were cold.

I turned to leave and said over my shoulder, "Don't wait too long. You have a time bomb up your ass."

As I passed Deputy Cline, I said, "Be careful."

Back on the street, there was a parking ticket flapping under my windshield wiper. That didn't bother me as much as the tow truck which had hooked up to my rear bumper. The driver was just lifting it when I yelled, "Hey!"

He turned to look and then went back to his winch control. He was used to this, probably. I walked around to hold my ID inches from his face.

"I'm a police officer."

He shrugged, "I've got a tow order. Doesn't matter."

"Really?"

"Yeah, really."

"Turn around and put your hands behind your back."

"Really?"

"Really."

"Bullshit."

"Oh. good, resisting. Another charge to go with interfering with a police officer in the performance of his duty. And I might get hurt and need treatment after overcoming your resistance. Another charge, a felony. It gets better and better."

He pulled the winch control the other way and my truck lowered to the ground. While he was disengaging the tow hooks, I considered the facts that I wasn't officially on duty, was out of my jurisdiction, and didn't have arrest powers in New Orleans, and that he didn't need to know any of that.

The driver stowed his gear, gave me a dirty look, and started back to his cab.

"Hey, Bud," I held out a ten dollar bill, "for your trouble." He took it and stuffed it in his shirt pocket. He laughed and waved. He'd made more not towing me than if he had, since he worked for the city and wasn't getting paid by the tow. At least he got lunch out of the deal.

XV

It had been a very long day and I was exhausted. I drove home, sat in a chair at the table in the den, stared at the vodka bottle for a while, drew some strength from not opening it. As I passed the bookcase converted to a shrine to Mae, with her *raku* urn, the framed photo, the wilted flowers, I remembered I had left the fresh bouquet in my truck. The flowers which had started the whole existential meander which had led to Booger, and more to come.

I went back out to the truck and retrieved the fresh flowers. I brought them back inside and changed them out in the vase with fresh water. I had originally bought the vodka after reading it made a good preservative for flowers, but I had never broken the seal. It had since become a test and an affirmation.

My phone rang. "Hello." It wasn't a number in Contacts or one I recognized.

"Travis Bowie?"

"Yes."

"This is Detective Cossich, Plaquemines Parish Sheriff's Office."

"Okay, what can I do for you?" I regularly got requests for assistance from other departments for information about inmates in our jail, so I wasn't particularly alarmed.

"You were down here today asking around about Clyde Cossich." It wasn't a question.

"Sorry, don't know him."

"He goes by Booger."

Uh-oh. Not good, not good at all. Same last name too. They were sure to be related.

"What can I do for you, Detective?"

"Could you come down to Belle Chasse and talk to me?"

"Now?"

"Yessir."

"Not now. It's been a long day, and I have to be in Federal Court in the morning. I can make it tomorrow afternoon."

"I really have to insist, Mister Bowie."

"Detective, I'm Lieutenant, not Mister Bowie, and we both know your insistence has no force of law. I'll be there tomorrow afternoon, is fourteen hundred good for you?"

He wasn't happy, but he managed to stay civil. The day was at an end, and it had just gotten longer. Well. I thought. If he had something to arrest me on, he would have just done it. So he was fishing. I had certainly left an evidentiary trail. I had had Booger's license plate run, actually the old man's. The traffic camera query. Asking for Booger at The Clove Hitch. My vehicle in the vicinity of Booger's place. Dropping the dogs at the shelter. Witnesses? And to make it even more worrisome, Booger's last name turned out to be Cossich, the same as the detective's. Cousin? Brother?

Plaquemines Parish had been settled partly by Spanish subjects during Louisiana's brief interlude as a colony of Imperial Spain, and later by Croatian fishermen, and by mixed-race Creoles who were partly black, Indian (feather, not dot), and who knew what else. With a population of only about 25,000, it was a relatively small gene pool. If Booger and Detective Cossich had the same last name, they were related somehow.

I was juggling too many balls. I didn't have the appetite for chaos I had once had. Andrea dumps me. I shoot a would-be mass killer. Someone tries to snatch her. Andrea gets arrested. Someone steals Kiddo. I rescue Kiddo and beat a guy down. Eddie's got a secret he won't share because it might interfere with his get rich quick scheme. Someone shanks Eddie. Were they random or connected? I can admit to coincidence, but…

I went to bed, sitting up against a back pillow and turned these things over in my mind until I finally fell asleep. Just as I drifted off, I remembered I hadn't fed Kiddo. I felt bad about it, but I didn't get back up.

XVI

I woke up early, at six, which was unusual, but then, I don't usually fall asleep as early either. I fed Kiddo, who didn't seem to bear a grudge. She was hungry and there was no food. Now there was food. Problem solved. I wished I were a dog.

I showered and shaved the guy in the mirror. As I did, I saw a middle-aged man, with what hair he had left turning gray, lean face with a little droopiness under the chin. Not a bad face, but the kind which makes people ask, "Don't I know you from somewhere?" The eyes were pretty sharp behind the glasses. I was always surprised when I saw myself on a video feed, because that guy looked older than this guy.

I dressed respectably, gray slacks, blue dress shirt and a black blazer, with black leather shoes. I let Kiddo out for a few minutes and then headed downtown to the Federal Courthouse at Camp and Poydras in New Orleans. I left almost everything metal but my belt buckle in the truck to minimize delay at the metal detector. Of course, no guns or knives allowed, even by law enforcement. If someone started shooting up the place, I guess I'd try to grab a stapler.

My wallet and watch glided along the rollers to the X-Ray box as I stepped through the metal detector portal. It was all civilized and polite. The checkpoint, manned by unarmed retired law enforcement officers, was nothing but a tripwire speed bump type of security. Anyone assaulting the courthouse could blow by these men and women in nothing flat, but I suspected that after that the going would get tough, with elevators shut down and stair doors locked at each floor. I wasn't thinking of breaking Andrea out of the place, merely musing as I had waited my turn at the metal detector.

82

Security systems were my business, after all. Not the electronics of the system, but the infrastructural, human and operational structures that make a jail secure.

I studied the wall directory and found the floor where the magistrates held court. Then I took an elevator. I already knew from previous experience that taking the stairs was not an option. Once in the stairwell, you were channeled to the first floor exit only, every other door locking behind you.

There was an information office on the floor, staffed with three women, one sitting at the counter. She was mid-thirties, dark hair, dark rimmed glasses, pretty standard issue bureaucrat, but polite in a way that said she would help you right up to the limit of her professional responsibilities and not a millimeter more. She smiled. I asked for the docket sheet and she passed it to me, where I found Andrea's name and the section she would appear in. The carpeted hall with its oak paneled walls and doors led to a small courtroom.

I took a seat in the second row behind the rail. My heart was beating fast and the pulse in my throat pounded. I could imagine the fear that Andrea must be going through, caught up in a system I served every day, albeit on the state side, not Federal usually.

At 0900 Andrea was led in by herself by a female marshal wearing the standard navy blue blazer and gray slacks, white shirt, dark tie. Andrea was dressed in the orange jumpsuit which reflected the fluorescent light onto her face and made her look older. She had scrubbed off most of her makeup from the day before. She looked like a jack-o-lantern. She cast her eyes at me as the marshal led her to the row of jury seats. There would be no jury here. This was just a first appearance for charges and bond. Then she looked down. She was shackled at her ankles and cuffed to a belt which kept her hands at her sides.

The prosecutor, a woman with severe red hair and a no-nonsense gray skirt suit consulted her papers from a stack in front of her. The public defender, a skinny fellow in a dark suit, who looked like he didn't eat enough or ran too much, studied his own folders. A daisy chain of three male prisoners entered from a side entrance and were escorted by a male marshal with gray hair to seats a respectable distance from the female, Andrea, to minimize fraternization.

I was well acquainted with the industrial aspect of the justice system, how it made nobodies out of somebodies, grinding them fine. In general, I had no problem with it, as I served it myself with no qualms of conscience, but I had always admitted to the possibility of an innocent being caught in the gears, and the horror that must be.

I watched Andrea. Her eyes darted around like those of a small wild animal caught in a trap. When they lighted on me briefly from time to time, I could feel her shame but no gratitude. She was trying to decide which leg to gnaw off to get out of here. The Feds were sure to give her that opportunity, at least the part about her leg, and offering the merest of hope in exchange .

As the magistrate swept in with a swirl of black robe, we all stood at the bailiff's command. He announced that the Honorable Susan Cohen was presiding. We all sat down again. The clerk at Judge Cohen's left below her lofty perch announced the docket. Andrea was first. It allowed the court to dispose of her case and, as the only female, get her back out of there without prolonged proximity to the males.

The prosecutor read the charges in shorthand: 18 U.S. Code 831, possession, misappropriation of hazardous materials, controlled radioactive materials, conspiracy, etc.

The defender, reading from notes he had obviously taken a few minutes before when he had first laid eyes on Andrea, described her accurately as a twenty year employee with a spotless work and criminal record, with community ties and a lifelong resident, a mother and grandmother. Judge Cohen gave herself a long look at Andrea, tethered like a goat, and asked for a plea. "Not guilty," Andrea managed to say. The judge then asked for recommendations related to bond. The Assistant U.S.. Attorney asked for remand. The defender asked for release on recognizance. The judge settled in the middle with a bond of one hundred thousand. I breathed a sigh of relief. That much I could do. Andrea, not understanding any of what was going on, was led away. I slipped out of the courtroom, and noticed a buttoned-down white man about forty, with close-cropped dark hair graying at the temples, sitting in the back row. He watched me with obvious interest as I left. He reeked Fed.

FBI Special Agent Carl Lewis, as he turned out to be, followed me into the corridor, and called after me, "Excuse me, Sir." As I stopped and turned to him, he continued, "Is it all right to speak with you a moment?"

"Sure," I said. I didn't want to talk to him particularly, but I also didn't want him hounding me, wire-tapping me, and otherwise wasting his time on me when he could be finding who really had stolen the isotopes in Andrea's care. He would probably do it anyway.

"Special Agent Carl Lewis, FBI," He identified himself. No offer of a handshake, but a quick flash of his ID.

"Lieutenant Travis Bowie, Sheriff's Office." I even pulled out my ID and showed him.

That seemed to surprise him a little, "Do you know Ms. Barrois?" He even knew how to pronounce it, *Bear-Wah.* Either he was a local or had done his homework.

I decided to take some control over this process and took a seat on a bench to signal cooperation. He stood for a minute so that he loomed over me, then evidently remembered his training about bonding with the subject, and took a seat himself.

"Yes, I do. Until Saturday night, we were going together."

He nodded, asked, "What happened Saturday night?"

"Someone tried to kill us in a restaurant in Metairie. It's in the news."

A piece in his puzzle fell into place, but not necessarily the same puzzle I was working. I wanted him thinking though.

"Oh, yeah. You were there?" I nodded in reply.

"You can check the news and get the police report."

"Were you the officer who took down the shooter?"

"I was."

"So you don't work with the lady?"

"No, and I don't know anything about any missing material either, but this lady's being framed. You should check into it."

"You would say that, of course."

"I might, I guess, but I'm trying to be objective here."

"Why did you two break up? The shooting get to her?"

"No, it was before, and that falls under none of your business."

He made an *okay* face. Cops don't get their feelings hurt easily. He shrugged for good measure.

"If you broke up, why are you here?"

"She broke up with me. I didn't break up with her. I'm here to bail her out."

He did the cop stare, and then stood. "Well, thanks for your time, Lieutenant. Maybe we can talk again."

"If I can help, I will, as long as you stay friendly. If not, not."

Feds didn't trust locals, locals didn't trust Feds, even though we worked together all the time. He watched me walk away. I had no doubt he'd be getting a work-up on me as soon as I was out of sight. He would find out about the terrorist incident in North Louisiana a year before, which involved, what else, radioactive material. I just knew he was going to put two and two together and get pi squared. He already had a suspect in hand, and he wouldn't let her go that easily. That would have meant he had made a mistake, and mistakes were not career-enhancing. I thought, why should I have radioactive materials in my life again? I knew next to nothing about them, but I was sure I was about to learn more than I wanted to.

I made my way to the Clerk's Office and pulled the deed to my house out of my jacket pocket. I handed it to the lady in her fifties with hair frosted to match her horn-rim eyeglass frames. I wondered which she had chosen first. I told her I wanted to bail out Andrea. She took the deed and went off to check the property value.

It only took two hours of waiting and signing to get it done. I then made my way back to the Orleans lock-up to wait some more. I took a seat on a bench which got harder as time wore on. Next to me was a woman in her forties, sporting tattoos including the obligatory *RIP* for someone who wouldn't need to get out of jail anymore. Several unruly children, a couple of whom were old enough to be in school instead of running around a jail lobby, I tagged as FCAs, Future Criminals of America. It was almost noon when Andrea emerged from the double door man-trap into the lobby. She blinked when she saw me, but I don't think it was from the bright light. They had lights inside the jail, but free light and air is somewhat disconcerting after a spell inside.

She walked to me. I kissed her on her cheek, but she didn't respond, other than to ask, "Is it over?"

"No, babe, not even close. You're just out on bail."

"Please don't call me that, Travis. Please. I just want to go home."

"Okay, and you're fucking welcome for bailing you out." I didn't raise my voice, but the tone cut into her, and she flinched.

I think she was about to say something independent about not asking me to, but she was beaten down and settled for, "Thank you, Travis. I am grateful." There was a *but* hanging loose there. She was wearing the same clothes she had been arrested in; they were wrinkled. Her always-perfect nail polish was chipped, and I wondered what the story of that was. I didn't ask. She smelled like jail, that odor of too many people in too small a space, with too few toilets and showers.

"Let's get you out of here, get you some clothes and a shower, and you can stay at my place." I took her hand and she didn't resist. She didn't respond either. I didn't take it personally. Who am I kidding?

We got my truck out of the parking lot across Tulane Avenue and drove to Andrea's apartment in Gretna. Andrea stared out the window as if seeing everything anew, the trees and cars and people walking around, all things she stood to lose, forever.

At her place, she immediately kicked off her shoes and made for the shower. I sat on the couch and listened to the water running behind the closed door. When she emerged, she was wearing a white terry cloth robe. Her hair was wet. She was barefoot. She looked lovely and sad and scared.

I patted the sofa and said, "Sit, Andrea, we need to talk."

She sat, curled her legs up beneath her in that endearing way women have, and let the tears roll down her face without even trying to stop them or wipe them away. She kept her hands in her lap. I left them there. This was no time for mixed signals.

"You do know you've been set up, right?"

She turned to me, her hazel eyes brimming, and asked, "Why? I've never done anything to hurt anyone." I could think of one right here on the couch, but I let it slide.

"It doesn't matter, you're convenient. If you had been killed Saturday night, or disappeared yesterday morning, you would have been perfect to pin this theft on, and a dead-end for the Feds looking for whoever did do this. Get it?" Finally, she nodded.

"You're not safe here. They're going to come back, and they're going to keep coming back. You need to pack some things and come with me."

"Where?"

"To my house, for the time being."

She shook her head, "No, I can go to my mother's, or my sister's, stay there."

"You don't think they'll come there? Let me guess, they're on your personnel contacts in case of emergency." She nodded.

"You want to put them in danger too? Do you?"

"Why are you doing this for me, Travis?"

"You really have to ask? I would have thought it was obvious." It made me wonder for a moment, though, why am I doing this? Love? The need to be a white knight? Cussedness?

****

Andrea tossed some clothes and women things in a tote bag, moving as if it were an Ambien sleepwalking event, and we left. As I drove, taking a circuitous route, with U-turns thrown in, and constantly checking the rear-view mirror, I quizzed her some more.

"Do you know if the FBI picked up anybody else?" I had to ask her twice.

"No, I don't think so. Larry's on vacation."

Larry was the supervisor of her section, and her boss.

"How long has he been gone?"

"He left last week. I made his travel arrangements."

"Had there been any activity in the vault last week?"

"No, the materials had been issued week before last for the camera operators. I just found the logs on Larry's desk and was putting them back when I found the shelves bare and reported it. I also had to check the dosimeters to get the old ones back and issue new ones for the month."

"Should they have been on Larry's desk?"

"No, but he forgets sometimes. He's always out sick, complaining, thinking about himself rather than the job."

"What kind of radioactive material was kept in the vault?"

"We had iridium, cesium, and cobalt isotopes."

"Did Larry have this trip planned for a long time or did it come up suddenly?"

"He said he got a last minute deal and asked me to confirm his hotel and flight." She was looking at me hard now and things were clicking behind her eyes besides her misery, "Are you saying…?"

"I'm asking questions. Someone took the isotopes, and I'm going on the assumption it wasn't you. Therefore, it had to be someone else with access. Larry had access. He takes a trip."

"All he ever talks about is retirement. He's lazy."

"Where did he go?"

"Costa Rica."

"Where?"

"Montezuma, at the hotel Casa del Sur, if I'm saying it right."

"Close enough."

By then, I was satisfied we weren't being tailed, so I drove home. Andrea clutched her tote bag between her arm and her side as we approached the house. Inside, I showed her the bedroom. She looked around for a way out.

"I don't want to sleep with you, Travis. I'm sorry."

"Don't worry. I won't be here." I had made up my mind. I was on my way to Costa Rica, but first I had an appointment with Detective Cossich.

"So you go visit an inmate friend, this Eddie character, who's costing us a gonad in medical expenses, bail out a suspect, take off for Costa Rica on your own authority, and stir up a cat rodeo in another country?" It was Capacolla, the short mean bookend, speaking, wanting to hammer in a nail or two himself.

I took a Buddha breath or two to stop myself from vaulting out of my chair and slapping him 'til he cried. While I was breathing, the Sheriff turned his head sharply in Capacolla's direction for a moment, and then fixed his gaze back on me.

I got my revenge by ignoring the little creep and asking the Sheriff, "Should I continue?"

The Sheriff punished him by just nodding at me.

XVII

I made it to my appointment with minutes to spare. I found the Plaquemines Parish Sheriff's Office building off LA. 23 in Belle Chasse and went inside to ask for Detective Cossich.

"Name?" The twenty-something brunette with too many ear piercings asked, and didn't care if I knew how bored she was.

"Yes," I replied. Her pen poised to process, then she looked up. I smiled. I know, I was wearing out the joke.

"Lieutenant Bowie," I said. She wrote it down and picked up the phone. She sent me upstairs, where Detective Cossich was waiting at the elevator. He was medium height, but thick,, like a fire hydrant. I think it was professional courtesy only that made him stick out his hand. His eyes met mine and held. So it was going to be like that.

Even worse, he didn't lead me to his desk, but to an interview room. So this was hostile. I had my story ready. He would have to prove otherwise. He motioned me to sit. He tossed the folder he had been carrying under his arm onto the table between us so that I could wonder about it and maybe confess to the Lindbergh kidnapping or something. If he thought I was going to admit kicking the shit of some dog-fighting, dog-stealing lowlife, he was going to have a long wait.

He tried the stare, until I said, "Detective, you obviously have something to discuss with me, and the suspense is just killing me." I thought I knew his type, fix a conclusion in his mind, find a suspect who fits and bully them into confessing.

"Do you know Clyde Cossich?"

"Never met him," I shrugged.

"Maybe you knew him as Booger."

"I would have remembered a stupid name like that. Kin of yours? "

He actually smiled at that, or maybe he had a cramp, "Cousin. Not our proudest moment."

"We all have relatives we'd rather not."

"You were asking around about him, but you didn't know him?"

Getting caught in a lie is the best way to get a policeman stuck to you like gum on your shoe, so I said, "I was. My dog went missing. Cameras picked her up in your cousin's truck. I traced him, but I never spoke to him. When I got to his place, my dog and these other two were running loose out on the highway. I picked them up and took the other two to PAWS."

"He's dead. My cousin, he was a bad man, bred fighting dogs, trained 'em, fought 'em. Likely stole your dog. Probably pissed you off."

"Whoa, are you saying someone killed him, or that he dropped dead and you're trying to find out who saw him last?"

"Oh, someone killed him, all right. Stomped his throat in for him."

I had not stomped him in the throat. I had stomped his face. Someone else had finished him off. I doubted Detective Cossich would be interested in the distinction. I sat, I thought, while he watched me think.

"I notice you haven't read me my rights."

"We're just talking here." Translation: the longer he could avoid advising me of my rights, the longer he could pretend he was just on a fact-finding mission and not treating me as a suspect, which gave him more latitude. It was supposed to make the subject, that would be me, less guarded. Right.

"I didn't see anyone else in the area when I was there. When did this happen?"

"Late yesterday morning, early afternoon." He let it hang, giving me an opportunity to blurt something out. I didn't take it. I could tell it annoyed him.

"You have anything to say about that?"

"I was waiting for a question. I already told you what happened."

"I'm going to take your statement."

"You mean if I decide to give you one."

"Any reason you wouldn't?"

"None at all," I smiled, "except you didn't phrase it in the form of a question. You know, a request?"

"You're kind of a smart-ass, aren't you?"

"All my life, Detective. And don't think I don't know that I make a convenient suspect for you. Sorry, you're going to have to find whoever really did this, instead of just closing the case and moving on to the next one. You said your cousin, the late, lamented Booger, was a bad man. Probably means he had bad friends, maybe even enemies, which means your list needs to be a lot longer."

"You telling me how to do my job?"

"No, we're just talking, remember? Just two colleagues discussing a case."

"Would you consent to a statement, *Sir*?"

"Of course."

"How about a polygraph?"

"Not a chance."

"Why not?"

"Would you?"

"Of course, if it would clear me."

I smiled at him with a gotcha' face, "I thought we were just talking. What would I need to cleared of?"

He took my statement, recorded, and this time he did read me my rights. When I left, we didn't shake hands.

XVIII

Detective Cossich had instructed me to be available for further contact, but I ignored him. I left his office knowing he wasn't going to shift his focus to anyone else unless I gave him a reason to, and now I was going to give him a reason not to. I went home to arrange my jaunt to Costa Rica, which he would interpret as making a run, if he found out about it.

Andrea was sitting on the couch, all the way at one end, while one of the cats, a ten year-old female who dominated everything in the house, sat on the other end of the couch and stared at Andrea without blinking her yellow eyes.

I asked her, "How are you doing?"

"Your cat won't stop staring at me," she gestured in the general direction of the tortoise-shell Toby, who swatted half-heartedly at Andrea's hand, missing by a couple of feet. Andrea withdrew her hand quickly and crossed her arms.

"She's trying to figure you out, and trying to intimidate you. She's smaller than you, don't let her."

"I don't know if I can take this, Travis."

I took a seat between Andrea and Toby and reached for her hand. She let me take it in both of mine. She turned to face me and smiled, but her eyes were glistening.

"How did my life just fall apart in a couple days, Travis? I haven't done anything wrong. I've always followed the rules."

"Sometimes it doesn't matter. You do everything right and bad things happen anyway," I shrugged, then continued, "You know I'm trying to help you, right?"

She looked down at her lap, said, "I know, I know. I feel so bad, I'm so scared."

"You should be scared right now. You have every reason to be. Being scared will help keep you alive until this thing sorts itself out, or we sort it out. You also need to get mad, so you can help fight

94

this. What you cannot do is ignore the warning signs. Someone you work with stole those isotopes. The questions are who and why. What are they used for? How do they work?"

"They're gamma ray emitters. They come in small sealed pellets, and they send out gamma rays to penetrate weld sections of pipe and the rays are caught on film or a sensor on the opposite side."

"Why would someone steal them?" I was half thinking out loud and not really expecting an answer, but Andrea answered anyway.

"We get bulletins warning that the materials can cause radiation sickness, burns, could cause cancer. That's why we have the dosimeters to measure the exposure the operators get. That's why we have to change out the dosimeters every month and log them, and issue new ones."

"And you do that?"

"Yes." She was looking at her chipped nail polish, and I could tell it really bothered her, since it was always perfect. It made her feel less, feminine.

"What about the isotopes? Do you issue them?"

"Not usually, but I did last week because Larry asked me to. He said he had a doctor's appointment."

"And then he went on vacation."

"Yes. Oh,"

"Yes, oh, he set you up. After you issued the isotopes, and put your name on the logs as the last one in the vault, someone, I'm guessing Larry, went in and stole them."

"What am I going to do?"

"You're going to hunker down. I'm going to Costa Rica."

"But…"

"I'm going to see if he can lead me to whoever put him up to this. If he decided to do this, there's money in it, which means there's money behind it. Larry doesn't strike me as someone who can tough it out, or he wouldn't have taken off in the first place.

He'll fold, and we can work backwards, or give the Feds something to run with."

"And I have to stay here?"

"Only if you want to stay alive."

I got up from the couch and grabbed the laptop off the desk across the living room. I pulled up flight information on the net. From what Andrea had told me, she had booked Larry into the Hotel Casa del Sur in the Puntarenas province. The closest airport would be the Daniel Oduber Airport in Liberia, but there weren't any flights until the next day, Wednesday. So I opted for the flight out that night to San Jose, which meant I would need a car when I got there. I booked online, including a car. I didn't get a hotel, since I wasn't planning on staying long.

Andrea had been sitting on the couch, staring at the television which was at low volume. The early news was on. I wasn't paying it any attention until I heard Andrea gasp. I turned to her to see what the matter was. She had her hand to her mouth and was staring at the screen. There was her picture and a caption with her name. I walked over and took the remote from her lap. I turned the television off. She looked up at me.

"It's not going to do you any good hearing things that you know aren't true. Look, let's go get your nails fixed."

"You really are too good to me, Travis." She smiled, but there was no joy in it.

I sat next to her, and said, "We never got to finish our discussion the other night. What changed?"

She waved her hand around her, "This. There's no place for me in all this."

"I don't understand. Explain it to me."

"The cats, the dog, that…," she pointed at the shrine to my dead wife, Mae, with the flowers in the vase, the eleven by fourteen photo with long-dead dogs and the Painted Desert in the background, the blue *raku* urn with the ashes inside, the Buddha figures. She had never said, but I think she found keeping my dead wife on a shelf ghoulish.

"Do you think we could have at least had a conversation about it, see if we could work it out?"

"I don't think it would have helped. We're just too different. I was hoping to find my forever guy before I'm too old, and you just aren't that guy. You're too self-sufficient."

I patted her on her knee, "Less than you think, babe, less than you think." I stood, took her hand, and said, "Let's go get your nails fixed. They're going to drive you nuts otherwise." And for the first time in my life, I sat in a nail shop, bodyguarding a woman who didn't love me. She did say, though, "You are very sweet, Travis."

XIX

I had grabbed my passport and the two credit cards I kept in it for travelling, packed two changes of clothing and underwear, my laptop and toiletries, into a backpack, and I was sitting in the Louis Armstrong Airport waiting to be called for the last flight to Houston. Costa Rica was a two-hop trip, which meant changing flights either in Houston or Miami. With a layover of eight hours until the morning United Airlines flight to San Jose.

We lined up by boarding groups and then filed down the retractable tube. The attendants smiled, I smiled, I took my seat. The flight was barely long enough for the attendants to hustle to get drinks served, pick up the trash and stow the cart before we landed. From New Orleans to Houston, the plane barely made it to cruising altitude before it began descending. I always like a window seat. I'm like Kiddo, I like to look out the window, even if all I could see were the lights of boats on the black Gulf of Mexico and then oil refineries and chemical plants as we made our approach.

We filed off. The attendants and the captain smiled. I smiled. Then I found my next departure gate and settled in. I had more time to review, since I had been moving pretty steadily for the last seventy-two hours plus. There was the attack at the restaurant, the attempt at Andrea's apartment, the apparent random theft of Kiddo, Andrea's arrest, the theft of radioactive material, the death of dirtbag Booger, which I had not caused. I had administered a righteous beat-down, but I had not stomped him in the throat. Someone else had. Why? Someone had tried to frame Andrea. The who part of that answer lay in Costa Rica with Andrea's boss Larry, I was sure. And maybe the why to Booger too. Coincidences were piling up, and to my way of thinking, and probably explained by game theory math which I could never understand, too many coincidences refuted the odds of pure chance.

Some things did not add up, some did. Larry, a guy making probably in the neighborhood of a hundred, hundred fifty thousand a year, would not steal material and take off to Costa Rica for a vacation unless there were retirement-sized dollars in it. The hit man at the restaurant was a low-life nobody, so was Booger. They didn't have the kind of money to pay Larry. That meant deep pockets were behind the operation. Arabs again? They had money to throw around for the Holy Grail, radioactive material which they could use for a grand-slam terrorist show. But so far, no Arabs in the picture, just white trash boys. And I wondered if Detective Cossich was bent. I doubted it. If he had killed his cousin, he could just write it off as a dog attack and close the case. He didn't need to drag me into it with all the complications, not the least of which would be that he would know arresting a cop would bring attention that he wouldn't want. So, not Cossich. He was probably just doing his job. That did not rule out someone else pointing him at me to tie me up, neutralize me, until what? Until whoever stole the isotopes had the chance to sell them or use them. I needed to get to Larry. He would have some answers, but almost certainly not all of them. I waited some more.

If there was big money behind this, then a big operation was the payoff. Surely the Feds were nervous too, with loose cobalt, cesium and iridium floating around. They would be on that, and I bet they were tracking me. Why? Were they letting me run to see where I landed? If I got jammed up along the way, not their problem. They never recruited me. I was a person of interest. Their hands were clean. In other words, I was on my own, until they decided to reel me in.

So, did they have a tail on me now, or would they just pick me up in San Jose? Neither, both? I was getting paranoid, which did not seem like an unreasonable frame of mind under the circumstances. And if the Feds were interested in me, would they reach out to Cossich, or my department? They might, without explaining shit. Feds weren't the sharing kind, but they sure could fuck up my life while they were at it.

I actually nodded off in a chair during the night in mid-conjecture. I needed the nap. When I awoke, with a clicking in my neck from sleeping sitting up with my head cocked at an unrecommended angle, morning had broken over the runways and taxiways.

I decided to check one of the food courts, but I went to another concourse, which was completely unnecessary, but if I had company, and they wanted to keep eyes on me, it would isolate the tail, since they wouldn't have any more reason to check out the food on a whole other concourse than I did, except to follow me.

First, I wandered through the food court on my own concourse, checking the various offerings from breakfast to pizza, stopping in front of each, doubling back to check out a place a second time. There were possibles, including two men at different tables with nothing in front of them, not even coffee. A woman pushing a stroller with a bundle so wrapped up I couldn't see if there was a baby in there or not didn't look quite right.

Then I wandered off to another concourse, taking my time as anyone with hours to wait would. I strolled through newsstands and window-shopped where I could see people filing by in the reflection off the windows, trailing suitcases or carrying duffels, and check out whoever had followed me. The woman with the stroller was definitely with me. She looked a little old to have a newborn, around forty. Her dark hair was cropped short, her nails had clear polish only, and she looked very fit for having an infant. I didn't believe there was an actual baby in the stroller, and for a moment, an image of an MP5 or an AK47 with a folding stock wrapped in a pink blanket flashed in my mind. I thought it was a good sign, bypassing paranoia and going straight to fantasy. I doubted she would get on the plane with me. Explaining a non-baby would be weird, and she couldn't very well just leave the stroller without blowing her cover. I liked her yoga pants, but they didn't go with the low heels. She must have been pulled in quickly for the assignment.

At the food court in the next concourse, I browsed some more until I decided on something called a Texas omelet on Texas toast, with green peppers and chili. It was pretty good. I ate while sitting at the edge of the food court closest to the shops, staring off into space and not even looking at the two men who had stuck with me along with the pretty Fed, as I was thinking of her now.

One of the men off to my right where I would have to turn to see him and give myself away was wearing a Rice University sweatshirt over the waistband of his jeans, so that he could conceal a firearm. The short hair, the fit look, screamed Fed. The other one sitting at another table, tall, about six one, and skinny, with tattoos crawling along his arms out of the sleeves of his black tee shirt, with long greasy hair and last week's beard sticking out from his face, was either deep undercover, or, I guessed, not with the Feds at all. He was too jumpy for an undercover guy. His eyes darted here and there, even at me when he figured I wasn't seeing him, and he talked on his cell phone several times. Two tails. I was popular. I hoped the Feds would notice him and not just be tunnel-visioned on me, but so far, there seemed to be lot of myopia going around.

Okay, next question. Did I want the Feds' company or not? I thought not, at least for the moment. If they followed me, observed me meeting with Larry, they would be convinced something was wrong, and would probably end up picking me up as well as Andrea and use the Patriot Act to drop us in a black hole. Hopefully, I could *interview* Larry without their interference and then feed him to the Feds. And what about the wild card, the guy who could have been Booger's uglier brother? He didn't look like he even had a passport, but he did have a phone. Were his people going to be meeting me along with the Feds in San Jose? It was a lot to consider over an omelet.

I wandered back after breakfast and took a seat in the waiting area for the gate across from the one I would be flying out of. I pretended to sleep while I checked out my fellow passengers. I was pretty sure I would have new watchers on the plane, and I was sure I would on the ground.

I could play the game with myself of spot the tail on the plane, but the truth was, it didn't matter. I would just work on the assumption that I had one or more tails and clear myself after I landed in San Jose.

When the boarding groups were announced, I queued up with my group and waited my turn. I found my seat and settled in.

All I saw below was the Gulf of Mexico, followed by the intense green of jungle, then green mountains. It was the usual boredom with the layer buried deep inside where I monitored the engine sounds to make sure everything was normal. Trying to be practical, I used the three hours to catch a nap as well.

XX

Filing off the plane in San Jose, I carried my only luggage, my backpack, and held my passport at my side as the line formed at Customs. I didn't notice anyone watching me overtly beyond the line of booths, but I didn't expect anything so obvious anyway. I had filled out my Customs form on the plane and it was in the passport. When my turn came, a polite Latina asked me a few questions and passed me through.

The airport terminal was clean, bright, and smaller than the monster airports like Houston or Atlanta. I saw the car rental agency ahead of me as the crowd channeled toward the exits. I bypassed it and continued to the exit. A line of taxis waited at the curb. I walked to the fifth in line and asked, "English?"

"Sure," he said. I had given up polishing my Spanish the last time I had been here, since everyone's English was so much better.

"Can you take me to the soccer, I mean *futbal,* stadium in San Jose?"

"Of course."

We passed residential, business, and agricultural areas, including coffee growing on nearby slopes. It took about a half hour in the early afternoon traffic. I paid attention to the small-engine motorcycles which passed to see if any matched our speed after passing. None did. Any tail I might have had was behind or maybe even non-existent after I had thrown the curves by not picking up the rental car and not taking the first available taxi.

When I spotted the soccer stadium a mile or so ahead, I told the driver to let me off. He looked confused, "But, sir, the stadium is up ahead."

"I know, sorry. I wanted to walk." I passed him a fifty, dollars, not colones. "Will that cover it?"

He pulled over, said, "Sure, thank you."

I got out, slung my pack over my shoulder and walked into the park nearby. I pretended to take an interest in the workers cutting down the imported eucalyptus trees to replace them with more bird-friendly indigenous species. Then, I continued walking, retracing my steps from time to time to check my six, and then left the park. I walked some more, into the city. San Jose is a city sprawling to fill a large valley surrounded by mountains. Half the population of Costa Rica lives there, about two million or so.

After a few tries, I was able to hail another taxi. All the taxis in Costa Rica are red, which makes them easy to spot. I asked the driver to just drive around. He set the meter and began a tour, mentioning points of interest as he drove. When I spotted the car rental office as we passed, I let him go another few blocks and asked him to let me out. He shrugged and pulled over.

"Senor, please be careful. That way, he pointed left, is not so good an area. Pickpockets are everywhere, but over there, drugs."

"*Gracias, senor,* for the warning. How much do I owe you?"

"Seven thousand, senor." It took me aback until I realized he meant colones, a little over ten dollars. I handed him a twenty and he started to make change in colones.

"Keep it, thank you."

I got out and walked in the same direction he had been driving until he disappeared from sight around a corner. Then I reversed direction and crossed the street by way of one of the many elevated footbridges used by pedestrians to keep from being run over in the traffic. The people walking in the same direction I was looked like locals, which didn't necessarily rule them out as followers.

I walked into the rundown area of shops and cafes and bars the driver had warned me about, browsing the cheap merchandise in the shop windows. I stepped past a white man in his late twenties folded against a wall. He had long stringy blond hair and a sparse blond beard. He was wearing cut-off shorts, a dirty Bob Marley tee shirt and cheap plastic flip-flops on his dirty feet. His head was cocked to the side, and he was unconscious, stoned on something, probably heroin. No one paid any attention to him.

Kids ran by in clusters and bumped me as they passed, but my wallet was twisted into my front pocket and I carried the pack in front of me. When I reversed direction the next street over, I stopped for a moment to check who made the corner with me. One black guy, maybe Jamaican, rounded the corner, and ran into me where I stood. He seemed surprised, and eased past me without a word. I couldn't know if he was a dealer, a would-be mugger, a spotter for the kid pickpockets, or a tail. He continued on without looking back and entered a bar. I thought about the guy for a minute. Blacks are less common in San Jose than on the Caribbean coast, so I found him interesting. Maybe FBI, DEA, CIA, maybe just a criminal or a lost tourist.

I walked another street over and repeated the routine. Then I meandered to the car rental office a few blocks away on a main street.

"Buena Dia, senorita," I said to the young woman behind the counter. *"Tengo un carro reservado, sed a la aeropuerto."*

"Would you rather speak English, sir?" She smiled without trying to be condescending.

"That bad, huh?" I asked.

"No, no, no, senor, it was pretty good."

"You're very kind. I was supposed to pick up the car at the airport, but I ran into friends and we went to a restaurant. Could I pick up the car here?"

"Certainly, sir."

A few minutes of form-filling and a swipe of my card after she confirmed the reservation on her computer, and I was off to the Pacific Coast and the Puntarenas region. The drive out of the bowl of San Jose was on a highway which had signs directing me to the beaches. The mid-afternoon sun told me I was headed vaguely west, so I knew I wasn't going toward the Caribbean beaches. The rental did not have GPS, but it did have a map. How quaint.

It was almost five when I found Larry's hotel, with tropical-themed bungalows with faux-thatch roofs, palms, and volcanic rocks placed just so. I parked in the limestone lot and went inside the lobby. There were two people working the counter, a young woman with long black hair and a figure that undoubtedly made women less gifted hate her, and a balding man in his forties with black strands of hair and a graying mustache. They both wore the uniform of maroon blazer and white shirt.

I had Larry's room number from Andrea, so I looked around for a house phone. My plan was a quick in and out, find Larry, corner him, interrogate him the old-fashioned way, which was to say, slap the shit out of him until he cried, and then slap him for crying.

I called his room, but there was no answer. I approached the desk. The young woman smiled. I didn't even try Spanish.

"Hi," I said, with my most sincere smile, "I was supposed to meet up with a friend of mine, Larry Spinelli, but he doesn't answer in his room. Have you seen him around today?"

The young woman, whose name tag identified her as Candida Flores, made a pretty pout with her lips, and said, "I'm sorry, Senor, I cannot say." I didn't know if she meant she couldn't say because of guest privacy, or because she didn't know. Her associate overheard us, however, and said, "I saw the *senor* go to the beach," and he pointed toward the Pacific Ocean. Apparently that information was not confidential.

"Thank you very much," I smiled at both of them and strolled nonchalantly toward the beach access at the rear of the lobby. Beyond the pool and hot-tub patio area, the beach stretched a hundred yards or so to the water. Small waves rolled in and finally gave up at the beach.

I took a chair and sorted out the swimmers and sunbathers. I was looking for a fat white guy, mid-fifties. I knew he wouldn't be too white, or too red from sunburn, as I remembered him as a swarthy guy, with short curly black hair. I ruled out the bikini-clad women and the young guys and several other fat guys, but I didn't see Larry. There were a few men and women in the water, but I couldn't tell at that distance if any of the men was Larry.

There was a boat anchored a couple hundred yards off the beach, with fishing rods sticking out from the sides, but I didn't see anyone manning them.

I waited. I wasn't going to talk to Larry on the beach anyway. The sun was hanging lower in the sky but it was still a couple hours to sunset. I even dozed a little in the chair under the awning as the sounds of the waves lulled me.

I was startled fully awake by screaming. People on the beach were rushing to the waterline, and three men waded in and then dove, swimming toward something which had grabbed their attention. I walked out into the sand, filling my shoes as I went. When I got closer, I could see the men hauling at something, which turned out to be a man, a fat man, a fat white man. Larry. I jumped into the surf to help pull him in along with a woman in her twenties who managed to stay inside her bikini top as she hauled on the dead weight along with the rest of us. When we got him past the surf line, one of the guys tried to roll Larry onto his belly and push water out of his lungs, while the other insisted on rolling him back and doing CPR. I could tell he was dead, so their argument didn't mean much to me.

I looked to the boat and saw two divers climbing onto it. I looked back to Larry and saw red marks on his ankles and wrists, bruises which would not have formed after death. Then I looked back up the beach. Some people had abandoned their personal items in the sand next to their towels, but were hurrying back to them. A couple were taking out their cell phones to record the event for Instagram or YouTube. There was one little zip-up blue vinyl bag all by its lonesome, and I made for it.

Before I could get to it, though, a kid about fifteen years old picked it up and started to walk away. When he saw me, he walked faster. It made for a slow pursuit in the soft sand, and I wasn't going to catch him. I reached in my pocket.

"Cien dolares," I called after him from about twenty yards away. He stopped. I stopped, and held the hundred dollar bill high.

He looked at me warily. Then, *"Dos cien."*

I nodded and dug another hundred out of my pocket. I held it out to him. He approached, ready to bolt. He snatched the bills and tossed me the bag. Then he began to run.

"Espera, por favor. Wait."

He stopped but kept his distance.

I struggled for the words, *"Quien te dijo tomar esto?"*

"Un hombre," he shrugged, which I guessed meant he didn't know him.

"Yanqui, *Tico, Anglo, Gringo?"*

"Yanqui, gringo," he confirmed.

"Que el dijo hacer con el?" What did he say to do with it?

"El me dio veinte dolares, dijo lo guarda." He gave him twenty dollars, said to keep it or guard it, I wasn't sure.

"No mas," the kid said and ran up the beach.

I did a disappearing act too, walking around the hotel rather than going back through the lobby. All I needed was to have Costa Rican police asking me why I was asking about Larry just minutes before he drowned. Unless they decided his drowning was an accident, something I couldn't count on.

And why tell the kid to keep the bag? I looked in it. An iPhone and an electronic room key in an envelope marked 132. I needed a look in that room before I went.

XXI

I walked among the detached bungalows until I found 132. I walked past it and then turned to see if there were any hotel employees around. I saw a man key his door and enter down the breezeway. I made my way back, slipped the card into the slot, and then removed it. The light blinked green.

The chair was swinging toward my head as I stepped in, and if the door hadn't caught most of it, I would have been out of it, maybe out of everything. Even so, the chair glanced off the door and caught me above my left eye. I ducked low and drove into the guy wielding the chair. He went backward and I lifted up both his legs, dumping him onto his back. I stomped him in the balls, then went for the other man who was holding a laptop in both hands, tying them up. I kicked him in the belly and he crashed into the television. Then I cup-slapped him on both ears. He dropped the laptop but managed to retreat through the open patio door. The guy on the floor tripped me and I went down. When I jumped back up, he had staggered out the door into the breezeway. I heard voices. I slammed the door shut, went into the bathroom and looked in the mirror. Blood was streaming from over my eye onto my face and my neck and shirt. I washed my face and grabbed two towels. I pressed one to my eye hard and then left by the patio door. I noticed the latch was bent. So they had jimmied their way in. I walked completely around the hotel on the lawn and between the trees and volcanic rocks to the car. Then I got out of there, taking the laptop with me.

I had to get out of the country fast. The police might have bought Larry's drowning as an accident before, but not after the brawl in his room. My identity would interest them, as would my DNA, in my blood, in his room. I also needed to take care of my face.

I considered the two guys in the room. They weren't Hispanic as far as I could tell.. They were taller than the average Tico, and paler too. Both had been dressed standard tourist, jeans and tee shirts. One had had long hair, the other had his head shaved.

I kept the towel pressed against my forehead until it turned red, then switched to the other. I found a pharmacy just off the highway and watched from the parking area as police and an ambulance flew by. I took some breaths and took the towel away from the cut. It wasn't actively bleeding, but it wouldn't take much to get it started again.

I went inside and found steri-strips, peroxide, and band aids. The clerk looked at me and I said, "Fishing accident." She shrugged. I paid cash.

I drove to a nearby pull-over, got out of the car, leaned over and poured peroxide over my cut and let it run pink to the ground while the peroxide bubbled and hissed. I then dried the area with the towel, got back in the car, and using the rear-view mirror, applied the steri-strips to close the wound and then band aids to cover it. I was going to have a black eye. I got back out of the car and changed my shirt. I threw the bloody one behind some bushes rather than in a garbage can which might be searched..

Next, I pulled up flight information on my phone, just imagining the data charges. The closest airport was at Liberia, and so was the earliest flight, but it was to Mexico City. I booked it, and a follow-up flight back to New Orleans.

I drove to the Liberia airport looking as much in my rear-view as in front of me. The hotel clerks had seen me asking for Larry. Larry ends up dead. That was too much of a coincidence for most policemen. Add in the brawl in Larry's room and it was beyond enough to make me, in the term of fashion, a person of interest. I just hoped I could make the flight and clear Costa Rican airspace before the police figured out who I was. I could just see the Feds getting interested as well, but they probably already were.

I turned in the car at the airport, made my way through Customs, printed my boarding pass at a kiosk, and settled into the seating area at the next gate over, where I could watch if anything unusual started to develop at my gate. Traffic was starting to thin in the terminal as I waited for the last flight of the evening.

They called the flight, I boarded. I held my breath. The plane rolled out on time and we were in the air. Next stop, I hoped, Mexico City.

When we landed at Terminal 1, flying over the city at night, I was spared the view of the infamous smog. I disembarked and walked past police and soldiers. They eyed me suspiciously, but then they did that to everyone.

I made the connection and was back in Houston for 0330. Waiting had given me time to go through Larry's phone. I was waiting to check the laptop.

I checked any notes he had made and his contact list. Most of the numbers had names to go with them, but several of his calls over the past week had been made to numbers not listed in contacts. If Larry had been taking care of operational security, he would have used a burner phone, not tied to any account. So far, I had been assuming Larry was responsible for the theft of the isotopes, and his death and the thugs in his room certainly seemed to support that. One of the numbers looked familiar, but I couldn't place it.

I intended to call those numbers when I got back, but not here, hundreds of miles away where I couldn't react quickly to anything I gleaned.

I started to call Andrea, but then decided I was too tired for a likely argument. So I took a nap until my flight was called.

XXII

When I pulled into my driveway, Kiddo was waiting at the front window. I let her out to water the lawn, she did her jumping thing, standing and leaping at my side until I told her to go pee. Then we went inside.

"Andrea?" I called out but there was no answer. In the middle of the kitchen floor, I found a pile of dog food, which, judging from the size, must have been the whole thirty pound bag. No Andrea.

There was no sign of disorder, other than my usual slovenliness. No sign that she had been taken. No note. The cats regarded me in their own inscrutable way.

I plopped myself down in a chair and dug out my phone, She answered immediately,

"Hello?" I had read that the word hello had been little used before the introduction of the telephone in the late nineteenth century. People needed to say something when they answered, and hello had become the default. Before that, it had not been a standard greeting. Now, with caller ID, it seemed less and less useful. She could have just said Travis. I didn't identify myself, which seemed superfluous.

"Andrea, what the fuck?"

"You're back?"

I held my temper, barely.

"Yes, and I'm wondering, what's with the pile of dog food on the floor?

"I'm sorry, I just couldn't take it any more with the cats and the dog. I had to get out of there. I called your daughter to come let the dog out. Amity called me a cunt."

"I'm sure she meant it in the nicest possible way." I was smirking at the phone. My daughter was never at a loss for the right words.

"Well, I've never been called that before, and it was a shock."

"Where are you?"

"I'm at my sister's in Lafitte."

"You're not safe. They're not safe."

"I think maybe you're exaggerating, Travis."

"Maybe I'm making up the fact that Larry is dead, too." There was a gasp at the other end.

"Oh my God, are you sure?"

"I helped pull his body out of the water."

"He drowned?"

"He had help holding himself under, and there were two men ransacking his room, whom I had to urge to leave."

Oh, my God, oh…," she didn't finish.

"Give me the address. I'm coming to get you before you get yourself and your sister's family killed."

She gave it to me without argument. I punched off the call. Then I called Amity.

"Hi, Dad," she answered, "did you see what that bitch did? She told me she broke up with you after the shooting the other night. After you saved her life."

"Actually, she was in the process of dumping me when we were interrupted. I was glad to have something to take my mind off it. Could you watch Kiddo and the cats until I get back?"

"Where are you going?"

"I'll be around. Just might not make it home."

"What's going on?"

"Too complicated to explain right now. Got to go, okay?" She agreed, sounding reluctant to let it go. I terminated the call. Kiddo was standing by, waiting, so I took her for a short walk along the canal.

***

I tossed the things I was going to need in a duffel and started out the door, but Kiddo was standing by, ready to go. I knelt down to her and hugged her big black Labrador body.

"I'm sorry, girl. I can't take you with me, but I'll be back as soon as I can. I love you." I know, it's sappy, but I never mind being sappy with animals and small children.

I placed the duffel in the back seat of the truck, got in, and plugged my phone into the charger so that I wouldn't use all the battery on the GPS. I had only been to Andrea's sister's house once for a crawfish boil, but I wasn't sure if I remembered the way there. I entered the address and drove toward Lafitte.

There was the community of Lafitte and the adjacent village of Jean Lafitte, both strung out along the bayou and various canals which were gateways to the offshore shrimping grounds of the Gulf of Mexico and the inshore shrimping grounds of countless bays and inlets. The gate swung both ways, however. When the hurricane winds visited, or even passed close, there was nothing to stop the storm surges from inundating the area. There was no high ground, and the tallest things were the cypress.

I drove through Harvey and Marrero on the way to the Lafitte-Larose Highway, where I carefully watched my rear-view. With the straight highway ahead of me and behind, there were few turnoffs. It gave me a chance to study vehicles behind me. As I approached the Crown Point turnoff, I signaled a lane change to the left and slowed. I studied the cars behind. One changed lanes. At the last moment, I turned off the left blinker and crossed to the right and made the turn toward Jean Lafitte National Park instead. I heard the horn of the car I had crossed in front of, and I was pretty sure I knew what he was saying about me and my mother.

At the T in the two-lane, I took a quick look both ways and powered my window down enough to hear the squealing of tires somewhere behind me. I took a right and pressed the accelerator slowly to the floor so that the sound wasn't as obvious as just punching it. At the turn-off for the Jean Lafitte National Park Visitor Center, I braked hard and pulled in. I had ignored the traffic signs on Barataria Boulevard, the old two-lane highway to Lafitte, warning that the area was under the jurisdiction of the park rangers. They would love to have the opportunity to play traffic cop, and I didn't know if my police ID would buy me any professional courtesy. I pulled around the oval parking area and pointed the vehicle toward the road, but didn't use a parking space. I didn't want to get boxed in. Just as a ranger vehicle pulled in, the car which I had noticed on the Lafitte-Larose Highway, which I now identified as a gray Ford Explorer, blew by, heading north. He caught the ranger's attention, who backed up onto the road and gave chase, activating her overhead lights. I smirked as I drove out of the parking area, turned right and headed back to the highway and Lafitte.

The thing that kept running around in my head was that they were watching me too. I called Amity.

"What now, Travis?" She called me by my name when she was being playful or was exasperated with me. She wasn't being playful.

"Go pick up Kiddo. Open an upstairs window."

"What the fuck, Dad?" Worried now.

"I've picked up a tail. I don't know if they're just watching or looking to get in the way, but I don't want them to burn the house down and kill the critters. If they do, the cats will break through the screen and get out."

"Are you serious. Never mind that, of course you are. Better question, are you crazy?"

"There's enough evidence adding up that I'm not, but I don't know who would be interested yet. It's complicated. Look, I want to hand this off, but I'm on a roller coaster right now and can't get off."

"I'm telling Steve."

"Not yet, promise me. Promise."

115

"I don't like it."

"What's not to like, total chaos? We've finally got our own Zombie apocalypse."

"You're too old for this shit."

"I sure am."

She laughed, the way cops do, a short bark, "Okay, for now, but not for long."

"Thanks, and kiss the girls for me."

"Don't say that. Don't you dare."

"Okay, don't kiss them for me." I punched off.

The GPS Emily voice had finally gotten tired of saying, "Recalculating," in that pissy English accent, after my detours and was once again directing me to Andrea's sister's house. Finally, after the Rosethorne Bridge and the turn onto Jean Lafitte Boulevard, state highway 45, the GPS guided me to the front door.

Andrea was waiting on the carport patio, smoking a cigarette. She must have recently started again, I thought. For a silly moment, I wondered if she had broken up with me so she could start again. I had never objected to her smoking, but she had quit while we were together, but always said she missed it and blamed quitting for gaining weight. Of course, I had hardly ever met a woman happy with her weight. Clearly, the stress of the arrest was getting to her. Of course.

I got out of the truck and took a look up the short street. There was nobody obviously lurking. Andrea's sister Carla stormed out the back door and up to me nose to nose. If she had been a man, I'd have head butted her into another zip code or kneed her in the balls.

"This is your fault, you son of a bitch. You got her in trouble, and now she's in danger." That was inaccurate on so many levels I didn't even reply.

"No, Carla, it's not Travis' fault. He didn't do anything," Andrea said with a flat affect. Depression and defeatism setting in, I diagnosed, courtesy of Dr. Bowie, cop.

"Mama says he got you arrested."

"No, that's wrong, she's wrong," Andrea nudged her sister back and kissed her on the cheek.

"You better take care of her, asshole."

I picked up Andrea's red overnight bag and put it in the truck next to my duffel. I got back in while Andrea embraced her sister. They were both scared. As Andrea started to get in, I thought of something.

"Tell Carla to watch for people following her. If she sees anything, she should call the police, or just use her bad attitude on them."

Andrea opened her mouth to say something, but turned to her sister and spoke out of my hearing for a few seconds. They embraced again. Really scared. I don't like it when citizens are scared. I needed to do something about it.

Andrea spoke little on the way back to her apartment.

"Larry's really dead?"

"Yes, he really is."

"I feel bad. I never liked him."

"He must not have liked you very much either, Andrea. He framed you for the isotopes. For his retirement package."

"Can you prove it?"

"Not yet."

That was the extent of the conversation for the drive back to Gretna. I took the time to think, and to ignore the repeated calls from the jail. How was I going to interest the right investigators in this? I had one Plaquemines Parish detective sniffing around his cousin Booger's death, which probably wasn't related to everything else. Costa Rican police were certainly going to be interested in talking to me if they figured out who I was. The FBI were apparently happy with Andrea as a suspect. Jefferson Parish had their horse tied to a tree, one restaurant shooter dead, end of case. When we pulled up at her apartment, Andrea looked confused.

"I thought it wasn't safe here."

"It's not. You want to put yourself in harm's way, you might as well be bait."

I looked at her evenly, and saw the tears welling in her eyes as she thought I was abandoning her.

"Come on, I'm not leaving you alone."

"Thank you," she said in a voice which came from far away.

"You didn't think of reporting this up the line?"

"I thought everyone would think I was crazy, Sheriff. I wasn't sure I wasn't."

The Sheriff didn't indicate that he agreed, but he did say, "Go on."

XXIII

I don't know what made me bring Andrea back to her apartment exactly. Maybe it was the notion that I could gather intel on whoever was after her and trace it back to the source, or better, give the information to the Feds, FBI and ATF, and hope to take the heat off her by giving them a viable alternative to their theory. The thing about theories, though, is that they tend to be self-fulfilling. It's like conspiracy theories, every fact fits the theory, and a lack of facts is just confirmation of how effective the conspiracy is. It would take some pretty good evidence to convince the Feds that Andrea was innocent. Maybe I was just being spiteful because Andrea hadn't cooperated with my earlier efforts.

I carried Andrea's red overnight bag and my duffel inside. I put her bag on the dining area table and my duffel on the floor in front of the couch. I unzipped it and began taking things out. Andrea interrupted me.

"What are you doing?" She had her hands on her hips and a frown on her face.

"Getting some things ready?"

"What, you're planning to stay here?

"What did you think, Andrea? You sure change fast. I told you I wouldn't leave you alone."

"But I thought you'd just…"

"What, sleep in my truck?"

"Well, I, uh, I don't want to sleep with you, Travis. We have to make a clean break. I've always found that's best in the long run, for everyone."

"I think I got that the first time. I don't think I'll be doing much sleeping anyway."

"I'm sorry. You've always been so generous and kind to me, but I just didn't see us headed anywhere. I'm not getting any

119

younger," she took a seat at the dining table and put her hands in her lap, "I was hoping to find my guy for the rest of my life."

"And I'm not him. I would have done anything for you, Andrea. But you never even mentioned it. We never even had a conversation about the future, so I left it alone. Until too late." There was an unattractive note of self-pity in my voice.

"I don't know why, I just don't like conflict."

"You don't like conflict resolution much either. Is that why you just walked out of your other marriages? You just cash in and move on. Starting over gets harder with age too."

She didn't want the conflict here, either, so she left the living room to me as she went into her bedroom and turned on the television. Luckily it wasn't loud and didn't interfere with me being able to hear suspicious sounds. When she returned to the living room and then into the kitchen, she picked up the remote control for the living room television.

"We need to be able to hear what's going on outside. Keep the TV off, please." She put the remote down on the counter a little louder than was necessary.

Andrea began puttering around in the kitchen, bleeding off the nervousness. She made us each a sandwich, turkey on wheat, and we sat at the dining room table. She had automatically locked the deadbolt and put on the security chain when she had entered. That wasn't going to stop a sledgehammer or a twelve gauge load, though, so I took one of the dining set chairs and wedged it under the doorknob. It might buy me a couple of seconds.

We sat and ate turkey on wheat in silence for a few minutes. Then she began staring at the family pictures on the wall opposite.

"Why would Larry do this to me?"

"Because he was a self-absorbed weak hypochondriac prick? And someone offered him enough money so that he could wait a few months, take a disability retirement or maybe even get fired for not managing things better to keep you from stealing the isotopes."

"But who would pay enough money to make it worth his while? And what would they use them for?"

"Keep thinking about it, that's good. Because those are exactly the right questions. And there is money behind this, enough to have me watched at the airport in Houston, to send people down to Costa Rica to snip off the poor dumb Larry loose end, enough to pay him off in the first place, unless he was dumb enough to do it without getting paid first, which I doubt."

She looked down into her lap for answers, and perhaps found one, "I haven't been grateful enough, Travis, I'm sorry."

I reached over and grasped her hand. She squeezed back. A minor thaw. Maybe global warming was real. The knock at the door made her jump. She started to get up, but I motioned her down with my palm out flat as if telling Kiddo to stay.

I moved along the alcove to the door, keeping close to the wall, then leaned over and took a quick peek through the peephole and pulled back again. I got a glimpse of a sixty-something black man standing in front of the door. I couldn't see his hands or face, or if there was anyone else there.

"I think it's your neighbor," I whispered, and told her to go down the hallway where a shot through the door wouldn't catch her. "Quietly," I said.

I went to the patio door, slid it open, looked out past the small patio to the courtyard and pool area, and made my way around to the breezeway. Edsel, the neighbor, was standing at the door with several newspapers in plastic sleeves in his hands. I moved my hand away from my pistol and covered it with my shirt tail.

"Hi," I said.

Edsel looked around to see where the sound was coming from and recognized me.

"Oh, hi," he said, "I was just checking to see if Andrea was home. The newspapers were sitting at her door for the last few days, and I didn't like to leave them there. Tells the bad people no one's home.

"You're a good neighbor, Mister Edsel. Thank you. Andrea's in the shower if you want me to take those."

"Sure, that'll be okay. You sure she's all right? I read about her troubles in the paper. Feel bad for her. And she told me you wouldn't be here anymore." I could tell he wasn't really comfortable leaving without seeing Andrea, since the last time they had talked, she had told him I wasn't going to be around her place anymore.

"Wait just a minute, I'll have her tell you herself." I went back inside by the patio door and called Andrea.

"Can you tell your neighbor I don't have you tied up in here, before he calls the police?"

She came out through the patio and around the corner. She embraced Edsel.

"Thank you for looking after me, Edsel. It's all right. Travis is helping me. I didn't do anything wrong."

"What I told my wife, Miz Andrea wouldn't do nothin' like that."

"Thank you again," I took the newspapers from him, carrying them all in my left hand to keep the gun hand free. I started to turn away, and thought of something, "Mister Edsel, you keep an eye out for things around here, being home all day. Have you seen anybody knocking on Andrea's door or hanging around in the courtyard?"

"You mean like reporters and such?"

"Well, yes, but anyone at all who might be interested in Andrea? There might be people who want to hurt her."

"Oh," he said, his eyes wide, "well, there was a guy just sitting in his car for hours and hours yesterday. I thought it was strange, he was parked in one space and then when a space opened up near the gate, he moved his car to that one. I remember thinking, how lazy can you be, waiting, for what, and then just having to have the spot closest to the gate?"

I thought, so he would have a clear view of her door and the breezeway through the wrought iron gate.

"This guy, young, old, black, white?"

"He was a young white guy, looked like one of those skinheads, you know, tattoos all over and his head shaved."

"The car, you remember it?"

"It was a gray SUV of some sort." Familiar.

"Have you seen anyone in the courtyard who doesn't belong?"

"There were two young black guys, gangster types, don't live here, I'm sure, passing through day before yesterday."

"Thank you again, Mister Edsel. Look, I don't want to alarm you, I'm probably going to move Andrea somewhere safer, but if you hear guns, you and your wife get to your bathroom and lie down in the tub. Promise?"

"Well, I don't know how me and that woman gonna' fit in the tub together, but I'll make sure she gets in. But I'm not afraid, Vietnam used up most of the fear I ever had."

"I can see you're not afraid, sir, but a little prudence wouldn't hurt." I waved and we backed away. I could tell he was still wondering why I was back at Andrea's after she had told him I wouldn't be.

"Let's go back inside," I said to Andrea, standing nearby. Looking at her, whatever spiteful feeling I might have had in using her for bait melted. She was a scared middle-aged woman completely thrown into an alternate universe.

I tossed her newspapers onto a chair with others from earlier dates.

"Edsel was telling me before you came outside he was sorry for your troubles. Read about it in the paper." The humiliation made her sit down and weep, quietly except for an occasional sniffle.

"I don't know if you heard, but Edsel saw people who were acting strangely, no good reason to be here. We're probably going to need to move again to keep you safe."

"Travis, please, can I just spend tonight in my own bed, and go tomorrow?"

I thought it would probably be all right. Whoever was out there was probably just keeping tabs on Andrea and wouldn't move until she was out in the open. I still can't believe I was so stupid.

XXIV

I took the binoculars out of the duffel and laid them on the table at the end of the sofa. I had already taken the twelve gauge with its collapsible stock and pistol grip out and propped it against the other end table before Andrea and I had lunch. The first aid kit went on the floor. The MAP 92 long pistol version of the AK-47 came next, with extra mags. I seated a full one, pulled the bolt back and let it snap back. Andrea jumped at the sound. I could tell she was horrified.

I continued. I held a thirty eight caliber revolver out to Andrea, grip toward her. She shook her head.

"They scare me. I don't like them."

"I'm not asking you to fall in love with it. I'm asking you to take it, put it on the table next to your bed and if someone gets past me, point it, pull the trigger and keep pulling it until it's empty."

"I don't think I can do that."

"I bet you can. Here," I thrust it at her again. She took it like it was a tarantula and hurried down the hall with it to her bedroom. At least she didn't try to flush it down the toilet at the end of the hall.

More mags for the MAP 92, empty for now. I would load them after. A Beretta 92, more mags for my Kimber, which I stuffed in my left cargo pocket. A Glock 27 in a paddle holster on my left and extra mags in my right cargo pocket. My department issue Beretta PX4 Storm was still held in the restaurant shooting, but I probably had enough. Of, and of course, my karambit knives which had served me well the year before in north Louisiana with the incident with radioactive materials. What was it with me and radioactivity? I did not need this nuclear shit.

Finally, there was the wakizashi short sword which I placed on the top of the sofa against the wall. If I needed the sword, we were definitely in the deep stuff. And one last surprise.

Andrea was still moping, hiding, whatever, in her bedroom. I checked the hallway and saw that the door was open.

"Andrea?" I called.

"Yes," a small voice answered.

"I need to go move my truck. They've seen it. We don't want to spook them, just catch one and make him talk.

"Okay."

"Can you come let me out the patio door and lock it back and put the bar in? I'll text you when I need to come back in."

She came into the hall, walking stiffly like a zombie. I took her hand and pulled her into an embrace. I just held her. She was vibrating like a crystal goblet being assaulted by a soprano.

"Hey, look at me. Really, look at me." She lifted her head until we were eye to eye.

"Okay."

"You need to believe, in yourself first, and in me. I'm not going to let you down."

"Why, after...?"

"Look, that's a whole other thing. I'm pissed that you have to go through this, that anyone would. One thing I've noticed, these guys have made mistakes, they're not masterminds, they'll make more."

"You're sure?"

"Yep. Now let me out, I want to do a walk-around and move the truck."

I removed the blocking bar and flipped up the latch. After sliding the door open, I stepped out, facing the courtyard. I slid the door shut and knocked lightly on the glass. I heard the latch snap shut behind me and the bar drop into place. I took my surprise with me, what looked like a two foot stick. It was a bang stick which didn't look threatening.

There was no one in the courtyard and the pool was closed now that the weather was getting cooler. I stepped off the patio and walked to the other side of the complex. Then I strolled the parking lot back around to where my truck was parked.

There were what appeared to be residents arriving or departing, but no one suspicious. I got in my truck, backed out, drove to the street, turned right and drove up a couple of blocks before turning left into a neighborhood. I looked for tails but there were no vehicles behind me. I found a place to park at the strip mall across the street from Andrea's apartment complex and left the truck there. I strolled along the street a block before crossing back over and making another circuit of the apartments.

When I got back to the patio door, Andrea was waiting. She had changed into another pair of beige slacks, red blouse, and her favorite flip-flops. When she opened the door, she asked, "Could I step out and smoke a cigarette? I'm going nuts."

"Sure, it's clear, as long as you don't mind me staying close."

She nodded and stepped out, her leather cigarette case and a lighter in her hand. She had never smoked indoors, always on the patio, until she had briefly quit. She lit up while I scanned the area.

"Tell me, did you break up with me so you could smoke again without feeling guilty?"

She gave me a look, but cocked her head to think about it, "You know, I'd hate to think so, but I was never happy not smoking."

"You know I never cared, right?"

"I know, but I thought quitting would bring us closer. Instead, it may have pushed us farther apart."

I shook my head that such a thing had come between us. True, I didn't like smoking, since my wife Mae had committed suicide on the installment plan, one cigarette at a time. There was more, of course, but cigarettes, really?

It was getting dark and I didn't want us standing around silhouetted nicely against the patio door. I stepped inside and turned the living room light out.

***

For the next two days, we sat around getting on each other's nerves. At least I got to walk around looking for surveillance. When Andrea looked like she couldn't take any more, I told her, "Get your smokes, lady. You look like you're going to turn yourself inside out."

She practically skipped to the bedroom and back, carrying her cigarettes. I stepped outside first and then motioned for her to come out too. We walked around, her feeling the freedom and probably worrying about how prison was going to be like the last two days, but a whole lot worse.

When she finished one cigarette, she lit another off the first one, something I'd never seen her do before. Making up for lost time.

"What's that you're carrying?" She pointed at the bang stick. I started to tell her it had a twelve gauge shell in it that would be discharged if I jammed it up against something, but I stopped myself. Instead, I lied to her.

"You ever hear of a cattle prod, one of those electric things, like a stun gun?"

"Sure, I've heard of them."

"You don't like guns, right?"

"No."

"You think if someone was coming at you that you could use this, give him a shock?"

"I think I could do that. It would be like the bat I keep by the door."

"Okay, then." I showed her how to pull the safety cotter pin affixed by a short length of chain. "You have to pull this out or the charge won't work. Can you remember that?"

"I think so."

"You have to know so to save your life."

"Okay, I know so."

"Good girl." I showed her how to thrust it horizontally, holding it with both hands, and she tried it, a cigarette dangling from her lips. I had to laugh. She reminded me of a photo of Bonnie Parker pointing a shotgun at Clyde Barrow. She even laughed too.

Since we hadn't seen any lurkers, I had finally decided we had to wait for them to show so that I could snatch one of them. It wouldn't do any good if we ran somewhere they couldn't find us. Not yet.

While we waited for something to happen, I went through Larry's phone contacts and looked at his computer. I read through the emails. Most were work-related or seemed to be, some were personal between Larry and his wife or daughter. I called to Andrea, "Can you look at these emails on Larry's computer and see if they look normal?"

"Don't you think it's kind of creepy, going through a dead man's personal communications?"

"I guess it is, but what I think is really creepy is someone stealing really dangerous stuff, probably to sell to really creepy people, and framing an innocent person, all for money so he can sit on the beach and drink pina coladas."

"You don't have to be so sarcastic."

"Sometimes I just do."

"Just give me the laptop." She held out her hands with an impatient gesture. I handed it to her and started looking at the phone call list again. There was a number, that one I had thought looked familiar, that appeared many times, including when Larry had been out of the country. I didn't know if he took work calls when he was off, but from what Andrea had said, it didn't seem likely.

"Do any of these numbers look familiar?" I handed her the phone. She looked at them, then up at me, and back down at the screen again. She had noticed that number too.

"No," she said, handing the phone back. She had just lied to me.

"What?" I asked.

"Nothing, I don't recognize those numbers," she insisted, and her eyes flicked away from mine. Andrea had always been honest with me, and I could see that she didn't lie well.

Well, I at least knew one thing, that there was something in the phone call list. I just didn't know what yet. I also realized it had been a week since the shootout at Vincenzo's.

XXV

I was starting to see probable spotters in the area on my walk-arounds and Andrea's smoke breaks. She now carried the bang stick, which I had convinced her was a long-handled stun gun, which somehow fit into her ethic or sensitivities. I had cautioned her over and over about not striking it on the ground or floor or wall when the safety pin was pulled, and had drilled her in pulling the pin and replacing it. I was glad she hadn't asked for a demonstration. The suspected spotters had been twenty- and thirty-something white guys whom I would have described as white trash dirtbags, either skinhead shaved heads and goatees or with long biker chic hair and full beards. There were motorcycles which cruised through the complex or pickup trucks or blacked out SUVs. Once, I had seen a pickup pulled way back along the back of the building which housed the lesbian biker bar and the laundromat, with a view of Andrea's gate, but when I tried to work my way around another building to have a chat with him, he spotted me and took off. They didn't seem to care that we knew that they were around. They had probably been given orders to watch, and maybe to snatch or kill Andrea. Of course, I wondered how long this game would go on.

On the night of the third day of Andrea and me getting on each other's nerves, when breaking up made more sense than before, my wondering ended. I had been napping on the couch during the day, reasoning that I would be able to find and grab one of the spotters more easily during their night shift, and also that I would be alert if they came, which I didn't expect, since they knew I was there by now. So I was awake.

Then, at 0300, the front door splintered at the deadbolt lock and the glass patio door imploded in a crystal shower. Probably sledgehammers. Then a smoke grenade came rolling into the living room. I remember thinking that it wasn't SWAT; they would have used flash-bang grenades, not a smoke grenade which would obscure their vision as much as mine. Some idiot's idea of a good idea. Just like criminals.

I dropped from the sofa to the floor and grabbed the shotgun as I did, yelling for Andrea to get down. I pushed the safety button to fire and caught the first one coming off the patio, silhouetted against the courtyard lights, low in the belly. He had been spraying bullets from an AK-47, and there was drywall dust and sofa stuffing dancing in the smoke. He just folded in half and blocked the entrance.

When the front door didn't fly open as they had expected, because the chair was still wedged under the door knob, someone let loose a volley of rifle fire through the door. I hoped Andrea was flat on the floor, since the walls were not going to stop even pistol rounds, much less rifle rounds.

"Pull the pin, lie down," I yelled over and over through the madness.

Bullets were sonic-boom cracking over my head as I racked round after round through the shotgun, alternating between the patio door and the front door, what was left of it. When I fired one load through the front door, the firing from the other side stopped for a moment. Stupid had been standing right in front of the door, evidently.

Another one stumbled in from the patio over the body of the first assaulter. He couldn't see for the smoke. I had it a little better on the floor as the smoke blossomed up toward the ceiling. I had tossed the shotgun aside after emptying the magazine and grabbed the MAP92. I fired my own 7.62 rounds into him, and he fell.

The front door had finally been reduced to splinters, and the chair wasn't holding anymore. Three figures rushed through the opening. I caught the first one with a swarm of bullets and he went to his knees. I had to roll toward the dining table so I wouldn't be where my last shots had come from and present a target. As I did, number two thug pushed past his fallen comrade and rushed down the hall.

"One coming your way, Andrea! Pull the pin!" I shouted as loudly as I could. I was desperate to protect her, but I had my own problems. Number three turned to the sound of my voice, and I fired from my position lying on my back as the dark figure pointed a pistol down. I fired until he staggered backward and hit the wall. He slid down.

I shifted my attention to the gunman making his way down the short hall. I saw him shoulder his rifle and point it down toward the bedroom floor. Toward Andrea. I could see by the light in the bathroom, which we had left on for minimal visibility, through the smoke which was a little lighter in the hall, a long cylindrical object, sticking out from the bedroom. I was trying to line up a shot when the thug stepped right into the end of the bang stick, making contact with his lower abdomen.

There was a muffled booming sound, and the thug momentarily inflated. Then blood and stuff blew out of his mouth and nose and ears and eyes, and bloody shit exploded from the seat of his pants. Then he deflated, in a heap.

It was suddenly quiet, except for the ringing in my ears. I got to my feet and screamed down the hall, "Andrea! Andrea!"

I heard, "Oh my God!"

Thinking she was hurt, I rushed along the hall, checking the doorway and patio first. "Are you hurt?"

She was sobbing on the floor, "Oh my God! You lied to me!"

"Yes, I did, and you're alive."

I regarded the heap at my feet. He looked like the worst case of road kill. His body had absorbed all the gas from the shotgun shell in the bang stick and the gasses had blown out all his natural orifices. I snatched a look back toward the front of the apartment, and then back at Andrea. Then there was the boom of a shotgun, followed immediately by another. I tore down the hallway and turned toward the front door. I almost shot Mister Edsel, who was standing in the doorway holding a smoking double-barreled shotgun. At his feet was a sixth gunman, still clutching his rifle, just inside the doorway.

133

I nodded to him, "Thank you, Mister Edsel. Is it quiet out there?"

"Is now."

"You weren't here, okay?"

He looked at me for several seconds, then nodded. He turned and went back to his apartment with his shotgun over his shoulder as if after a day of rabbit hunting.

I switched on the vent fan in the kitchen and the AC fan to clear the smoke which was wafting out the blown-out doorways anyway. The AC fan made a constant ticking noise from where a bullet must have nicked it.

I could hear Gretna PD responding, and from the chorus of yelps and wails, there were a bunch of them. I put my MAP92 on the floor and took out my ID and stood there, holding it high. When the first light mounted on an MP4 flashed in my eyes from the front door, I yelled, "26!" Code for police officer. Code for *Don't shoot me*.

The officer took a quick look down at the bodies heaped just inside the entrance and stepped over them after probing them with his boot. Another officer covered me from the patio. Backup arrived and they entered, keeping their weapons pointed at me and Andrea, whom I had sat on the shredded sofa so that they wouldn't have to go looking for her and maybe make a mistake and shoot her as a threat. She was picking at loose upholstery stuffing in a daze.

The apartment quickly filled with police, some with shotguns or rifles, others with pistols. The first officer who had arrived took my ID from me and read. Someone had turned the lights on, the ones that were working anyway. I read his name tag as M. Dupre.

He lowered his rifle and asked, "What the fuck, L.T.?"

"Long story, getting longer. Is there a detective responding?"

"Oh, yeah. Take a seat." I took a seat next to Andrea, who sat with her hands in her lap, staring at the floor and holding stuffing delicately between her fingers.

Gretna determined that two of the gun thugs were still breathing, for the moment. They called for medical. EMTs arrived and fitted the men with oxygen and IVs, and took them away on gurneys. I looked at the men who had assaulted the apartment. They were all black. As the EMTs were cutting away their clothes, I spotted a GMC tattoo on one's neck. A gang tattoo. I was more confused than ever. First white skinheads and now black bangers, not a common combination outside of drug deals.

A Gretna P.D. sergeant was standing near the dining room table which had been chewed up by bullets. He was talking on the radio, his cell phone, and giving instructions to officers. Crime Scene arrived to start processing the scene.

The sergeant, Williams, flicked his hand at me and Andrea, who wasn't looking at him. I took her hand and we stood.

"I'm going to put you in a unit to wait for the detective." I knew what he meant was he was going to put us in two different units so we couldn't collude on our stories. I would have done the same.

I nodded, asked, "Do you know who's responding?"

"Lieutenant Mather, know him?"

"Yes, I do."

We were led out to two of the units outside the gate. Andrea was put in the back seat of one and I in the other. She gave me a big-eyed look before she was put in the back and the door closed her in.

I sat in the backseat of the other unit with my legs out and feet on the ground. The officer said, "Put your feet in, sir."

"No, I'm not under arrest and I'm a cooperating witness. You're not locking me in. And open the lady's door too."

He wanted to argue, but he wasn't clear on his instructions. Usually, a police officer will seek guidance or try to push his authority. This one walked off, probably to talk to his sergeant. When he returned, he opened Andrea's door. I waved a thank you at him.

A few minutes later, Jerry Mather arrived in his black Crown Vic, found a spot to park. He walked over to me when an officer pointed me out. I stood up and we shook hands.

"What the fuck, Travis? Wait, don't say anything yet."

"Sure, Jerry, you want to go take a look around and get back to me, read me my rights and talk?"

He looked at me eyeball to eyeball for a few seconds and nodded. He walked off to survey the scene. Jerry and I had worked on cases through the years. He had retired with thirty-something years from Jefferson Parish and was working on another pension with Gretna P.D. We were friends, but that wasn't going to stop him from doing his job.

I waited, sitting in the back seat of the unit for about half an hour until Jerry came back. He opened the other rear door and took a seat next to me. He opened his portfolio and started to fill in a form. I knew it was a waiver of rights and Miranda warning.

"Give it to me to sign when you're done, Jerry. We're victims here, even though the bad guys didn't come out so well."

He finished filling in the date and time and gave it to me. I signed and handed it back to him.

"Okay," he said, "what's this all about?"

"Well, the first thing it is not about is a drug rip. I saw the ink on one of those boys, GMC, and you know and I know they're about dope and shooting. There's no dope inside, never was, because this isn't about dope. They were hired. Oh, and get the lady to give you a consent to search. There's nothing there."

He waited, good interview technique, let the witness/subject talk as long as they will. I smiled.

"Someone is trying to kill the lady over there. You heard about the shooting at Vincenzo's last Saturday?"

"Yeah, saw that was you. How many shootings you been in?"

"Well, not many, but in the last two years a few."

"How do you know they're not trying to kill you?"

"Because they only try to kill me when I'm with her."

"Why?"

"Theory, but she was arrested by the Feds because her name is on the sign-out logs for some radioactive isotopes used by her company in oil industry testing. The isotopes went missing."

"Shit. What can that stuff be used for? Some kind of nuke?"

"No, not in a real way. I don't know if you heard about the thing I was involved with last year up in the north of the state. Some Arab bundled regular explosives with some radioactive material to contaminate the aquifer. A radiological bomb. I guess that could be what this is about. I do know she didn't do it, but she makes a great scapegoat, especially if she's dead or disappeared."

"Yeah, I heard about you working undercover with the locals up there."

"That was just the department covering their asses because I was on suspension at the time and it wouldn't look good if I did something while I was on suspension. Better that I was undercover."

He laughed the cop laugh, a short bark, and then gone.

"You tell anybody about this?"

"I'm telling you, and I'd tell anyone who'd listen. The department is happy with the restaurant shooter all wrapped up, he's dead, end of story. The Feds are happy with Andrea as their thief. I knew they were watching us here, and I hoped to grab one of them and make him talk, hand him over to the Feds or the department and have them work him. I did not think they were going to do this," I pointed back at the apartment.

"What a fucking mess. Look, I don't have anything to hold you on. It's clear the bangers used sledgehammers on the doors, left them outside, and that they assaulted. It's self-defense, really noisy and messy self-defense, but still…"

"Self-defense. Look, Jerry, I'm going to need my weapons back. If they're sitting in property, only my heirs are likely to see them next, because I'll be dead. Because I'm not leaving that lady to get herself killed."

"You too must really have it bad for each other."

"She dumped me last Saturday night right before the shooting started."

"Then you must be an idiot."

"I think you're right."

"Okay, look, what weapons did you use?"

"I used the MAP92 chopped assault rifle and the Remington shotgun, that's it. Andrea used the bang stick."

"A bang stick? That's what made the mess in the hallway?"

"Yep. All the charge went inside him. He blew up like a balloon and then blew out everywhere."

"Jesus H., why use that?"

"She was afraid of guns, and I told her it was a stun gun."

This time he laughed hard and long, "Oh, man, she's not going to forget that sight. She still talking to you?"

"No."

"Okay, I'm going to have Crime Scene process the weapons you used, take them back and test-fire them, and give them back to you. The others I'll give back now. This isn't going to come back and bite me in the ass, is it, Travis?"

"No, Jerry, it's all righteous."

"Maybe the lady would be safer in jail."

"Maybe, but then, there she would stay and probably get convicted on the charges she's not guilty of."

"You think. Maybe she is, and someone's just cutting off loose ends."

His comment made me think of Larry in Costa Rica. And the fact that she had lied to me about not recognizing the phone number on Larry's phone.

"Yes, I think."

"And one guy in the front doorway looks like he caught two rounds in the back from outside. Know anything about that?"

I wasn't going to get Mister Edsel involved in this mess, so I just said, "Must have been friendly fire."

"Okay, then," and he held up his digital recorder, "statement time."

The Sheriff asked, "Don't you think this would have been a good time to get us involved?"

"Looking at things from inside the bubble, Sheriff, I wasn't sure what to do. We were running for our lives, and a lot of what was going on was happening outside your jurisdiction. I didn't think anyone would be interested." I kept my hands on the chair arms. I didn't want to be seen as a supplicant.

I could tell he wasn't convinced.

XXVI

After we gave our statements, we were allowed to go, after picking some things up from inside the apartment. It was ravaged. Crime Scene tape still festooned the perimeter from the patio, all around the pool area and courtyard, and back around to the front door. The scorch mark on the carpet marked where the smoke grenade had cooked off. EMTs had already taken away the two breathing thugs, and the coroner's ghouls had gathered up the bodies. Blood was everywhere.

"Take anything valuable, like jewelry," I told Andrea. "It won't likely be here when you get back."

"You think the police will steal it?" She asked.

"No, but there aren't any doors on the place anymore."

I heard the rattling as she emptied her jewelry box into her overnight bag. I tossed things into my duffel. The sergeant on scene supervised us as we packed. I could tell he didn't like me taking my other weapons.

We schlepped our stuff across the street to the parking lot where my truck was parked. Before we got in, I checked underneath and popped the hood to check the engine. I didn't see anything that was obviously a bomb. We got in and I started the engine, holding my breath in case it was my last one. I looked at Andrea and figured she would be the best last thing to see.

"Where to now?" Andrea asked.

"Good question. I think we avoid any place connected to us. Plan A didn't work out so well." So I drove all the way out to New Orleans East and found a chain hotel with a vacancy.

We settled in, which consisted partly of Andrea turning on the television as soon as we were inside. I think it was a Hallmark Channel movie with has-been actors going through one of those paint by numbers romances that Andrea had probably already watched a dozen times. She kept the volume low and I didn't object.

Then I returned some of the phone calls I had been avoiding. The first was to Sergeant Heath at the jail. She had called me seven times in the last two days. I was drunk from no sleep the night before and precious little the previous three days.

I called Central Control and waited for the deputy to find the sergeant.

"Hi, Lou," she picked up.

"Hi, Sarge. What's up?"

"It's Eddie," she sighed. "He's driving us all nuts at the hospital demanding you. Only you."

"Okay, thanks, Sarge. I'll make it over to see him later today."

"Thanks."

I decided to take a nap and go see Eddie before returning the call to Major Head in IAD. I knew that was not going to go well and that I would likely be barred from seeing Eddie after I met with him. I stretched out on one of the double beds, taking off only my boots. I propped up some pillows so that I was half-sitting, took my Kimber from the holster, and laid it by my side. The last thing I remember was Andrea running the shower after I had watched her look at some photos of her children she had grabbed from her apartment on the way out.

When I awoke, it was a little after noon. Andrea was on the other bed, under the covers, facing away from me. I took some clean clothes out of my duffel, grabbed one of the unused plastic bags lining a wastebasket to put my dirty clothes in, and headed for the shower.

I let the water beat on me until I felt a little more alive, brushed my teeth, and shaved. Appearances. When I came out of the shower, Andrea was awake and staring at me.

"Are you leaving?"

"I have to go see some people. You should be safe here for the time being."

"Could you come hold me for a minute?" I thought she'd never ask.

She sat up and the covers dropped to reveal her breasts. She didn't seem self-conscious about it. The blood was pounding in my, ears, and making its way to other places. I sat on the bed and wrapped her up. She presented her open mouth and I covered it. I hadn't put my shirt on yet, and I hadn't put on my socks and boots. Our breathing got more rapid. She unsnapped my pants and yanked the zipper down. I was out of them in a flash.

I pulled the covers back and pinned her for a three-count. I wouldn't let her mouth go even as she writhed. She broke free for a moment and breathed in her husky smoker's voice, "I think I may hate you."

"You have a funny way of showing it," I breathed back.

We wrestled as we had never done before, slapping against each other with sounds like the gunshots of the night before. I inserted three fingers inside her and she gasped. I found her spot. I bit her nipples the way she always demanded. Finally, she ordered that I "get inside" her. I did, and we thrashed to exhaustion, and even then we didn't let go of each other. We kept undulating likes waves until there was no more. This was different, it was combat more than tenderness. I knew then we were truly over.

We lay there holding hands for awhile, and then I got up and finished dressing. No time for another shower, so I took her scent with me as a memory. She turned her back and looked out the window.

****

I drove downtown to University Hospital, where our inmates were treated since Katrina had destroyed Charity Hospital.

Eddie was in a room by himself, one thin white leg shackled to the bed rail, although by the looks of him, he couldn't have run anywhere. A shoelace could have held him.

"Lieutenant," he smiled.

"How you feeling, Eddie?"

"I'm feeling pretty bad. They cut the tumor out, but I'm messed up inside. I'm gonna' sue these people. They shoulda' caught this earlier."

"Maybe you should have told them you had a bunch of raisins hanging out your ass, give them a heads up, you know." Eddie had been HIV positive as long as I had known him, and never looked the worse for it, until now.

He waved my comment away like smoke, said, "I'm gonna' tell you what I have, Lieutenant, in case I'm not, you know, competent later. You got to promise me you'll do everything you can to get me a good deal, and a reward too. I don't want to die in jail."

"Hey, who's dying here?" I didn't sound convincing even to myself.

"Hey, not me, Lieutenant," he forced a grin. "Just covering my options. If the DA thinks I'm dying, they'll let me out, right?" Always the optimist, always the hustler.

"Okay, Eddie, what can you give me to bargain with?" Then he told me a story that changed everything.

"Listen, Lieutenant, two friends of mine and me, we were watching this storage place over on Causeway. We'd figured the blind spots in the video so we could get in, cut the locks on the units that were in the blind, and take the stuff that was easy to carry.

Well, one day we were watching from an empty house behind the place, and this van pulls in with some guys who looked like they were in the life, you know what I mean. They start unloading boxes into the unit, looking around, you know, like this ain't the usual family items and junk. We figured drugs, electronics, jewelry, something hot,

When they left, we waited for dark, went under the fence at a spot we'd cut that was covered with weeds, and crawled to the unit. We cut the lock and went inside. We found the boxes. There was these little cylinders in them. They were heavy, like lead or something, and they had decals on them, DANGER, and RADIOACTIVE MATERIAL, and had these black and yellow triangles on them.

We figured it was valuable stuff, but what we gonna' do with it? So we decided to shake them down for a payoff. Not much, just something for our trouble, like a thousand, each."

I thought, typical Eddie, always thinking of a score, and always thinking small. I also thought, Holy Shit, the isotopes.

"So what did you do?"

"We had the plate for the van, so Abe, he was with me, had a pen, don't know why. I wrote a note with my phone number on it on one of the boxes and told them we needed three thousand to keep quiet. Then we grabbed one of the boxes and took it with us."

"And then what?"

"They called, and I set up a meet with them on the bike path at the foot of the Causeway."

"And?"

"Cosey, he was the other one with us, he lost at rock paper scissors, so he was the one to stand on the bike path with the box. We watched from behind the rocks."

"What happened?"

"Two guys showed up, one was kind of short, black hair, I think, and a light beard. It was getting dark, we didn't want some cyclist to come by getting there too early. The other one was tall and skinny with a shaved head. The short guy was dressed better, dress shirt and khakis, the other one a black tee shirt and jeans."

"Then what?"

"They checked inside the box to see if the cylinders were there. Then the short guy brought out an envelope and started to hand it to Cosey. The other guy shot him with a pistol he took from his back."

"What did they do next?"

"A van, I think it was the same one from the storage place, looked the same, white, came tearing up the bike path. They put the box inside and put Cosey inside too. Then they started looking for us, walking along the path. I was already running, Abe too."

"What did you think was going to happen, Eddie?"

"I don't know," he said, running his hand without the IVs through his thinning sandy hair, "I mean, we wasn't asking for that much. They didn't have to shoot Cosey."

"What was the number of the storage unit?"

"It's right here," he said, reaching for his Bible and not quite making it. I handed it to him. Good place to hide something, since it was one of the few things allowed an inmate. He had written it in the margins of Leviticus. No one reads Leviticus, unless they're Jewish.

"That's part of the van plate I remember and the storage unit number."

"What about the phone number the guy called you from?"

"It's in my phone."

"Is it in your property at the jail?"

"No, it was a burner, and I ditched it after so they couldn't trace me."

Who did he think these guys were, the NSA?

"Okay, Eddie, thanks, I can work with this." I left him with a squeeze of his hand. His response was feeble

. I felt bad that the only friends he really had in the world were his jailers.

****

My next stop was in Metairie, to IAD. I didn't call first. I figured they would fit me in without an appointment. They did, but not before making me wait a half hour. Standard procedure for IAD,

145

treat everyone with the disrespect they think they deserve. While I waited, I tried to call Special Agent Lewis, but I got his voicemail.

Major Head himself came out to greet me, with his usual cheery self. He always seemed to think people were glad to see him.

"Hey, Bud, come on back." I followed him to his office.

"Have a seat, have a seat," he waved me to a chair.

"Seems we have a little problem, Bud."

Okay, I thought, what does he expect me to do, slit my wrists or something? Instead, I just waited, which seemed to annoy him.

"Did you call Criminal Information Center on Monday to ask for license plate camera information?"

"Yes, sir."

"For what purpose?"

"Someone had stolen my dog, and I wanted to get a lead on who took her."

"So it wasn't for a case you were working?"

"It most certainly was. The theft of my dog and the burglary of my truck."

"But not for a case to which you were assigned?"

"No, sir."

"So it was for personal reasons."

"It was personal, but it was still a crime. And I'm still a police officer."

"On administrative leave."

"Yes, sir."

"Well, Bud, you seem to have stirred up Plaquemines Parish, and it's made its way to the Sheriff."

"Yes, sir."

"But that's their investigation, and I understand you were in another shootout last night?"

"Not of my choosing."

"Well, Bud, that's a whole other thing. Not my purview." He seemed to inflate a bit at the word purview, almost like someone had unloaded a bang stick in his belly.

146

"Did you write a report of the theft of your dog and the burglary?"

"I'm on administrative leave."

"I'm sorry to tell you, Bud, but as of right now you're not on administrative leave. You're suspended, pending the outcome of the different investigations."

"Figures."

"What?"

"Never mind, Sir."

"I'll need your weapon and ID."

I pulled the ID from my back pocket, took my driver's license and credit cards out, and handed it to him. "The range still has my weapon from the shooting. I haven't gotten it back yet."

"Do you have any other weapons, Bud?"

"That's really none of your business, Major," I stood and left the office.

XXVII

I took the card from my pocket again and got the number I needed. I punched it in on my phone and waited. I realized while it was ringing that I already had the number in my phone. I must have been a little off my game.

"Special Agent Lewis," the voice on the other end said.

"This is Lieutenant Bowie, we talked outside the courtroom the other day, on the Andrea Barrois case."

It took him a second to sort through his caseload in his mind, then, "Oh yeah, what can you do for me?" Arrogant prick.

"Well, since you put it that way, I wanted to let you know people are still trying to kill your prime suspect in this thing, and you might want to widen your scope of investigation."

"Maybe you shouldn't have bailed her out."

"Great idea, Lewis. I should have left her in custody so she could get shanked in the shower instead."

"Let me ask you, do you know a Lawrence Spinelli?"

"No," I answered.

"Well, it's kind of curious, he was your girlfriend's boss, and he turned up drowned in Costa Rica. Didn't you just make a quick visit down there?"

Oh, shit, one more brick in the wall.

"Are you accusing me of something, Agent Lewis?"

"Not yet, but I'll take your advice and, as you say, widen my scope."

"Agent Lewis, you're looking through the wrong end of the telescope. The lady didn't have anything to do with your missing stuff, and I didn't have anything to do with this guy's death. And before you start sizing me for a lying to the FBI charge, I met the guy once, and only knew him as Larry."

"So you say."

"I do have something you might want to check, though. An informant of mine came across some radioactive material at a storage place on Causeway Boulevard. Unit 321 had some stuff in it."

"Wait, when was this?"

"Last week."

"Does your informant still have the material?"

"No, the knucklehead took a sample and tried to ransom it back to the people who put it in the storage. They killed my informant's friend and took it back."

"Where is this place again?" I gave him the information again.

"Call me if you find your isotopes, okay."

"All right." He hung up.

I found that whole conversation a little strange. Why didn't Lewis want me to come in? Why didn't he want to talk to me further about being in the same small foreign country with Larry when he was killed? The only thing that made sense to me was that he was letting me run, thinking I was part of the theft and might lead them to the isotopes. Okay, I guessed I was the rabbit. It occurred to me that I hadn't given Lewis the license number of the van which Eddie had given me, or the phone number contact for the thieves. I guess if I was going to be the rabbit, I would have to follow these leads on my own.

Next, I called Jerry Mather on his cell.

"Hey, Travis," he answered.

"Hi, Jerry, checking in with you. Did you find anything on the shooters?"

"One is critical and on a respirator, not in any shape to talk. The other one did admit they were hired for the job, but didn't give any more than that. And I talked to the Chief. He agreed that you might need your weapons." The fact that Jerry had consulted his Chief told me our friendship only went so far. He wasn't willing to risk his job on his own decision. I didn't blame him. It was good that Gretna was a smaller department, with shorter lines of communication.

"Thanks for speaking for me, Jerry. I appreciate it."

"Okay, so if you want, you can drop by and pick them up at the lab."

"Thanks again."

Finally, I made a call to the communications center. I hoped two things: that the news of my suspension had not made it that far yet, and that the log of my inquiry did not come to anyone's attention for awhile, long enough to get this mess sorted out. Better to ask forgiveness than permission.

I got my information. The van which Eddie and his friends had seen at the storage place was registered to an Elgin Garrity at an address in Livingston Parish, north and west of Lake Pontchartrain.

I went back to the hotel to get Andrea, but first I picked up my weapons from the Crime Lab.

"Come on, let's take a ride."

"Why?" She was sitting in the easy chair staring out the window.

"To get you out of here for awhile for one, and so that I don't have to worry about you being here alone for another. I have something to check out."

"I'm very tired, Travis."

"What you are besides tired is stressed and depressed. You need to move. You can nap in the truck."

I took her hand to help her up. She let me, then reclaimed her hand. I took the duffel with me and grabbed my spare ID, which the department didn't know about, out of the bag, sticking it in my back pocket. A couple of years before, I had lost my ID, filed a report, gotten a new one, and then found my old one. I had kept it, just in case. This was that case.

"Come on, bring your cigarettes. You can smoke in the truck, I don't care."

She gave me a weak smile and picked up her purse.

We exited the hotel through a side door rather than the lobby where there were more eyes. We were living in a shadow world while all around us, people were going about oblivious that there was someone out there planning some unknown atrocity.

I watched for watchers as we made our way to my truck. I didn't see any lurkers, but I wouldn't have been surprised if there were a drone orbiting somewhere high above. The age of privacy was dead. We were all caught on cameras every day. It was becoming almost impossible to be invisible. Even if there weren't a drone above us, traffic cameras would track us. There was no use driving myself crazy over it. After all, I was a rabbit, meant to run, in the eyes of others, but not in my own. To the bad guys, we were just running and hiding. To the FBI, we were evidently bait. I decided we were going on offense.

We drove east on I-10 to Slidell and connected with I-12 toward Baton Rouge. Outside Hammond, we picked up U.S. 190. It was a two-lane highway running east from Baton Rouge. On the stretch between Albany and Holden, we found the address.

It wasn't what I expected. It was a junkyard. It was surrounded by a chain-link fence topped by barbed wire. There were about four acres of automotive carcasses of various species, some so disemboweled and cannibalized that their original provenance was not immediately identifiable. The two most notable oddities I noted, which did not fit with junked cars and trucks, the trailer office, the two obligatory junkyard curs roaming the lot, and the flatbed tow truck with a winch on the front and a crane boom on the back, were the castle at the gate and the fleet of serviceable-looking white vans parked all the way at the rear of the yard. I drove by without stopping and then pulled over at a residential road half a mile up.

"Are you sure that's the address?" I asked Andrea.

"The address on the mailbox on the road is the same as the one you gave me," she said, clearly not liking me questioning her accuracy, a point of professional clerical pride apparently.

I pulled up the notes file on my phone and showed it to Andrea. She nodded.

"That's the address on the mailbox," she glared at me.

"Okay, okay, I'm not questioning you, just verifying, okay?"

"Okay, I'm sorry."

I gave her my cell phone, pulling up the camera app.

"I'm going to pass again. Can you video the yard as we go by?"

"Sure."

"Okay, hunker down so that just the camera is up, instead of you obviously sitting up holding the camera."

"Got it." She settled herself with her back against her door. She stretched out, first touching my leg with her knee and causing a thrill through my groin, then she kicked off her flip-flops and put her feet in my lap. I looked over at her in surprise, and she laughed. I laughed back and stroked an ankle once as I turned the truck back up the road.

"It's good to see you getting your spunk back. We're both going to need it," I smiled at the windshield.

"I do feel better, doing something."

"Told you."

As we approached from the other direction, I got the confirmation I needed, a sign facing west which read EG Salvage. EG, Elgin Garrity, the name on the registration of the van seen by Eddie and his cohorts, maybe one of those very vans parked in the yard.

I continued on into Albany and pulled over in a church parking lot with a message board which read in eight-inch letters against a white background: CHRIST OR NOT? LIFE OR NOT? YOUR CHOICE.

I took the phone back from Andrea and cued the video. It was pretty good, considering that Andrea's idea of a phone was that it was a phone, and hers was so old I wouldn't have been surprised if it had commands in cuneiform.

We watched it together. There was the castle, of course, which had no conceivable purpose. It was evidently made of sheet metal painted white. The lines of rust running down from screws which held the thing together were clearly visible in the video. It was only about ten feet square at the base, and had no recognizable purpose. It did have crenellations cut in the top as if for a tower for crossbowmen, but the Gothic windows were just black-painted shapes. There was no door on the highway side, or a moat and drawbridge either, but there was a painted-on portcullis. Maybe it was for storage, or marketing, or just something stupid.

Of more interest than the curiosity of the faux castle were the five vans parked abreast at the rear of the yard.

"See that?" Andrea pointed with a freshly painted nail, which was burgundy or some other exotically named shade.

"Yeah, curious, isn't it?"

"Why would a junkyard need five nice-looking vans, and why would they park them all the way in the back if they were using them? They'd waste a lot of time walking back and forth. And look, they're all up on their tires, so they're probably in use." Andrea knew van and truck fleets. They were part of her job, with the dispatching of testing crews to different sites. Little details made all the difference.

"And they don't seem to have any signage, just white."

"Something we need to take a closer look at, if those dogs will let me."

A soft sigh escaped Andrea's mouth, and she relaxed visibly.

"What?" I asked.

"Nothing. I just feel we may be on to something which will end this, this nightmare, and I can get back to my job, to normal."

I was used to a certain level of chaos in my professional life. Police swim in a sea of chaos and are expected to calm it, often impossibly. It is unbelievable how many calls for service come in on school mornings from mothers whose kids refuse to go to school, or from people arguing with cashiers about their change or the price of an item. These wasteful calls are outside the area of police action, but still people call for petty grievances like the neighbor blowing leaves on their lawn or the neighbor's dog taking a dump in their yard. Police are the ones to call when something needs to be done or settled, not the perfect solution, *something*. It's why the courts, not the media who never gets it right, have issued a whole body of law to protect police "acting in good faith."

Andrea's world was completely different. Her job was clerical. Her world was about orderly function, not chaos. She lived to keep a system running smoothly, but a system which was already sane to begin with. I didn't think Andrea should be so relieved just because we had run down a lead. I hadn't forgotten that she had lied to me once already, that I knew of. Pressing her on it wouldn't lead to anything yet, I figured, but it was always there lurking. I was convinced that Andrea had nothing to do with the theft, but she knew more than she admitted. I just didn't know what yet. That hurt as much as the break-up.

I decided to make something happen. I stepped out of my truck behind the church message board and on a whim, flipped my middle finger into the sky just in case there actually was an FBI drone overhead. That was just a tangential gesture. The real idea was to call Sheriff Susan Hadley, formerly Police Chief Hadley, my partner in the terrorism incident the previous year and short-term lover.

I changed my mind and sat back in the truck so that Andrea could hear the call after all. I tried her old cell number, but it had been reassigned to an old lady. I bet she got a lot of calls. Next, I pulled up the number for the Sabine Parish Sheriff's Office and called.

"Sabine Parish Sheriff's Office, how may I help you?" The operator asked.

"Sheriff Hadley, please."

"Hold, please."

I got a secretary next, working my way up the line. "Sheriff Hadley's office," the pleasant voice answered.

"Travis Bowie for the Sheriff, please."

"I'm sorry, but she's not in. May I take a message?"

"Could you contact her on her cell and ask her to call. I'm pretty sure she'll want the message."

There was a pause of reluctance from the secretary, and I let it hang. Didn't want to appear needy.

"Well…"

"Remember the terrorist incident last year?"

"Oh, Lieutenant, I'm so sorry, I didn't place you right away. I'll call the Sheriff right now. You just stay by your phone."

"Thank you so much, Ms….?"

"It's Miss Annie Greer, Lieutenant."

"I think we might be cousins, I had a great great grandmother named Annie Greer."

"Oh, Lieutenant, that would be wonderful. Let me get the Sheriff for you, and you call back some time so we can visit."

"Thank you, Ma'am." I punched off the call.

"What was that about?" Andrea asked.

"I'm going to have to spend some time watching this place and I'm trying to find some place safe for you."

"Don't you think you should have discussed this with me first?"

"Well, it seems we've established a tradition of not discussing things, like you deciding you didn't love me anymore."

"That's mean, Travis."

"Sorry," I said, not meaning it.

"I'm not going anywhere."

"I can't watch over you and work this at the same time, Andrea."

"I'll work it with you."

155

"How?" I knew her aversion to sweat and dirt, and I didn't envision her crawling through the woods. We already knew she wasn't a shooter.

"Whatever I can do, driving, stuff like that."

We sat in silence until my phone rang.

"Susan?"

"Travis, I'm glad you called. I had hoped you would call me sometime."

"I'm sorry it's not social. I wish it were, Susan."

"Did you get into trouble again?"

"I did, and I have fires all over the place. I was looking for a safe place for a lady because it's hot down here, but she's refusing to go. So thanks anyway."

"Girlfriend?"

"Ex. She dumped me too. It seems my charm comes with an expiration date."

She laughed, "You're so mean, Travis. Your charm didn't expire with me. I was just an ambitious bitch."

"Don't be so tough on yourself. I never thought of you like that."

"That's because when it comes to women, you are hopelessly idealistic."

"More like naive, I think, Susan."

"Whatever it is, Travis, it is so sweet. So you don't need a haven for the lady?"

"She's refusing," I shrugged at the phone.

"If you change your mind, just call. This number is my cell. Call any time, I mean, any time, and call me just to talk. Come see me. I miss you."

"I will, promise. Thank you."

"Wait, what is going on anyway?"

"Guess what's loose again?"

"No, not radioactive stuff."

"Yep. This time they think the lady in question took it, but people keep trying to kill her. The FBI's suspicious of me, and I think they're letting me do their dirty work, since they won't listen to what I have to say. And careful what you say, they're probably listening."

"You getting paranoid?"

"As Yossarian said in Catch-22, if people are trying to kill you, you'd be crazy to think any other way."

"Still quoting, Travis." She laughed.

"Goodbye, Susan, I miss you too." I ended the call.

Andrea was fuming. "That was embarrassing. Making me listen to a call with your old girlfriend."

"She's not old."

"You know what I mean."

I did. I also knew what I needed to know. Andrea wanted to stay close to this. Now I just needed to find out why, and also figure out if she intended to sabotage my efforts.

XXVIII

I needed a busier and more anonymous place to park and check the junkyard area on Google Earth, so I drove to the Berry World country store between Albany and Hammond. While I searched my tablet, Andrea did me the courtesy of stepping outside to smoke.

She seemed a little calmer, since she wasn't lighting one cigarette off the fag end of the previous one. It seemed that she had turned a corner, was more resolved to fight back. I wondered what she was holding back.

Google Earth showed me the area around the junkyard. The only road access was by way of Highway 190. To the west were woods, but they could only be accessed through people's yards and acreage on a nearby country road. To the immediate east was a cleared pasture with a line of trees separating it from the junkyard. Good access, but little cover. To the north were acres of woods, but with little access close to the junkyard. I thought about it.

Andrea finished her cigarette and sat back in the truck.

"You must be really disappointed in me for smoking again," she said, looking out the windshield.

"None of my business now. It never was. I'm still curious, though, did wanting to smoke again have something to do with your decision to call it off between us?"

She turned to me quickly, waited a beat, said, "That would be so, so, superficial."

"Smoking can be a powerful draw. Mae chose to die rather than quit."

"I'm not your wife. And that's another thing." There always is.

"What is?"

"You would bring up your wife in conversation a lot."

"You do know she's dead, right?"

"Don't be sarcastic."

"Well, I'm glad we're finally having a discussion. Let me clarify, it was insensitive for me to mention my wife, but it was not for you to mention your ex-husbands?"

"I don't know." That was probably a signal to end this particular conversation.

"Well, did it?"

"Did what?"

"Did not smoking become a problem for us?"

"I wanted to smoke again, I liked it, and I felt inferior with you, you know, giving up drinking. You were strong, and I was weak, and it felt unequal."

"One thing I learned from sobriety is it isn't a matter of willpower, and you can't try to change other people's habits, even their bad ones."

"It still made me feel bad."

It made me feel bad too, that we destroy not just our bodies with addictions, but also all the beauty we have in our lives, in order to avoid the pain that is in them too. I wasn't judging. I had been there. I didn't have anything else to say.

I thought I had a plan. I drove to the street west of the junkyard and proceeded slowly along the gravel road. The houses and trailers along it were well spaced on yards that varied from a half-acre to an acre. The road was about a quarter mile long and dead-ended at a fence with a pasture to the front and a wall of trees to the right.

I checked the rear-view mirror to see if anyone had been interested in our passing. A couple of people had noticed as we drove down the road, who waved as we went by, since we were out of the city and in waving country, but there was no one standing in the street looking in our direction. Maybe the FOR SALE sign off to the left had people coming by from time to time.

"Let's get out," I said.

159

When she got out on her side, I walked to her and took her hand. She gave me a funny look.

"Just go along, okay?" She didn't pull away. We walked to the property with the FOR SALE sign hand in hand and inspected it. It was a cleared acre and a few trees. We walked up the drive which ended at a concrete slab where a trailer might have been before. From there, I could survey the screen of trees to our right. They were mostly pines without much undergrowth. The area had evidently been cut and replanted probably ten or fifteen years before. This would be my entry point. We were a little west of the junkyard. I would make my way through here to the north edge of the junkyard where I could take a closer look at the white vans. As we returned to the truck, a man wearing shorts, tee shirt and a big straw hat was driving a lawnmower on the street toward us. He was about a hundred yards away. When he saw us, I waved and he waved back before pulling onto another property.

"See, just a couple looking at land," I said.

"You're sneaky," Andrea said and pulled her hand away.

"Sometimes."

"Makes me wonder."

I wasn't even going to get started again. We returned to the truck. As we drove back to the highway, I waved at the man on the lawnmower. He waved back.

"Where to now?" Andrea asked.

"Wal-Mart."

At the intersection with the highway, I Googled Wal-Mart locations and found the closest one in Hammond. I bought bug spray and a headband light with both white and red LEDs. Then I found a motel.

"Why are we here?"

"There's no point in driving all the way back to New Orleans and then coming back here tonight."

"But my things, my bag, I don't have a change of clothes, my makeup."

160

So we drove back to Wal-Mart. I should have mentioned the motel before. Andrea had to shop, not just throw some things in a cart and go. While I waited, I tossed some things in another cart: black cargo pants, a black tee shirt and fresh underwear, also black though I hoped it wouldn't matter what color my underwear was. I also got some black nitrile gloves and a ski mask, in camo since they didn't have black.

When Andrea was satisfied, we checked out, again, and finally went back to the motel.

XXIX

I lay on the double bed closest to the window and took a nap fully clothed. Andrea took a shower, but since I would be getting dirty and sweaty and would be doused with bug spray later, I didn't see the point.

When I awoke a half-hour later, Andrea was still in the bathroom. Whatever women took so long to do to themselves in the bathroom, I liked it. I took Larry's phone out of my khaki cargo pocket and looked once more at the call list. That one number nagged at me. Two points of intersection. It looked familiar. Andrea recognized it, and had lied when she had said she didn't. What was her part in this?

When Andrea emerged from the bathroom, she was perfectly put together as always. Her hair, her make-up, her clothes, were perfect. I felt a twinge in my heart and other places.

"You look wonderful," I said, taking in her new blue slacks and aquamarine blouse.

"Thank you," she smiled. She saw Larry's phone beside me on the bed.

"Is that Larry's phone?" She knew it was.

"Oh, yeah, it is."

"What are you going to do with it?"

"Still thinking about that. Any ideas?"

"No."

"Maybe I should call some of these numbers and just see who answers."

"I don't know, wouldn't that warn them?"

"That's what I've been considering too." I could see the pulse in her throat. She didn't want me to call that number. It meant I would have to. I also knew I couldn't let her have access to the phone. She would likely delete the call list or disable the phone.

First things first. The peek at the vans. I just knew they were key to this whole thing. I stuck the phone back in my cargo pocket and took another nap while Andrea watched the TV. Through the slit of my slightly opened eyes, I caught her worrying and occasionally stealing glances at my pocket.

After another hour nap, I used the bathroom, to lighten the load. Changed into my ninja outfit. And brushed my teeth.

It was ten o'clock, 2200, when I packed my binoculars, bug spray, headlamp, and pepper spray into the day pack.

"Okay," Andrea asked, "what now?"

"I had an idea. Back to Wal-Mart."

"Again? Well, there was another blouse I looked at." I laughed and she stuck her tongue out at me. Whatever she was keeping from me, it had to be important. I couldn't believe she was bad.

And so back to the all-night Wal-Mart. I bought ground meat and Benadryl. Outside at the back of my truck, I pulled the plastic wrap away, dumped all the Benadryl capsules on the tailgate, separated them one by one, and dumped the powder onto the ground meat. Then I worked the mixture with my hands and rolled little meatballs. I placed them in the plastic shopping bag. I threw the plastic ground meat tray and empty pill bottle and capsules in the trash, then went back inside the store to wash my hands. When I came back out of the restroom, Andrea was standing in front of the check-out area looking around. I walked up on her blind side unintentionally.

"Waiting for the bus?" I asked.

She jumped at my comment, "Jesus, you scared me."

"Sorry, I should have been more obtrusive. You get something?"

"Yes, I don't usually shop for clothes here, but there was a nice blouse. I hope you like it."

"Why?"

She shook her head with that *men are idiots* look and walked away, leaving me to follow like a puppy.

Back in the truck, she asked, "What did you have to get anyway?"

"Meatballs for the dogs, with a little something in them?"

"You're going to poison them?" She didn't like dogs, but didn't want to poison them either.

"God, no, just some Benadryl to make them sleepy."

"Does it work?"

"It does with Kiddo."

"So what now?"

I sat there for a moment, then said, "Let's switch. You drive, and drop me off at the end of McCullen Road. I'll make my way in from there."

We switched places. I had to direct her back to Highway 190, since, as a passenger, she hadn't paid much attention. As we crossed the intersection with LA. 43, I saw the lights of a tow truck, as well as the yellow safety lights stuck on the old Chevy pickup it was hauling behind it. Andrea started to pull around him to pass, but I put my hand on her arm.

"Wait. Let's see if he's going to the junkyard."

When the driver pulled partly into the drive, still blocking part of the highway lane, his headlights lighting the locked gate, I gave Andrea a quick kiss on the cheek, figuring I might be able to save a lot of slogging through the woods in the dark, told her to drive on once I was out, grabbed my pack, opened the passenger door as little as possible, then pushed it shut without slamming it, and rolled out into a crouch on the blacktop. I didn't want to cross my headlight beams and make a shadow, so I ran in a crouch to the ditch on the side of the road and then crawled toward the tow truck. The driver, wearing a greasy jumpsuit with the sleeves cut off, was unlocking the gate. I lost sight of him as I got close to the vehicle.

I thought, in the pickup bed or the tow truck bed? I decided and stepped up on one of the dually tires, rolled onto the flat bed

164

next to the boom, and lay flat. I heard the gate rattling back, and then the crunch of the driver's boots on the gravel as he returned. I saw Andrea's headlights swing away as she pulled into the eastbound lane and around the truck. I heard her voice.

"You're working late," she shouted at the driver.

"Yes. ma'am, late pickup, sorry for the delay."

"No problem. Take care." And then she drove away. Bless her little diversion.

We rolled and bumped through the uneven gravel of the junkyard. Then the dogs started barking and chasing the truck. I felt like an idiot. In desperation, I reached into my pack and started dropping meatballs over the side. I peeked over the side and saw the dogs stop momentarily to snag a treat, then resume chasing and barking. More treats.

Toward the back of the yard, the truck swung in a wide arc, then started backing the towed truck into an empty space. Wait. Wait. Then, as I heard the driver's door creak open, I went over the side, out of sight. The dogs were still barking, but not snarling, thank God. I looked under the truck and saw the driver's boots headed to the back to break loose the tow. I tossed some more meatballs far ahead of me and the dogs, one a Lab/Catahoula mix by the look of him, and the other a white Pit/American bulldog mutt, went to fetch. They weren't retrieving though. They were gulping them down as quickly as they could. I crept around the front of another wreck and low-walked a few hulks down to a rusted sedan with no doors.

I clambered inside onto the floor behind the front seats and sat facing in the direction of the tow truck. The dogs were looking for me, barking their excitement. They seemed to be enjoying the game.

"You dogs'll be sorry you corner a coon in one of them wrecks," the driver yelled at them over the sound of the winch lowering the tow. I thought, oh please, don't let there be a coon in here with me.

The dogs found me, barking. I tossed them each a meatball. I hoped they were getting sleepy. I was running out of meatballs. I could hear the driver stowing his gear, putting his tow hooks back in their slots.

"Awright, dogs, I'm goin'. It's late." I heard his door slam and the diesel make a throatier rumble. Then he drove off, leaving me in the dark with the dogs.

I sat in the dark, my only company the panting of my new friends. When I had first spied the dogs from the highway, I didn't figure them for trained dogs, just junkyard mutts. From time to time, I tossed a couple of meatballs in the direction of their panting. I caught an occasional flash of their eyes in the moonlight. I finally heard one of them yawn with one of those little squeals dogs make, and the sound of them patting down the gravel in a circle.

When all was calm for half an hour, I placed the headband light on my head over the ski mask I had pulled on. Then I pulled on the black nitrile gloves. I slid on my butt to the edge of the door sill where there was no door. I started to place my feet on the ground and encountered a hump. In the red light of the headlamp, I saw it was the Catahoula mix, sound asleep on his side with his tongue hanging out. I felt his body to satisfy myself that his breathing was good. Nearby the pit mix lay with his head on his forepaws. As I stood in a crouch outside the wreck, he lifted his head as if with a great effort and then laid it back down again.

I called Andrea. She answered right away, "Are you okay?"

"I'm in. That was a nice touch distracting the driver. Don't hang around in the dark. Go back to the motel. You shouldn't hear from me until sometime after sunup. Get some rest. Smoke some cigarettes."

"Okay, please be careful."

"I will, thanks."

I took my time. There was no hurry. If there was anybody around at night, which it didn't look like, they probably relied on the dogs to raise a ruckus. The office trailer was dark. Nevertheless, I made my way carefully from row to row of junked vehicles, not even using the red light most of the time. Even red light can be seen, even if it's a little harder.

It was nearly two when I reached the vans. I walked along the fronts of them, which were pulled up close to the fence line. As Andrea had noted, their tires were full of air. I kicked them and got the strong resistance. They were all Fords, work vans with no windows in the cargo area. I looked through the windshields. The dashboards were all clean and clear, no papers or trash. All had up-to-date inspection stickers. As I made it to the fifth one, the last, I walked around and checked the door. Locked.

Slowly, carefully, I checked every door, the two passenger compartment doors, the side cargo door, the rear doors. All locked. The only windows were to the drivers' and passenger doors. Every one was clean, but each one had one or two white plastic rectangles on the passenger seat, about twenty by thirty inches. Only the van in the middle of the line had the rectangle facing up. It was evidently a magnetic sign, or decal with the backing still on. I couldn't read it in the red light.

I went around to the front and stepped on the bumper. I leaned over as far as I could and took a chance on the white light setting on the headlamp. I switched them on and shielded the lamp with my hands while balancing on the bumper, channeling as much light as possible through the windshield. The sign read, NEW WORLD ALARM CO., INC., with a phone number and website, nwa.com. I switched off the lamp and dropped back down to the ground.

I squatted out of sight in the dark. I knew more than I had, but I didn't know what it was I knew. Also, I had saved myself hours of stumbling in the dark woods with my little trick with the tow truck, but now I had hours to wait. Would someone come in the morning to check the vans? Were these vans even significant? Would anyone ever come? How long should I wait? What could I do to make something happen? Was I an idiot? Should I wave to some drone which might be orbiting overhead with FLIR, already reading everything in bright infrared? Fed pricks, I thought. At least, if they were watching, they would have to know I was investigating, not conspiring. Right?

By the red LED lights of the headlamp, I took photos with my phone of all the license plates. Then I scurried back to the fence line to check them. They weren't good, but I could read them.

Then, before trying to figure out how to get over the eight-foot fence topped by barbed wire, I let the air out of two tires, the left front of the middle van, and the rear right of the right-most one. No particular reason on the choice. Hopefully, it would look normal.

Finally, I found a floor mat in a piece of junk nearby. I walked well away from the vans before climbing the fence. With my torso clear of the top of the fence and its three strands of barbed wire, I placed the floor mat carefully on the wire and pressed it down hard so that it would catch on the barbs. Then I lay on top of it. The barbs were trying to get through to my belly. I had my pack on my back, so my hands were free. I reached over and grabbed the fence on the other side. I let myself fall over the top and caught myself with my hands and feet in the fence holes. Hanging there, I pulled at the floor mat until it came free, then dropped to the ground and rolled to keep from breaking an ankle. I stepped into the woods and hoped I didn't step on a nocturnal snake looking for a rabbit. I took the floor mat with me.

It would be a long time to dawn.

XXX

Stepping carefully into the trees beyond the narrow cleared area on the other side of the fence, I felt the same atavistic fear that lives deep in our brains, evoked in Hansel and Gretel and Little Red Riding Hood. I was a city boy after all. Whereas dark streets and alleys didn't cause me undue fear, the prospect of stepping on a hunting snake or spooking a big bad wolf made me move slowly.

Using my red lights, I found a stout pine deep enough in the woods so I could not be seen from the yard. I settled myself with my back against the trunk and slid down into a sitting position. I removed the ski mask because it was hot, although the night was cool, in the high sixties. I stripped off the nitrile gloves since my hands were sweating inside them. The consequence was mosquitoes swarming my face and hands, so I sprayed myself with DEET, including my clothes.

As the night wound slowly toward dawn, I dozed off from time to time, catching myself awake when my head dropped to my chest. I tried to keep awake by eating a nut bar along with some mosquitoes which flew in my mouth. Protein.

Around six, I could detect a lightening ahead of me in the junkyard as the pre-dawn twilight made individual objects identifiable. Before the sun was fully up at seven, I moved a few trees farther back into the woods, but where I could still see the vans.

Although I could see activity at the trailer office in the junkyard beginning around seven thirty, and vehicles coming and going on what appeared to be regular business, it was after nine when a blue Mustang rolled toward the back of the yard. A white male, about thirty, with shaved head and a chin beard that reached to his sternum, got out and inspected the vans, walking around them and noting the flat tires. He kicked them as if that would make a difference. Then he checked every one of the doors to make sure they were locked. He looked around the yard and into the woods where I stood behind a pine trunk. He made a phone call. I couldn't hear what he said, but he shook his head at one point and nodded at another.

I noted the man's clothes. He wasn't dressed like a mechanic or someone prepared to get dirty working in a junkyard. He was thin, wearing clean black jeans and a collarless black shirt with three buttons at the top. When he turned, I could see a black automatic in the rear of his waistband. Now I knew the vans were important.

Mustang Guy made another call and stayed with the vans. A few minutes later, a work truck with a compressor, gas cylinders and a welding machine on its flat bed arrived. A fat guy in a baby blue jumpsuit with old oil stains got out and walked around to Mustang Guy, who pointed to the flat tires and seemed to be giving the yard worker orders. The truck driver didn't seem to like his tone, but he reached over and flipped a switch on the compressor. Then he uncoiled a hose from the back and filled the tires. Mustang Guy just watched and made another call. When the truck driver was finished, he tossed the air line back and walked back to the driver's side. Mustang Guy yelled something at him. I could hear it but not make it out. The truck driver took something out of his jumpsuit breast pocket, a tire pressure gauge, and tossed it to Mustang Guy. Then he drove away, around the back of the yard and on to the front. The two men didn't seem to get along, and it occurred to me that the truck driver was probably just a working man, who had nothing to do with whatever the vans were about.

My inferences were bolstered when a half hour later another young white guy probably in his late twenties arrived in a gray SUV, which looked a lot like the one I had seen following me earlier on the Lafitte/Larose Highway on the way to pick up Andrea from her sister's. Mustang Guy pointed to the vans, then at SUV Guy, then got in his Mustang and drove away. In the distance, I could see him exiting the yard. SUV Guy repositioned his vehicle and stayed. I figured he had been put on watch over the vans.

I considered how long I wanted to watch these vans. They could sit for days, or weeks, or forever, for that matter, while I gathered moss. If I didn't watch them, they could disappear and I wouldn't know where or why. I had made something happen, and now I knew the vans were important, and connected to the storage unit where Eddie had seen the isotopes offloaded. I decided I was done here for the moment.

I looked around for a branch to probe ahead of me as I made my way to the road where I had originally intended to enter the woods, and where I now intended to exit. I had just started to step farther into the woods when I heard two car doors slam. I turned to the sound, but couldn't see the vans well, so I had to retrace my steps. Back at my pine tree, I saw that another man had arrived. He was out of his vehicle. I saw him do that handshake chest bump abrazzo popularized by the hip-hop generation, which seemed so alien to my generation wherein men didn't embrace unless someone had died or was dying.

Then a whole lot more things began to come together.

XXXI

I knew now why the number on Larry's phone had looked familiar. The other vehicle which had arrived was a small pickup truck with the logo from Inspections Safety, Inc., which happened to be the company Andrea worked for, and the company from which the isotopes had been stolen. And the little less than medium height man with the dark hair and beard was Brent, Andrea's son, who also worked for the company. He was the one in charge, judging from the body language, as he talked to the other man.

I drew Larry's phone from my pocket, powered it up, and got to the call list. I took out my own phone and went to the Contacts, punched in Brent, and there it was, the same number. I had had it all along. I called the number using an app I had which simulated a phone number other than my own. When I heard the ring faintly in the yard, and Brent pulled out his phone, another pin fell into place. I wondered why he was still using the phone until I realized it was almost certainly a company phone, and people expected to be able to get him at that number. I hung up. Andrea had some explaining to do, but I thought Brent was far past that point. He should have used a burner phone, not his company phone. I was grateful he was an idiot.

There was no way I was going to make it out of the woods undetected in time to follow Brent to wherever he went to when he left the junkyard, but there was also no point in hanging around. I waited for Brent to leave in his company truck and for the guy watching the vans to settle back into his vehicle. Then I faded back and began picking my way west through the trees, probing with my stick. When I was far enough away, I called Andrea.

"Hi, can you meet me at the end of McCullen Road in about an hour? I'll be at that property we looked at yesterday if I get there before you."

"Okay. I'll leave now."

"No, wait, we don't want you having to hang around at the end of the road and attracting attention." I thought, I also didn't want her running into the company truck on the highway with Brent driving.

As I picked my way along, in places the underbrush was thin, with a light covering of dead leaves and pine needles on the forest floor, with occasional muddy low spots where a fallen tree had dug up a giant root ball and left a depression which would fill with water when it rained. I considered the life cycle of the forest. Trees grew tall, then old, and died, or were struck down by wind or lightning. Termites and ants reduced the dead tree. Rain eventually weathered the root ball of dirt until the soil was rearranged. I passed a pine which bore a slash of a lightning strike. A flash of white revealed a magnolia, blooming late in the year.

Eventually, I came to the western edge of the woods, pursued by a cloud of gnats and mosquitoes the whole way. The cleared field ahead of me was bordered by a barbed wire fence. In the field were a black horse and a brown over white donkey. Both seemed apathetic to my presence until I climbed over the fence. Then the donkey ambled over to investigate. She sniffed at me and nudged my cargo pockets. I pulled out a fruit and nut bar and opened it up. The horse then came over. I shared out two of the bars and then walked to the southern edge of the field while the two munched happily. I climbed the fence again to get to the road and saw my truck heading toward me. It was a nice scene, but it promised to get less idyllic pretty soon when Andrea and I discussed what I had found at the junkyard.

Andrea got out of the truck and walked around to the passenger side. We both got in. I drove back up the road.

"Well, did you find out anything?" Andrea asked.

"I did. I think we should relocate up here until we find out more. So, we can drive back and get our things from New Orleans East. There's no point in staying there any longer."

"Tell me what you found. Is it going to help?"

"The vans are definitely part of whatever is going on. The van seen by my informant is there, same plate. I've got to find a way to run the others, but I'm betting they all come back to the yard owner."

"What else?" Man, she could smell the deception and I hadn't even said anything.

I had hoped to avoid this conversation until we were both in a more relaxed setting, but it was unavoidable, so I asked, "Why didn't you tell me that number on Larry's phone was Brent's?" I stole a glance across at her as I drove east on Interstate 12, back toward New Orleans.

Her mouth was set hard, and her lips were mashed together like a fault line about to slip, and it did. The quake came in the form of tears, the sobs which wracked her body. The tension which had been building for days was breaking out all over. I pulled off at the next exit and stopped on the shoulder of the road.

I waited for the storm to subside, then asked again, "Why?"

She spoke through her tears, which is a skill or a talent I've always marveled at in women, that they can cry and talk at the same, while a man trying that sounds like he's being garroted while choking on a chicken bone, "It's a company phone number. There could have been a good reason Brent and Larry were talking."

"If that's the case, why not just tell me it was Brent's number?"

"I was scared."

"Scared? Of me? What have I done to scare you?"

"Scared Brent was involved with this?"

I nodded, then, "And if he was involved in this, then he is involved in framing you, and with trying to kill you, right? Not the sort of thing a mother wants to contemplate."

She buried her face in her hands and sobbed. I reached across and drew her to me, my arms around her as she cried it out. Finally, she managed to ask, "How did you know?"

"I knew you were lying when you said you didn't recognize the number, but the clincher was when I saw Brent, in a company truck, at the junkyard this morning."

She was done crying for the moment, but her eyes glistened, "Brent has had troubles trying to find his way. I talked for him to get the job. They must be using him."

"I don't know how to tell you this without it being harsh, but he was giving orders, not taking them. He's involved in a big way."

I drove on to Slidell, and then transitioned to Interstate 10 back to our hotel in New Orleans. On both sides, Lake Pontchartrain stretched to the horizon. From time to time, I caught Andrea shaking her head as if to empty it of the realizations which were crowding in.

Finally, she said, "But...," and left it hanging.

"Yes, if he's involved at the highest level, he knows about people trying to kill you, to frame you for this theft."

"I'm his mother," she protested.

"Apparently that doesn't matter."

She held both palms out in front of her, as if to ward off an attack, or some unimaginable evil, which was of course what she was facing.

"How could he do that to his own mother? I've always loved him with all my heart."

"Are you going to try to warn him? Because if you do, we'll never get as good a chance to clear you as we have right now."

I left her to think it out as we approached the south shore of the lake, and passed through the marshes and wetlands of New Orleans east. We didn't speak as we pulled up to the hotel on Read Blvd, packed our few things in the truck, and checked out. Andrea had a lot to think about. After loading the truck, we drove back to Hammond, which was closer to the junkyard and the focus of my counter-operation.

We settled back in the hotel room. I took a much-needed shower after checking myself for ticks. I didn't find any. Hopefully they were done for the year. Then I took a nap, leaving Andrea to stare out the window. I kept one ear attuned to her movements in case she tried to warn Brent. I would have to prevent that, even if I didn't know how far I would go to achieve it.

I slept for two hours, lightly. When I awoke, I didn't see Andrea, and I panicked a little. Then I heard her in the bathroom. She could have gone in there to make a phone call, but then I saw her phone on her bed. When she emerged, I watched her for signs she might have made a decision. She watched me watching her as she sat in a chair. We continued to hold each other's gaze.

"Well," I kicked off. Her ball.

"I want my life back. If that means helping you, so be it. I want you to promise me you won't hurt Brent. I've seen you at work. You're a very violent man, Travis."

"Only when I have to be. I don't want to hurt anyone. I don't want to hurt Brent, but in the end, it will probably be his decision."

"Promise me anyway."

"I promise to try."

Evidently she thought that was the best she was going to get, and she nodded, "What now?"

"Has Brent called you since you were arrested?"

"No."

"That right there is odd, don't you think? You work for the same company. It's natural that he would have heard about your arrest and call you to see if you're all right. Where does Brent live?"

"He has an apartment in Baton Rouge on Essen."

"Then that's where we start. Does he live alone?"

"As far as I know."

"We have to take a look inside, and we have to find out who the money is behind this, money to buy vans, pay soldiers, send a crew to Costa Rica to shut Larry up, hell, to bribe Larry in the first place."

"How can we do that?"

"Brent knows. We don't know if this is about some sort of whacko cause they're fighting for, or if it's about a crime for profit."

She nodded, apparently resolved.

"You do know Brent is your enemy, right?" It was a horrible realization for a mother who doted on her three sons to embrace, but again, she nodded.

I took another nap, and then we headed for Baton Rouge.

"So there you were, running around like a one man army," Andy Landry, the Sheriff's Office counsel, "and not passing anything along to the department. Didn't you consider the potential liability of a sworn member, keeping things secret?"

The other bookend bobbled furiously.

The Sheriff was as impassive as a Buddha.

"You mean an indefinitely suspended member, Sir? With no authority anyway?"

My little revenge, which might cost me more than I gained.

XXXII

We drove to Baton Rouge by Highway 190, past the junkyard, until we got to Holden and then took I-12. As we passed the yard, we could see all five vans in their usual place, and the gray SUV with its driver standing watch. Brent's truck was gone. Andrea seemed deep in thought.

"Why do you think Brent would do this? Money or politics?" I asked.

She turned to look at me for a moment, as if I had just pulled her back from a faraway place, then said, unhelpfully, "I don't know."

"Think, please, Andrea. Does he have strong political views? Money problems?"

"He's had money problems for years, paying child support to two different mothers for three children. When he started working for Safety, I thought he had turned things around. He knew Larry from when he was a kid, they were friendly."

"What about his political views?"

"We never talked about politics exactly, but he has made comments about the government and police. He hates them, from back when he was seventeen and got busted for marijuana."

"I don't like the government much either, and I work for it, but this is a step beyond."

"I know he has some friends, they say, he says, the government has no authority, no right to do all the things it does, taxes, jails, snooping. He says the citizens are sovereign, not the government, something like that. I don't pay attention to politics"

"Well, sometimes politics pays attention to you anyway. Does he know anyone with money who could bankroll something like this?"

She shrugged and said, "Not that I know of."

178

I transitioned to the interstate, then took the exchange from Interstate 12 to 10 and then took the Essen exit. I pulled over at a gas station.

"Have you been to Brent's apartment before?"

"No, he just moved up here for a job that's scheduled for three months. The company is paying for it. I found it and rented it. It's down near Perkins Road."

"Maybe you should pay him a surprise visit."

She gave me a look that communicated fear, alarm, conflict, so I followed up with a partial lie intended to appeal both to her sense of self-preservation and her motherly instincts, "If we're going to help Brent get out of this mess and get you out of trouble, we need to find out what we can. She gave a nod which didn't convey much enthusiasm, but I think she was pretty incapable of anything like enthusiasm at that point. The truth was I intended to stop whatever Brent and his co-conspirators had planned, and if he got burned down in the process, I didn't care.

"Okay," she said.

"So here's what we do. Let's check if Brent is home. If he is, you drop in for a visit unannounced, catch him unaware. I'll watch to make sure no one grabs you. While you're inside his apartment, notice anything lying around which might indicate what he's working on. Notice the locks on his doors. He'll probably have a patio door, so look to see if there's a locking bar. If there is, take it out when he's not looking. Can you do that?"

She sat staring ahead without speaking.

"Go ahead," I prompted, "say what's on your mind. Let's talk it out."

She sighed, "I'm so confused. This makes me so sad. I've always done whatever I can to help my children, and now I'm supposed to spy on my own son, to help you."

"To help me help you, remember. I don't really have a dog in this fight. I'm not the one who was framed and facing prison, I'm not the one who is dodging killers."

"I know, that's why I'm confused."

"It is confusing." I let the situation percolate, sitting silently. The only accompaniment was the engine sound and the air conditioning.

Finally, "Okay."

"Okay, show me the apartment complex."

She pointed vaguely south and said, "I've never been there, but when I was looking for a place with good access to the plant where the job is, I checked maps of the area."

I drove south on Essen toward Perkins Road, while Andrea watched to our left. As we passed an apartment complex, she leaned toward me to get a closer look and said, "That's it."

"Are there any other company people staying here? Would there be any other company trucks?"

"No, the other two guys live up here, so there was no need to find accommodations for them."

"What job are they working on?"

"They're photographing welds on some pipe at an expansion at one of the refineries."

"So they're using the same radioactive stuff? How are they doing that if the isotopes have gone missing?"

"The cameras they're using are already loaded, so they wouldn't need new ones right away."

"Oh. So what does Brent do?"

"He's a supervisor, talks to the plant people, sets up shoot schedules. They have to clear a safety zone when they're shooting, things like that."

"Does he know how to handle the isotopes?"

"He knows safety procedures. He's trained as an operator, though."

I made a U-turn and proceeded back to the complex. I took the risk of driving through the parking areas which fronted the several buildings. The buildings were sited so that the driving lanes wound in curves, probably to discourage speeding, with islands planted with trees and shrubbery. It contributed to a certain esthetic sense, and it offered some concealment, so that if Brent or one of his associates who might recognize my truck were outside, I could hopefully stop behind one of the islands and reverse course before being spotted. It was a risk, but there was no SAFETY INSPECTIONS truck.

"Which is his apartment?"

"37C."

I parked and walked to Building C, but actually took a look at it from the breezeway of the building opposite. The blinds on the front window were closed. There were no vehicles parked directly in front. I made a long loop around the building next to C, and walked behind. Each apartment on the ground floor had a small patio bordered by a low wooden fence to imply privacy. Blinds were drawn at the glass patio door as well. I returned to the truck before residents could notice my suspect activity.

"Okay, not home, I guess," I drove out of the complex.

"What do we do now?"

"Wait, go shopping, get some lunch, dinner, whatever."

"Shopping?"

"You'll see."

First we needed to eat. Living alone, I often forgot to eat, and wouldn't notice until I started feeling sick. I drove back to I-10 and pulled off on Acadian to TJ Ribs. It was decorated throughout the interior with LSU sports memorabilia. The food was good, and not so exotic as to offend Andrea's mainstream appetites.

"I don't know if I can even eat," Andrea said.

"At this point, it's about filling a hole. We're not dining, we're just eating, because we have to, to keep going."

I got the ribs and sweet potatoes, she got barbecued chicken and a baked potato. We shared a salad.

"I do feel better," she said afterward.

"Me too."

Next, I pulled up the location of a GOODWILL store on my phone. When we found it, I bought an old green fabric raincoat and a straw hat. Andrea looked her question. Finally, I rented a gray Ford Fiesta at Enterprise. We drove separately to a parking lot across Essen from the complex.

"To make me look as little like a cop as possible while you visit Brent."

It was nearly five when we got back to the apartment complex. I parked in a space near the office and did a walk-through until I saw the company truck parked in front of 37C. I returned to Andrea in the truck.

"Looks like he's home. Ready?"

"I'm   nervous."

"I know, but sell yourself the story. Believe it. You came up to Baton Rouge with me. I'm at a police workshop downtown. You decided to drop in. Give me your phone." I called my number, put her phone on speaker, then blanked the display. I answered the call on mine, then muted it.

"I'll be able to hear everything you say, but you won't hear anything from my end. If anything goes wrong, I'll be close, okay?"

"Okay."

"You borrowed my truck to visit while I'm in a meeting. They know my truck already, so we won't be able to follow him in it anyway. When you leave, drive back toward the interstate, but make a U-turn and come back here. I'll be able to see if anyone follows you." She nodded again. I took her hand, kissed her quickly.

"You're on. Give me a smile." It wasn't much as smiles went.

XXXIII

Andrea drove across the street after taking a deep breath. Before driving into the complex, she spoke into her phone, "Wish me luck," and I waved at her to let her know I could hear her. She couldn't hear me since I had muted my end.

I heard the engine noises, the sound of the truck door closing, the knock on the door of 37C, the sound of a leaf-blower in the background. I heard the sound of a security chain being disengaged. So he kept that on when he was at home.

"Mom! What are you doing here?"

"Hi, baby, give me a kiss." I heard it along with the rustle of fabric as they probably embraced.

"Really, Mom, how did you end up in Baton Rouge?"

"Travis, you remember Travis, he had some workshop, some police thing up here, and I borrowed his truck to come visit you until he's free."

"Well, that's great. Really." When people say *really,* they often mean the opposite.

"Are you going to invite me in, or do you have a naked girl in there?" She laughed. Brent laughed.

"No, no, come on in." More laughter, his sounding more nervous than hers. No obvious sounds of footsteps, so I assumed carpet on the floor.

Brent's voice again, "I didn't expect you. I've got this stuff I've been working on. Let me clear it out of the way. Oh, this is my friend, uh, Robert, he lives nearby."

"It's so nice to meet you, Ms. ...?" I heard a damaged voice.

"Hello, I'm Andrea, Brent's mother." I heard the sound of something scraping and things being dropped.

Brent said, "Let me put this stuff in the bedroom out of the way." I heard his voice from a distance.

"It's so nice to put a face with the name," the other voice again. He sounded not just older, but old.

It was a full minute between hearing a door close, and then close again, more than long enough for Brent to drop his "stuff" and return, but about the right amount of time if he wanted to make a phone call.

"Pardon me for saying it, but you don't look old enough to be Brent's mother." I rolled my eyes, even though it was true.

"That's very flattering, Robert, even it is a lie." They both laughed. The other door closed.

"So what stuff are you working on?" Andrea asked.

"Just hobby stuff in the evenings. Keeps me from getting bored, stuck up here on this project."

"Well," Robert said, "I should be going, let you two have a family visit."

"Oh, don't leave on account of me. I can't visit long. I'm just hanging on to my phone waiting for my friend to call so I can go pick him up."

"No, really, I need to be going. Just dropped in on Brent. Are we still playing golf this weekend?"

"Oh, golf, sure," Brent said, as if he'd never heard of golf.

That was my cue. I had been sitting on the bus stop bench, wearing my straw hat and coat like some down on his luck guy so that I could be close in case Andrea needed help, but now I needed to know more about Robert, if that was his real name. I risked my life running across the two northbound lanes, the turning lane, and the two southbound lanes, almost getting clipped by a young woman pulling into the turning lane while talking on her phone. I dodged her by turning sideways like a matador. She went by me without ever seeing me. I made it to the rental Fiesta and watched for cars leaving the apartment complex.

Less than a minute later, with Andrea and Brent's conversation still coming in on my earbuds, I saw a black BMW 700 series pull to the street. His right blinker was on, so I jumped the two southbound lanes into the turning lane and waited until the BMW was clear. I observed a man with thin white hair cut short, with big eyes. He looked to be in his seventies. When he turned into the street, I followed only long enough to get his plate number. I couldn't leave Andrea unprotected, so I made a U-turn and returned to my spot.

I had been listening to the conversation as I followed the old man the short distance. I hated letting him go, since I had the feeling he might be the money man. He had sounded cultured, and he drove an expensive car. He might be the money man behind this thing. Or he might be a rich guy romancing young Brent for all I knew.

"Why haven't you called me, Brent? I know you heard about all the trouble I'm in," the conversation had continued.

"I'm sorry, Mom. I just didn't know what to say." He was going to have to practice lying. They both knew it, and silence hung like a bad odor. I thought it was a good time for Andrea to leave.

I terminated the call, and then called Andrea's number back, making sure the mute was off. Her phone rang. The new call cancelled the speaker option, I hoped.

"Hi," she answered with what I heard as false brightness.

"Time to go," I said.

"You're right, I'll be right there. I'm leaving Brent's now."

"Drive toward the interstate, then make a U-turn so that I can see if anyone is following you, then drive to Perkins and turn right. I'll be behind you. I'll call you to pull over."

"Okay, love you too." That was unexpected.

I didn't think Brent would try anything close to his home, but I'd bet he would have her followed. I watched my truck leave the complex, Andrea driving north. Another of those SUVs, this one dark blue, followed after a beat. I called her and she answered.

"Put your phone on speaker."

"Okay." She did and said, "Okay," again.

"You've got a fan. Pull into the turning lane and then left into a lot or one of the fast food places, then go the other way. I'll tell you when to turn and where."

"Right, I mean left," and she laughed. Good girl.

She switched lanes without a blinker, nice touch, and turned into a Wendy's, drove around the back and to the front past the drive-through and then back out again to the south toward Perkins.

"Good, turn right on Perkins. I'll be behind the dark blue SUV following you."

I heard horns as the SUV took a risky U-turn and followed Andrea, with five cars between them. I pulled into the right lane behind the SUV. I could see two men, both white, both young, in the front seats. I caught a glimpse of a long barrel in the passenger's hand, for just a second.

"At some point, they're going to try to jack you," or worse, I thought, "so do just what I say, okay, babe?"

"Yes," I heard the nerves vibrating in her voice.

"Take some deep breaths, I'm serious. Do it now." I took my own advice and practiced combat breathing, getting oxygen, calming the nerves. I slapped the stupid old man driving a Ford Fiesta straw hat on my head.

I heard her breathing quickly and told her, "No, not quick breaths, you'll hyperventilate, deep, slow breaths."

"I'm scared."

"That's okay, you should be. Breathe. I know what I'm doing," I said, hoping it was true.

"I'm turning right."

"I see you, stay in the right lane."

The SUV had jumped two cars closer by pulling around those which had made the turn with Andrea and then pulling in front of them, just clearing metal as it did so. I followed along through the lights on Perkins. One of the cars between Andrea and the SUV peeled off and there was only one separating them. Up ahead I saw the light for South Acadian. I pulled into the left lane.

"When I tell you, put on your right blinker, but be ready to pull in front of me and then turn left at the light."

"Got it." She sounded as if the combat breathing was having its effect.

"Okay, left lane now."

She changed lanes. The light turned red ahead.

"Left turn lane, now." We both transitioned to the turning lane while the SUV bullied its way across. The left turn arrow flashed green.

"Go, go, go!" She did, I didn't. The SUV was blocked by me in the turn lane and by the other cars in the through lanes at the red. Horns were playing a one-note symphony as the other drivers became enraged at the stupid old man (me) and the reckless young hotheads (them).

"Take your first left into the neighborhood. Drive around slowly until I call you. You're clear."

But she wasn't, quite. The SUV driver drove into the oncoming lanes, which were clear because the traffic was stopped for the turning vehicles. The light changed again, and the oncoming cars crowded the intersection. The SUV slammed into a work van and they both stopped. Like the rest of the cars in the turn lane, I worked my way back into the through lane and drove on. No one was making a left turn there for awhile. As one of the cars shot past me, the man driving shot me the finger, blaming me for the mess. When you're right, you're right. I had to make my way around the small recreational City Park Lake by way of Dalrymple to get back to Andrea, who was still driving around. I directed her back to Acadian and then south to Highland Drive. We met up just inside the gates on the LSU campus.

XXXIV

We hung out in the super-sized parking lot next to Tiger Stadium, which was virtually empty, but we did find a couple of vehicles to snuggle between for concealment.

"How are you doing?" I asked. It was the first chance we had to talk. I had parked the Ford Fiesta and gotten into the passenger side of my truck.

"Not too bad," she said, but the tears streaming down her face contradicted her words.

"Talk to me." I held her hand, and she didn't pull away.

"I'm a mess. The whole world is upside down. My whole life has been about work and family, with a relationship thrown in here and there between marriages. I walked away from two marriages because they weren't good for my children, and now..."

I waited silently for her to continue, and she did, after a breath, "Now my own child has betrayed me, why?"

"It usually comes down to love, hate, money, religion, politics."

"I don't have any of those things, except for love of my family." It still stung when she dismissed me like that.

"Then hang on to that for now."

"But Brent," she almost wailed.

"I heard what you said pretty well for awhile, but what did he have to say after I called you?"

"He asked me, twice, where I was staying. He asked it casually, but, he asked twice."

"What did you say?"

"I told him I was getting another apartment, but I didn't know the address yet, that I would call him with it."

"That's good. Did you notice any locking bar or a broomstick on the patio door?"

"Yes, there wasn't anything."

"Could you see what it was he was tossing in the box that he was so careful to get out of sight?"

She thought a few seconds while I contemplated Tiger Stadium ahead of us, "All I saw was some smaller boxes and some loose wiring. I noticed the word ALARM on one of the smaller boxes, but I couldn't tell what kind of alarm?"

"What about Robert, did you get the impression that it was his real name?"

"Maybe. Brent seemed pretty surprised to see me at his door, maybe too surprised to come up with a lie. Maybe not."

"No last name?"

"I couldn't exactly ask to see his driver's license."

"It wasn't a criticism."

"Sorry."

While we were still sitting in the parking lot, I called FBI Agent Lewis. It was time for him to do a little work.

"Special Agent Lewis," he answered.

"Agent Lewis, Travis Bowie."

"It's Special Agent, Mister Bowie."

"It's Lieutenant, Special Agent. Now that we've gotten the honorifics out of the way, and could you explain to me some time just what makes you guys so special anyway. I need a favor."

He either laughed, or snorted, or sneezed, I wasn't sure which, but then he said, "You need a favor. Why would I do you a favor?"

"Because you've got me running around doing things you can't or won't do. You've stuck me and the lady next to me out in a swamp full of alligators with chickens tied around our necks. That's why. So why don't you take down this plate number and see what you come up with?" I read off the license number of the BMW Robert had been driving and repeated it.

"I don't know what you're talking about. I haven't asked you or authorized you in any way to take any action on behalf of the Bureau, and I'm not your personal NCIC operator."

"Excellent deniability, and very special, Special Agent."

"This conversation is over," and then it was, with me trying to hold a rope out straight by one end.

"That useless prick," I said at my dead phone.

"He's not trying to help at all, is he?" Andrea asked.

"No, we're cannon fodder, bait, nothing more. Let's head back, return the car, and get to Hammond, and Holden. We've got to keep an eye on those vans. Wait a minute, " I slapped my forehead hard enough to hurt, "you said there was Alarm printed on one of the boxes. The sign I managed to see in one of the vans was for an alarm company. Okay, we know something else, but still don't have any idea what it means.

I looked at my watch. It was too late to call the Secretary of State's Office to check the ownership of the NEW WORLD ALARM COMPANY name printed on the sign. It wasn't too late to check the website, however. A GOOGLE search came up with nothing, likewise with BING. Then I remembered I didn't need the Secretary of State's Office to be open. I could do an internet search. No such company listing. Those signs were as phony as a televangelist's hair.

As we drove back to the rental agency, Andrea followed in my truck because we couldn't have her driving and violating the rental agreement. God forbid we do that in addition to shooting people, trespassing and a laundry list of other felonies and misdemeanors. My phone rang. It was an unfamiliar number, but I answered because I didn't know what I didn't know.

"Travis, Lewis."

"Would that be Special Agent Lewis?"

"Cut the crap. We need to meet. I don't trust the phones. This is a burner. I won't call on it again." He sounded, well, scared, and pissed off too.

I did cut the crap, with no more wisecracks, "How about Gonzales, the Cracker Barrel, what could be more innocent than that?"

"Good, an hour?"

"Good for me, maybe a little longer for you coming from New Orleans."

"I'm FBI, I'll drive fast."

I hung up and called Andrea with the change of plans. We stashed the truck at a Wal-Mart and kept the Ford Fiesta.

XXXV

Gonzales is a small town of about ten thousand about twenty-five miles south of Baton Rouge. I wasn't much of a shopper, but still all I really knew about the town was the large outlet mall that sat at the side of Interstate 10, and the giant Cabela's sporting goods store. I drove there and waited at the Shell station so that I could see Lewis arrive. I didn't know what he would be driving, so I would have to watch everyone who turned in from the highway. It would be tedious, but I wanted to see if he had a tail, or back-up to arrest us for something.

It was easy to dismiss most of the vehicles which entered the outlet mall lot. Most of them were driven by women, or the vehicles didn't look like they'd be driven by an FBI agent, special agent, whatever. It was easier when all the cops drove Ford Crown Vics, but since Ford had discontinued production of the iconic police car, agencies had switched to SUVs, Chevys, Dodges, and there was no consistency. I didn't think he'd be driving a compact or foreign or pickup, though. I watched the time, too.

Lewis made it in thirty-five minutes, which meant he must have been rocketing. The dark blue Ford Explorer had heavy window tint, so that I couldn't have seen a searchlight from inside, but it looked cop. I watched the SUV pull into the CRACKER BARREL parking area and Lewis get out. I watched follow-on vehicles but didn't see anything to alarm me. I drove over and we got out.

We found Lewis looking around the store area for us and walked up to him. We didn't shake hands. Andrea gave him a scared dirty look.

"Let's get a table," I suggested. "It'll make us look normal, or at least the two of us. You look like a Fed." He didn't say anything. Maybe they didn't issue smart-ass attitude at the Bureau.

Local cops pretty much all have it, along with creative obscenity and bowel humor.

The earnest but friendly young man showed us to a table and turned us over to the care of a fresh-faced twenty-something blonde. I ordered unsweetened ice tea, Andrea water with lemon, and Lewis sweet tea. Lewis was tall and fit, his blue knit shirt with collar just making room for his muscles, so he could afford the sugar in the tea. I could too, but I didn't like sweet tea. Of course Andrea was probably on a diet, like almost every woman I met, including the ones who didn't need to be and the fat ones eating a bag of pork rinds.

Lewis kicked off, which surprised me. He pushed a sheet of paper across to me, turned around so I could read it. It showed that the vehicle Robert had been driving was registered to a ZBA Trust. I shrugged.

"First of all, I apologize to you, Ms. Barrois. I no longer think you stole the isotopes from your company. There was evidence, and I had to arrest you."

"Thank God," she let out a breath she'd been holding for a week.

"What changed your mind?" I asked.

"Coincidences. That storage unit you pointed us too. It was empty. I thought you'd sent us on a hunt for Bigfoot, intentionally or not, and I decided to have you monitored to see where you led us. But just for due diligence, I checked who had rented the unit." He stabbed a finger at the paper he'd shown me, "ZBA Trust."

"Okay," I said, waiting for another tumbler to drop, though that was a pretty big one.

"And that's when things started to get weird," Lewis said.

"Weirder."

"Yeah, that. I found that the trust is for the heir of a fortune back in New York, a kooky guy named Robert Sturdevant. He's reclusive, has extreme associations, is suspected in three murders. So I write up my report, turn it in, and then I'm told to leave it alone."

"That is weird," I agreed.

"It took a couple of days between the time I submitted my report and the SAIC, that's the Special Agent in Charge, called me in, jumping my supervisors. He said I should drop this line of investigation, that the locals, that would be you, were just fumbling around as usual."

"Funny, that's what we say about you guys."

He waved the comment away, "I figure this went up the chain and back again, so I'm thinking this guy Sturdevant must have yank up the line."

"We call it stroke."

"Whatever. So I do some more research, but not on Bureau servers, find out he contributes money, lots of it."

"To who, whom?"

"Everybody. He doesn't care which party. His money gives him access to everybody."

"What does he do with it?"

"I don't know, but one thing his money does is make authorities think three times about messing with him."

"So now, you're using us to do what you can't officially."

"You know I can never admit that."

"I understand. I really do." He looked for sarcasm in my remark, but he didn't find it. It wasn't there. He nodded.

"But yes, if you lead us in a direction we can't ignore, without following up on Robert directly, oh well."

The waitress came back. We couldn't just take up space at her table, costing her and the restaurant money, so we each ordered something. I was hungry. I got the pot roast with biscuits and cornbread on the side, and the others ordered too. When she had gone, we continued the conversation, or council.

"You haven't asked where we got Robert's license plate. Does that mean you already know?" I stared at him and he stared back. Cops can do that all day long.

"I do know your movements in general, but no, I don't know that. I was getting to it."

I felt Andrea stiffen beside me as I said, "At Andrea's son Brent's apartment this afternoon, where she met Robert."

Lewis took a long hard look at Andrea and processed the family connection. I was trying to figure out what his Fed calculus concluded when he asked, "Your son?"

She nodded with obvious reluctance, "He works for the company."

"Did he have access to the vault? Records don't show that."

"No, just the material which is issued for use at the job site."

"So…," Lewis prompted.

I butted in, "So Larry probably took the stuff and gave it to Brent, or Robert."

Lewis nodded his agreement.

I filled Carl Lewis in on the junkyard, the vans, the magnetic signs, flattening the tires, seeing Brent at the junkyard, the box of whatever it was in Brent's apartment, and my intention to break into Brent's apartment when he was at work the next day.

"You know I can't authorize something like that."

"You are kind of limited in what you can authorize right now, Carl," I used his first name to soften the comment. He got it and nodded again.

"But you can use evidence recovered by a free agent not acting at your behest," I lectured.

"Right, and you are not acting at the Bureau's behest."

"Got it."

"So what kind of nightmare do these anarchist assholes have in mind?"

"These are short-range gamma emitters, these isotopes. They could cause cancer, radiation sickness, birth defects," Andrea said.

"Or terror," I said.

With that, we all ate dinner. I was still hungry, even if there was a small apocalypse looming.

XXXVI

It had been a very long work day. I was tired enough to fall asleep in the motel room without even thinking much about why Andrea wouldn't have sex with me anymore, or the loss of the emotional underpinning to it. I did manage to take a shower first.

I am not an early riser by nature, but falling asleep at eight in the evening made it easier to get up at five. I saw Andrea, already drinking coffee she had made in the room's coffee maker and mostly dressed for the day. She still had to do her hair and makeup, and was barefoot, which was her default choice when inside anyway.

"Sleep well?" I asked.

"I would have, except for your snoring."

"You never complained before."

"I'm not complaining now, and you didn't snore much before. I think you must have been exhausted. Snoring was the only way I could tell you were even alive." She smiled as she said it, so I guess we were still friendly.

"Well, thanks for listening so I didn't swallow my tongue."

"Anytime." We both felt weird, sharing a room but not together. I found it sad. I think she might have just found it inconvenient. I was glad to have a task to relieve the mutual embarrassment. I brushed my teeth and threw on some clothes. I waved at her as I made for the door.

"Wait," she said, "where are you going?"

"To break into Brent's apartment when he leaves."

"Aren't you going to need some help?"

I gave her a look that must have conveyed my surprise. Andrea was hardly the adventurous or risk-taking type. She followed up by saying, "I know, he's my son, and it breaks my heart what he's done, but I need to know where this leads. I have to see it through."

"I could use a spotter."

"Let me get my shoes."

We took the rental with Andrea driving. I know, it violated the rental agreement. We got there before six, and cruised just far enough into the complex to see Brent's company truck parked in front of his apartment. Then we took a position across Essen to wait for Brent to leave.

"Why are you really here, Andrea?" I asked while still watching the exit to the apartment complex, staring out the windshield.

I saw her in my peripheral vision turn to me, "I'm trying to help you help me get myself out of this mess, and I'm sticking close to you so you don't kill my son."

"I don't want to kill him."

"You kill people, Travis, I've noticed."

"I haven't killed anyone who wasn't trying to kill me first, and I wouldn't mind not killing anyone else ever again. I don't like it. It makes me feel, heavy, weighted down, maybe with their souls." I didn't mention Booger, who I might have accidentally killed, though I had doubts about that.

"I'm sticking close anyway."

At six seventeen, Brent's truck exited the complex and turned toward the interstate. I could see Andrea following with her eyes as she watched her son, her betrayer and fruit of her womb, disappearing up the street.

"How do we do this?" She asked with a resolve and a little relief that he wouldn't be in my way. I think she thought of me as an inherently violent person. I didn't see it that way, but others' perceptions of us are often more accurate than the self-deceptive cocoon we weave for ourselves.

"We'll wait until most of the people who are going to leave are gone, to minimize suspicious eyes." More vehicles were queuing at the exit, forming their own mini-traffic jam. Baton Rouge had the worst rush hour traffic for a city its size that I'd ever seen, so maybe people were getting an early start.

"Around eight, you'll drive up and knock on the door. I'll go around back and force the door, hopefully without breaking anything. I'll put myself on a timer, so that I'm in and out in five minutes. By the time anyone starts to get suspicious, we'll be gone and they'll convince themselves there was nothing to be concerned about."

"Okay, wait, are you going to ride in with me or walk in?"

"Good question. I think I'll just ride up with you, stand around a few seconds and then go around the back like I'm looking for Brent. Probably better than wandering in." I could see her nod in my peripheral vision.

From time to time, a police car would pass on Essen, but they had no reason to be interested in us, nestled among the other cars in the parking lot. Just before eight, I reached in my backpack at my feet and pulled out a small pry bar and a large screwdriver. I leaned over and stuck them in a cargo pocket.

"You actually carry stuff like that around with you?"

"I got them out of the truck this morning while you were doing your hair."

"Is that a comment about my hair?"

"It's worth every moment you spend on it. It looks lovely as always."

"Thank you." She even smiled.

Traffic coming out of the apartment complex had stopped, so at eight, I asked, "Ready?"

She took a deep breath and said, "Yes. Go?"

"Yes." There was nothing else to say. The next few minutes would decide if we went to jail in Baton Rouge for burglary. Andrea put it in gear and drove out of the parking lot, across oncoming lanes to the turn lane in the middle, and waited her chance to merge and then turn into the complex.

We got out of the rental car in front of Brent's. Andrea knocked on the door and waited. I stood near the car door. She turned to me and shrugged for the benefit of any observers, and then I mimed going around the back. It wasn't great acting, but it looked believable, I hoped.

I walked around the edge of the building, through the breezeway, around the back and counted off apartment patios as I walked past them on the grass verge separating the apartment building from an eight-foot fence bordering the property. When I got to Brent's patio, I stepped onto it through the opening in the three-foot wooden fence which enclosed it. It had the suggestion of privacy without being the actual thing, it being an apartment complex and all. I hoped it would afford me enough concealment, however. I knocked on the glass door. Right above me was a balcony for the apartment above, and while anyone who might be up there couldn't see me without hanging over the railing, they could hear.

There was no answer, but I didn't expect one, and would have been surprised if there had been. I slipped the pry bar out and inserted it into the jamb and leaned into it. The door flexed a little after it had slid back a few millimeters on its track. Then I stuck the screwdriver into the space I'd created and pulled up. The latch was under stress from me prying the door back, so I released a little pressure on the pry bar and tried it again. There was the satisfying click as the latch popped. The door slid open.

"Hey, Brent, how you doing?" I said to the empty room. I stepped inside and glanced at my chronograph watch. The stopwatch was running. One minute gone.

I looked around the living room/dining area and kitchen quickly for anything of interest. Nothing. I walked down the hallway to the bathroom, opened the door and saw it was empty. The bedroom was next.

Inside, I saw a box, large enough to hold a microwave oven, on the floor next to the bed. On a side table, there were pliers and screwdrivers. I looked in the box. There were smaller boxes and a

199

couple of loose units inside. I picked up a unit. It was a fire alarm, the kind of industrial or commercial application which wired into a central command and monitoring station. I didn't know anything about fire alarms, but the wires and the coax connector told me this wasn't a free-hanging model that could be found in any home. The housing was utilitarian clear plastic, so that said commercial or industrial too. The other boxes indicated they were the same according to the pictures and printing on them. One of the units had been taken completely apart and was on the side table. Next to it was a wheel-like device with a slot in it. It was heavy, as if made of lead or some other heavy metal. None of this gave me a *Eureka* moment. I photographed everything in place with my phone, without touching anything but the wheel thingie. I looked at my watch. Three minutes fifty seconds.

I had to decide how to leave. If I left by the patio, I wouldn't be able to latch the door back, and Brent would be suspicious. The security chain was on the front door, and I was sure the deadbolt was locked too. I went to the patio door, latched it back, and thought, I'm trapped. But then, I did what I had to, and hoped no one would see me.

I ran back to the bedroom, opened the window, popped the screen out after looking out to each side as far as I could, and rolled through. I pulled the window back down and replaced the screen. I looked around, and there was an old woman on a balcony to my right. She was staring at me. I waved, but there was no response. I waved again, and saw she was in a wheelchair. She probably was only seeing her past life through those eyes. I felt bad for her, and relieved at the same time.

I walked around the front. We got in the car and were gone.

"I notice your report kind of glosses over how you found out about the devices the son had in his apartment," Andy Landry said.

I wondered, what kind of idiot did he think I was, that I would document my burglary? I opened my mouth to say something non-committal, but the Sheriff interrupted.

"I think we're trying to contain this thing, not create more problems."

He knew, and he was telling Landry to shut up.

XXXVII

I needed more coffee, so we ended up getting drive-through coffee and sausage biscuits at a McDonald's outside the neighborhood where we had just pulled off a burglary. Then I drove to a park area on the lake. We sat on a bench and watched ducks that came to share our bounty. I ended up taking one bite and gave the rest of the biscuit to them. After wiping the sheen of oil from my hands with a napkin, I passed my phone to Andrea so she could see the photos I had taken inside the apartment.

She scrolled through them as I watched her face for any recognition of or reaction to any of the photos. When she got to the last one, the wheel-like device, she stared at it for several seconds. Then she said, "Oh my God," quietly, as if a prayer and not an oath.

"What?"

"How many of these did you see?"

"The alarms? Maybe ten."

"No, these, she pointed at the slotted wheel."

"There was the one on the side-table, and let's see," I took the phone from her and scrolled back to a photo of the inside of the large box, "these in the box."

"Oh, Brent, what have you done?"

"What, tell me."

She shook her head as if to clear it of something unpleasant, then said, "Those are shutters."

I shrugged in response, but I wasn't sure if she saw it, so I repeated it, "Shutters?"

"For X-ray cameras. The radioactive source goes inside. It's shielded by the lead lining. When the operator is ready to take a picture, the wheel rotates to line up the openings and the gamma rays exit through the slot in a beam. It's aimed at the object, like a weld and the image is collected on the other side."

The ducks, as oblivious to the threat we were trying to understand as the few people about, running, or throwing sticks in the water for their dogs to retrieve, started to wander away when the free food ran out. I stared at the water ahead.

"Okay, we have alarms, we have shutters. They're in the same place, but the isotopes are not. How dangerous is it to handle this stuff?"

"If you don't know what you're doing, you could end up exposed."

"What's the safety zone for this stuff when the operators are working? A few feet? Several yards?"

"Oh, at least. There would be a pretty large exclusion zone, but probably bigger than is actually needed, just to be sure."

My phone rang while we were pondering. I didn't recognize the number, which meant it could be Agent Lewis calling on another burner phone. I started to let it go to voicemail, but decided he might not leave a message, and might not answer when I called back. I answered it, and instantly wished I hadn't.

"Yes?"

"Bowie?"

I didn't recognize the voice, but knew it wasn't Lewis.

"Yes."

"Detective Cossich. I need you to come back in to talk."

"Detective, and it's Lieutenant Bowie."

"Not for the time being from what I hear, and I still need you to come in to my office."

"I didn't hear a *please* in there."

The air was dead. I let it hang. I guess he was doing the audio equivalent of the cop stare. I let him. After all, he called me, he wanted to talk to me, not the other way around. Finally, he blinked.

"Well?"

"Well, I'm out of town at the moment, with all my free time, thank you very much (I wanted to add *you rat bastard* but restrained myself), but," I raised a finger as if he were there to see it, "I'll be sure to call when I'm free. Thank you so much for calling, and try to work on your people skills." I punched the virtual End Call button harder than I needed to. He'd probably start pinging my phone soon. Good luck and get in line with the FBI, who were almost certainly already doing that. Maybe he'd end up explaining himself to the Feds. That should keep him busy for awhile. I had more pressing matters on my mind than his little case with Booger the dirt bag dog-stealing sack of shit. Of course, a murder is no small matter, and Cossich seemed to be trying me on for size. One thing at a time. I wished.

Andrea could see I was more worried than my smart-ass attitude with Cossich had pretended. She said, "I've been so wrapped up in my own troubles. What's wrong?"

"Some guy stole Kiddo. I tracked him down, got Kiddo back. The guy ended up dead, and now his detective cousin thinks I killed him. And before you start on my homicidal nature, I didn't, I think."

"You think? Why don't you know?"

"I hit the guy, but I didn't stomp him in the throat, which was apparently the cause of death. I'm convenient though."

"Oh, Travis," she said, but I had apparently reached the limits of her sympathy. I felt the distance between us widening, but she had already made that clear.

"Back to these shutters. Who would know how to load them with the pellets, whatever, safely, for himself?"

She didn't want to answer, but said in as small a voice as she could and me still hear her, "Brent."

"What I figured."

She too was staring at the shallow water of the small lake which decorated the urban space of Baton Rouge. I don't think either of us found any answers there. We packed up our fast food trash and tossed it in a barrel. The ducks ignored us as we left. I wasn't sure where to go at the moment, so I headed back toward Holden. At least we could check on the vans at the junkyard and wait for Agent Lewis to call.

At least the maniacs' plan was not operational yet. The alarm boxes were still in Brent's apartment, and the isotopes were not with them. Watch Brent? Watch the vans? Try to find Robert's location? Then what? I didn't like being reactive rather than proactive, but we still didn't know enough.

XXXVIII

I called Sal Baker in Homicide. When he answered, I said, "Sal, Travis Bowie."

There was a pause while he processed how much trouble he would get in for talking to me now that I was suspended, but he said, "Sorry to hear about your suspension. That's bullshit."

"Maybe, Sal, I need to ask you something. I'm not asking you to step over any lines here, but I need to know, anything more on the shooter from that night?"

Another pause, then, "I think I can tell you that. It'll be public information anyway, sooner or later."

Good, I thought, figuring the guy was tied up with the Livingston Parish crowd, but what he said threw a curve, "He seems to be originally from Plaquemines Parish, somewhere around Myrtle Grove."

"Plaquemines, and Tangipahoa?"

"Yeah, why? You got something to share?"

"Apparently not, thought I might, but this is a surprise. If I have something to help you, I'll call, thanks."

"Okay, take care." He hung up, apparently glad to distance himself from a departmental pariah. Like most detectives, Sal was a careerist through and through. I think every detective saw himself as a Deputy Chief one day. There was only so much room at the top, and being a second-class jail policeman, even if I was an investigator, I didn't harbor any such illusions.

I was driving back to Hammond on Highway 190 when my phone rang again. I was still holding it after the surprise Sal had delivered. I checked the number, and saw it was Cossich again. Persistent, like gravel in your shoe.

"Yes, Detective," I answered after sliding the virtual answer switch on the screen.

"Lieutenant, I want to apologize for being so abrupt earlier. I would like to have your help finishing my report, and I was wondering if I could meet you and get your input on some details, since you were a witness in the area around the time the victim died." What I heard between the lines was the translation: he was going to go the good cop route, interviewing, not interrogating, me as a witness, not a suspect. That way, he didn't have to advise me of my rights, and then be *surprised* if I made incriminating admissions he could then use to fit me for the murder of Booger. There's a difference for a detective between focusing on a suspect, and getting tunnel vision. From his perspective, he would call it focus. I would call it the other, especially since I knew, or thought I knew, I hadn't killed Booger.

"Okay, Detective, I'll meet you if you're willing to come to Slidell, where I am at the moment (I wasn't)." If he was pinging my phone, he would know I was lying, but he didn't let on one way or the other.

"That would be great, Lieutenant," he said immediately, laying it on a little thick, I thought. "Where?"

"How about the old train station on Front Street? You know it?" I thought it would give me and Andrea a view from Old Town to see him arrive. I didn't trust him, and it was more than just the fact that he was a detective. Was he in with the conspirators?

"No, not really, but I think I can find it. Two hours?"

"Fine, see you then."

I had no intention of meeting him there.

"What was that about?" Andrea asked, at least feigning interest in problems other than her own.

"Well, I found out that the guy who tried to shoot you, the first time, is from Plaquemines, with history on the north shore of the lake, which makes me think that stealing Kiddo was maybe more about getting me away from you than some opportunistic shitbird out to steal a dog for his fighting operation. And this detective is really eager to meet me, maybe because he's a detective, and maybe because he's trying to set me up for his friends to take a shot. We'll play it out a bit."

"This is dangerous."

"Very."

We passed the junkyard on the way, and saw that the vans were still in the same place, with a watcher vehicle, a shiny pickup which didn't fit in with the junked vehicles in the yard, sitting nearby.

"We're spread really thin here," I said. "We don't have enough to tell locals, and Agent Lewis is being handcuffed by his superiors. We're still on our own, and I don't know if that's going to be enough."

"What if we just tell the police what we know?"

"Maybe they even believe us a little bit, maybe not, and they start trying to play catch-up. Without probable cause for warrants, and our say-so doesn't make it, they start asking questions, the bad guys go to ground, and we have no way of finding them until they pull off whatever they're planning. We're kind of riding the tiger and can't get off without getting eaten." I saw her nod out of the corner of my eye. She was being braver than I expected.

We drove out of Livingston Parish, into Tangipahoa onto Interstate 12, and the sixty miles to Slidell in Saint Tammany Parish. We didn't speak much on the way, both lost in our thoughts, including, at least for me and probably for her, the real imminence of mortality.

When we reached Slidell, a small town which had grown to a city across Lake Pontchartrain from New Orleans as white residents fled the racial politics which black Democrats had imposed on New Orleans beginning in the 1960's and had made whites feel less and less welcome, it was early afternoon.

We took a position parked on a narrow street among other parked cars from which we could watch the old train station, a dark red brick building no longer used for the original purpose, which housed a restaurant as well.

I saw Cossich get out of the maroon Crown Vic, as another stocky white guy in his late twenties got out the passenger side. They were both wearing dress shirts with ties and dress slacks, with their pistols and badges on their belts. They looked around, I guessed for me. The other detective walked around the building and went inside. When he came back to Cossich, he shrugged. I called. He answered, pulling his phone out of his shirt pocket with an impatient snatch.

"Lieutenant, we're at the train station."

"I'm sorry, Detective. I got tied up on something. Can you meet me in Mandeville?"

"This is bullshit."

"I'm really sorry, Detective. If you would like to reschedule?"

"No, no, I drove all this way, what's another thirty miles?" I noticed he said he, not we. I wondered if he was planning to arrest me, though on what evidence I didn't know.

"Okay, sorry, I'll meet you at the Koop Road trailhead for Tammany Trace in half an hour. Will that work?"

"Yeah, I'll be there. Where is it?"

"Take the Highway 59 exit off I-12, south, look for the sign a few miles down the road.

"Okay," he hung up. It was funny to watch him give the middle finger to his phone and kick a trash can before they got back in their car.

We followed at a distance north toward I-12. I didn't see any other vehicles that looked to be part of a convoy. I began to think he hadn't come ready to arrest me, because arresting a policeman without more backup isn't smart, or safe.

I knew where we were going, so I passed him on the interstate, even though he drove like a policeman, but then, so did I. I got to the trailhead for the hiking and biking trail before Cossich and his partner, and parked at a nearby office building about a hundred yards away. We got out.

"I want you to walk on down the trail a ways so that you can't be seen, in case something goes wrong." I gave her the keys. 'You can watch, but don't expose yourself. If things go bad, they arrest me or bring in some goons, wait until everyone is gone, then get the car."

"Then what?"

I gave her my phone, "Hope that Lewis calls. If he does, tell him you need help."

"I'm supposed to trust him?"

"I guess so."

When Cossich and his partner arrived, I was sitting on a swing in the children's playground area, lightly kicking my way back and forth. They approached at angles on each side of me, watching my hands. Andrea had already disappeared some yards down the trail. I didn't know if she was watching.

"What's going on, Bowie?" The respectful tone had worn off.

"You probably know this already, but people keep trying to kill me. I'm trying to prevent that."

"And you think I have something to do with that?" His fists clenched.

"I don't know you, so I don't think anything. I'm just taking precautions. You're already stalking me for something I didn't do." I waved him to a park bench and table combo. He took a seat. His partner, whom he didn't introduce, stood to my side. I continued to swing slightly.

"You look ridiculous. Come sit down," he said, his jaw clenched. I thought he would probably have blood pressure problems later in life.

I got up and walked, slowly so as not to concern either of them, to the other side of the table. I sat at the end of the bench without putting my legs through the space between the bench and the table where I would be trapped. I turned my body to face Cossich. I opened my hands palms up.

"Are you carrying?"

"Maybe."

"We need to hold on to it while we talk."

"Bullshit, not going to happen."

"What if I insist?"

"I'll insist back."

The cop stare, but that goes two ways. The partner started to move to my side of the bench, but Cossich held up his hand, his gun hand, I was glad to see. The partner held his position.

"You're a witness, maybe the last person to see my cousin alive."

"Already told you I didn't."

"You did, but there are, uh, inconsistencies, between facts we now know and your statement."

"And you're not reading me my rights because?"

"You're a witness, not a suspect."

"Right, let's go with that. It will play well with the DA when I make some incriminating admission without you reading me my rights. I'm just a witness. You were as surprised as I was when I incriminated myself." I looked up at the partner and caught a smirk on his face, which he quickly made disappear. "Your partner thinks that's funny too."

Cossich gave his partner a dirty look, then turned back to me.

"I have a question, Detective."

"I'm here to ask, not answer."

"Two questions, actually," I said, ignoring him. "Who's Janathan Kruger?"

"How would I know?" His eyes narrowed. He knew.

"Answering a question with a question, a sign of deception, as I'm sure you were taught in interrogation school. As was I. Second question, what kind of work did your dear departed cousin Booger do?"

"You're not on the job in your own department right now, and you sure the fuck ain't on the job in mine."

211

"Answer my questions, and I'll decide whether you deserve answers to yours."

I could tell he wanted to reach across and snatch me, but it wasn't going to happen, and he knew it. After the required stare down, he took a breath. He let it out.

"Kruger is a multiple felon, did time, robbery, batteries, attempted murder pled down, hangs with motorcycle gangs, skinheads, kluxers, you name it."

"And Booger, what did he do besides dog fighting?"

"I knew he used to drive a tow truck north of the Lake somewheres."

"Livingston Parish?"

"Fuck if I know."

"Okay, Detective, you pass. I don't think you would have told me any of that if you were dirty. I hope I'm not wrong."

"Oh, great, I was never good at tests."

"Ask your questions."

"You said you picked up your dog, and the others, on the highway, but guess what? A witness across the road saw your truck parked behind the old fruit stand. The witness also saw you head across the highway and into the woods, then saw you come back some time later with the dogs out of the woods, from the direction of Booger's place."

He waited. I spoke first. He was close to his necessary probable cause, so my only hope was to tell him a story, a true one, and hope for the best. It was my turn for a deep breath.

"Let me tell you a story first. A week ago, Janathan Kruger came into a restaurant in Metairie and shot some people. They were a distraction. He was trying to kill my soon to be ex-girlfriend. I killed him first. You should know this." I stopped, he nodded.

"People have been trying to kill us ever since. I don't think Booger stole my dog just as an opportunity. I think he was trying to distract me from trying to help my friend. There's a junkyard in Livingston Parish, with tow truck drivers by the way, that is being

212

used as a base for some kind of terrorist attack or maybe a shakedown for money. The details I don't know."

Cossich had the natural cop's skepticism, but he wasn't dismissing me either.

"Go on," he said.

"I've been working with FBI Special Agent Carl Lewis. I hope he'll confirm that. Here's what happened at Booger's. I traced him to his place from the bar he hung out at, telling the bartender I was looking for a fighting dog. I made my way to his place through the woods, I found my dog, and was getting her loose when Booger came out. I hid, I hit him. I freed the other dogs and we made it out of the woods. I did not stomp him in the throat. He was alive when I left him."

"A good story."

"I'm trusting you here. You arrest me, some bad things are going to happen. I'm under the radar right now and I intend to get closer to these guys, figure what they're up to, and turn it over to anyone who'll do something about it."

"I read about what you got into in north Louisiana last year. It was good work. You were a good cop."

"I still am, just suspended for accessing the license plate cameras for personal reasons."

"Now I feel bad about the trouble I got you in."

"Good, you rat bastard," I smiled when I said it.

"Okay, I'm going to trust you for awhile, and I'll look into who else might have been by Booger's after you left."

"Thank you."

"You need some help?"

"I just might."

Cossich turned to his partner, who just shrugged. Cossich stuck out his hand. I took it.

"Call me, or I'll call you."

I nodded and they walked back to their car. That went better than expected.

"You involved everyone BUT us," the Sheriff said.

"Everything at the time was happening outside of Jefferson Parish, Sir."

"You could have told Detective Baker." He was seething. I could see it in the pulse throbbing in his throat.

"Maybe I shouldn't have been suspended, and no offense, Sheriff, I like Sal, but he's a drone who couldn't find his ass with both hands."

My answer did not improve his mood.

XXXIX

When I found Andrea on the trail, actually a walking and bike path of light blacktop, nearby, she was talking on the phone. She handed it to me, "Lewis."

"Yes," I answered.

"Look, things have gone from bad to shit," he jumped right into the middle.

"What?" I asked.

"My supervising agent called me in this morning, asked if I had accessed Robert Sturdevant's record after being told not to. Then he told me I was being tasked to a special assignment, in Alaska."

"I'd heard stories, but I didn't know they really did that."

"Oh, yeah, it happens."

"So you're out of it. We're on our own."

"Not exactly. I'm having chest pains, so I'm checking myself into the hospital for tests."

"They're gonna' be pissed."

"Hey, when you're sick, you're sick."

"You're putting your career on the line, Carl."

"I don't think I have much of a choice here."

"You just raised my opinion of Feds. I always saw you guys as career first. What's with your supervisor? Is he stupid, or dirty?"

"It's not him calling the shots, it's the SAIC, Special Agent In Charge. He's political, sees himself as a future U.S. Attorney, so he sniffs asses to smell which way the wind breaks. Sturdevant makes a complaint that his shoes are too tight, the fundraisers start making phone calls. He obviously has people on his payroll inside."

"Who is this guy, and why does he have such stroke?"

"He comes from a big real estate family in New York. They own a lot of Manhattan, and you can imagine what a square foot of that costs to stand on. Robert is the bad boy, but the rest of the family doesn't like getting embarrassed by his behavior, so they cut him loose with like a hundred million, but they still send out the lawyers and PR people when Robert pops up in the news. Political contributions along with threats."

"What's this guy about?"

"Thinks he is a law unto himself. His wife disappears thirty years ago, the police don't even drag the lake next to his house. One P.I., ex-NYPD, looked into the case for the family to shadow the police investigation, dropped it like a hot skillet when inconsistencies showed up, won't talk about it, because his license wouldn't last if he breached confidentiality."

"Jesus, he is used to getting what he wants."

"And he's not afraid to get his hands dirty. An old girlfriend ended up shot in the back of the head in California when people in New York starting taking a fresh look at his wife's disappearance. And Robert was in California at the time."

"So what is he planning?"

"I'm thinking maybe revenge. He could go after people he thought did him wrong, or he might just like the idea of chaos for the thrill of it. This is a guy who cut up his neighbor and threw him in the Houston Ship Channel and got acquitted of murder. He's rich, he's crazy, he's lethal."

"If the Bureau finds out you're talking to us, you're toast."

"You mean talking about a case that doesn't even exist as far as the Bureau is concerned?"

"That's true."

"Call me back with a fax number so I can send what I do have. I'll use this number a little longer. I'm feeling those chest pains. I think I'm going to need an ambulance from the office."

"Take care. I'll call with the fax number."

We punched off. Andrea was looking at me waiting for me to fill her in.

"Brent's friend Robert is a very bad guy. *Mucho peligroso*. We have to get back to the hotel and get Lewis to fax us what he has on him. We need to know where he is staying. He's calling the shots on this thing. The question is, will he even get close to the operation or run it through Brent."

"So what do we watch? And are we going to get any help?"

"I don't know. The Bureau is trying to send Lewis to Alaska to get him out of the way, but he's going to play sick. Cossich might help. At least he didn't arrest me."

"Do we even have a chance?"

I didn't answer, because I didn't have one. We were going to need some luck, but as the saying goes, the harder you work, the luckier you get. Maybe it was even true.

We were driving all over southeastern Louisiana, pulling on strings. We stopped at our hotel to shower and change. While Andrea was in the shower, I got the fax number of the business center and called Lewis. Then I went downstairs to wait for his fax to come in. The pages I collected as they came out of the printer had some public information and some from law enforcement databases. Robert didn't seem to have any permanent address that was confirmed. He had moved around the country a lot, living in cheap apartments, cheap hotels and high-end hotels. He was known to use disguises. He had high-priced lawyers on speed-dial for the various troubles he found himself in, from the suspected murders to shoplifting and urinating on the snack aisle in a store for the hell of it.

I went back upstairs to take my shower. Andrea was out, with a towel wrapped around her head and another towel around her body. I still felt a tug of desire as I saw her, but I was starting to get the message as she nonchalantly went about getting dressed as if I weren't even there. I asked myself for the hundredth time, why am I doing this, but the only answer I got was that it was just pure doggedness. Enough, I told myself, it wasn't like I was going to quit now.

We drove the rental car back and turned it in, and reestablished ourselves in my truck.

217

"The way it keeps coming down to me is, we can keep a watch on the vans and try to prevent whatever it is that they're planning, or we can watch Brent and Robert to gather evidence, but we don't know that they will lead us to the isotopes, or even be involved in the operation. They might just be planners."

"Can we do both?"

"Not for long, I think, but let's watch Brent, see if he leads us to Robert, and monitor if their activity level changes. If they start moving differently, or disappear, I think we'll know it's about to happen." I looked at her, and she nodded without much conviction.

We were tired, and it was starting to show, with long silences and staring out the windshield, a loss of appetite as we lived on drive-through burgers, and frequent bathroom stops for upset stomach. It had been a week and a half since Vincenzo's and we were ragged. Adrenaline eventually runs out.

"I don't know how much longer I can keep this up," Andrea spoke for both of us, but I was being a guy, unwilling to admit weakness. I didn't say anything.

I called Lewis. He was still using the same phone.

"Yeah, Travis," he answered.

"Are you in the hospital?"

"Yeah, I'm set for a battery of tests over the next couple days."

"Can you slip out?"

"I just got a visit from the supervising agent. I think he wanted to check that I was really here."

"Do you think they'll keep checking?"

"Probably not. He probably reported back that I was safe in the hospital, which is almost as good as being in Alaska."

"We need eyes in more than one place. Can you do me a favor?"

"What?"

"There's a Detective Cossich in Plaquemines, who has been trying to fit me for the killing of his cousin, a low-life nicknamed

Booger who stole my dog. I found him, hit him, got my dog back, but the asshole ended up dead. No, I didn't kill him. The thing is, I thought it was a random thing stealing my dog, but it turns out Booger used to be a tow truck driver over here north of the lake, and he was supposed to have gotten a job with an alarm company. I think someone snipped another loose end. Cossich is letting me run for the moment, but it would help if you could give him a call and tell him I'm working with you."

"I guess I can dig my hole a little deeper, what's his number?" I gave it to him.

"When you talk to him, ask him to go over Booger's place, see if there is anything that might connect him with the people up here."

"Okay, I'll call you back."

It was late enough that Brent should be getting back from work. We decided to check on him. We were only a couple of miles from Brent's at the rental car agency, so we drove over. We took a peek from the entrance to the apartment complex and saw Brent's company truck parked in front of his apartment. We waited. And waited. Nothing happened. It got darker.

Lewis called back.

"Well?" I asked.

"Cossich is going to take another look and call me back. He's eager to cooperate with the FBI. I gather that he's ambitious and wants to look good."

"It's fine with me if he looks like a genius when this is over. What about getting some more eyes up here? We're trying to watch Brent and the junkyard and find where they've got the radioactive material, all without knowing what they plan to do with it, Oh, and find Robert too."

"I'll slip out of here after this afternoon's test and shoot up there to watch Brent's place, but I'll need to be back in the morning. I'll tell the nurse on the floor I'm taking a walk."

"You know they're going to come in your room about fifteen times to take your temperature."

"Well, I won't be here, will I?"

"Okay."

"I'll be in touch." He punched off the call.

Exhausted, we returned to our hotel to get some sleep. I was nervous and strung out on caffeine, but I still went out like a switch had been flipped.

XL

I woke up early, while it was still dark, which was still an unfamiliar experience for me, but Andrea was already awake, sitting fully clothed in her bed, staring out the window into the darkness.

In the darkness, on the way to Baton Rouge, we passed the junkyard, and could see the white vans at the back glowing in the late moonlight.

We made it to Brent's and saw his truck was there. I drove slowly around the parking lot across the street until I found Lewis' vehicle. I pulled up to it slowly with the interior light on so he could see it was us. Driver's side to driver's side, we powered our windows down.

"Anything?"

"Like a tomb."

"We're here, so you can take off, go get your heart checked."

He laughed and started up.

"Call me," he said. I waved.

It was a weekday, and we expected Brent, if he were keeping his regular schedule, would go to work at the plant. We were looking for a change in his routine which might indicate that things were about to go live. We waited. For five more days we waited, checking back and forth between Brent's place and the junkyard. On Saturday, Brent stayed in his apartment, probably working on his devices. On Sunday, he drove to the junkyard, checked the vans, and then went back home.

Lewis had managed to get himself diagnosed with exhaustion and sent home from the hospital on sick leave. He would slip out of his house in the evening and make the run up to Baton Rouge to take the overnight watch of Brent's and we would relieve him early in the morning. Our handover conversations were much the same.

"The same?" I asked Lewis who had weathered another night sitting in a car, but he looked more or less well, considering that he got to go home each early pre-dawn morning and be there if someone checked to see that he was being a good boy on sick leave.

"The same," he answered. "Are you sure this is going to pay off?"

"I'm not sure of much, but we're still stuck with the facts, and as John Adams said, facts are stubborn things. We've had people trying to kill Andrea here, isotopes missing, fire alarms being modified to hold radioactive material, a fictitious alarm company, and on and on. And don't forget a crazy killer millionaire."

Lewis nodded, "So we keep at it?"

"Do you have an alternative, because I'm willing to consider it. Andrea and I are worn down to lint, we're nomads on the run, we're tired."

"I know, I know, life's not fair," he commented, but I could hear more sympathy than his comment indicated.

"This would be a lot easier if we had electronic resources available," I wished.

"Yeah, but my SAIC's got his head up his own ass, or up somebody's."

"What have you heard from Cossich?"

"He checked his cousin's place, a dump from what he told me. What he found were some internet pages on sovereign citizens, anti-government, anti-police stuff. What was interesting was that there was a piece of paper with what turned out to be your address and Ms. Barrois' address. So your theory that you were targeted makes a good bit of sense."

I nodded at this bit of information. "So Cossich is convinced that Booger was part of this?"

"Yep, and he figures that you tracking him down got him killed."

"Probably true."

"And Cossich is ready to help whenever we call."

"Good."

Then, Brent's truck exited the apartment complex. I stole a quick glance at my watch. It was still dark, five thirty, much too early for Brent's normal routine.

"We follow?" Lewis asked unnecessarily.

"Of course." And we did.

Brent drove north to Interstate 10, then went west, then to I-110 and out of town north of Baton Rouge as we convoyed. Lewis and I read each other's moves, switching lanes and positions so that Brent never got too long a look at either of our vehicles. It was easier that it was still dark since we were just sets of headlights in his rear-view.

It became more challenging as we followed Brent off Interstate 110 and then onto U.S. Hwy 61, the original north south artery running from New Orleans to Baton Rouge and beyond. The highway was still multi-lane, but that changed as Brent exited after a few miles onto a street just outside St. Francisville. I didn't catch the name in the dark, but it was a winding, tree-lined residential street. Telepathically, almost, Lewis, who was in the lead position at the moment, held at the entrance to the neighborhood while I followed at a distance, waiting for Brent to disappear around a curve or take a turn at a stop sign before continuing.

It was starting to get light, with the barest of color starting to manifest in a kind of watercolor wash, but street lights were still on. Ahead, I saw Brent pull into a semi-circular drive behind a black BMW like the one which we'd previously seen Robert driving. I stopped and hit the switch to turn off my headlights. I picked up my phone from the console to call Lewis, but he called first.

"Yes," I answered.

"There's a plain white van entering the neighborhood now. Maybe nothing, maybe something."

"I was just picking up the phone to call you. Looks like Brent is at Robert's, if the black BMW is any indication. I'm up the street. Rather than tell you how to get here, why don't you just follow the van. I think it's coming here. I think they're moving."

"Okay. Coming."

I saw the van in my side-view mirror coming along the street and scrunched down so that the headrest blocked any view of me sitting there. I motioned Andrea to do the same. It pulled into the driveway behind Brent's truck. I was still on the line with Lewis.

"Stop behind me on your right, the van's at the house."

Lewis, running without lights, pulled in behind us. A young white guy, wearing a dark blue jumpsuit with the top unzipped and the sleeves tied around his waist to reveal the black tee-shirt and his excellent pecs and lats, and with his head shorn to dark stubble, got out of the van.

Brent had been standing next to his truck. When the other guy got out, they shook hands which went from the standard handshake, rotated into the thumb-lock grip and morphed into the chest bump abrazzo. How hip-hop. I looked in my rear-view and saw in the dawning light Lewis studying the scene through binoculars, using my truck as cover.

Another figure emerged from the house. It resembled an old woman, wearing a blouse and baggy slacks with long blond hair.

"You see the woman?" I asked Lewis on our open line.

"That's Robert Sturdevant."

"What the fuck is that about?"

"It's part of his known M.O., disguises, including dressing as a woman."

"This guy's nuttier than a pecan log, which probably means this scheme is too, which doesn't make it any less dangerous." Lewis didn't seem to feel the need to reply. The air was dead for a few seconds, then Lewis did say, "Uh-oh."

I looked, and saw the tall young guy carrying what appeared to be a heavy cardboard box from the van and Brent carrying the box I had seen before in his bedroom from his company truck. Robert in drag issued them inside.

"Yeah, shit, they're assembling their devices."

"Do we have enough for a warrant?" I pleaded.

"Not even close."

I glanced over at Andrea. She was pale in the early morning sunlight and she had chewed the lipstick off her lower lip, staining her teeth, I could see, as she breathed through her mouth. Her look was how I felt, and my guts gurgled in dread. It was like watching a horror in a nightmare in which you could only witness but were paralyzed. I was ready to storm the house and stop this, whatever it was, but I knew if we did, all the evidence, assuming we found what we thought was inside, would be lost. I could hear Robert's attorneys now, Why didn't you get a warrant? Wasn't there enough time? Oh, you couldn't get a warrant because you didn't have enough probable cause, but you thought you had enough exigent circumstance to justify an assault on the property? And Robert and his gang would walk as the case went up in smoke. So we waited.

"You're right," I said, "no probable cause." Not to mention that I had no legal authority to get a warrant in West Feliciana Parish, and Lewis wasn't going to get a Federal warrant with his SAIC running interference.

"Nope. You want to wait at the highway while I keep eyes on the house, see where the toys end up?"

"Right." I made as tight a U-turn as I could to avoid passing the house, leaving some tread marks on the lawn on the other side of the street, and feeling apologetic about it for about a second.

Back at the highway, I looked for a good spot to surveil the entrance from the neighborhood. I found a nice stand of oak trees where I could pull off the road and still see.

"I'm so nervous I could throw up, and I never throw up," Andrea said. My guts were still gurgling and I didn't want to talk about it. I wondered if I was going to have to find a nice tree.. And of course, if I did, that would be the moment things would start to happen, and I didn't mean in my guts.

I maintained my state of denial as long as I could, then gave in, "I have to find a tree. I'm sorry." I felt like I looked green. Everything in my vision had a greenish cast to it. Andrea gave me a look that said it was too much information. I staggered from the truck and checked sight lines to the highway. When I couldn't see the highway, I figured no one could see me. I loosened my belt, leaned against an oak, pulled down my pants, and fertilized the tree base with a foul stream. I cleaned up with baby wipes I kept in the truck to clean the seats when Kiddo had been inside. I felt better as I made my way back to the truck.

"Anything?" I asked as I squirted hand sanitizer over my hands. She just shook her head.

The phone rang. I didn't remember when we had disconnected.

"Yeah,"

"The company truck pulled into the garage. The van's pulling out." We had been waiting two hours and it was full morning, eight thirty. A new morning, but it felt like Armageddon.

It wasn't the rousing speech from Henry V. All I said was, "Okay."

XLI

The van turned south onto Hwy 61, back toward Baton Rouge. I followed after it passed our position in the oak trees. In my rear-view, I could see Lewis pulling out onto the highway. The van travelled the speed limit, and not one mile per hour over. The driver evidently didn't want to risk being pulled over for speeding. He also stuck to the right lane, which made it harder to follow, as the other traffic was passing us. It made us stick out behind the van. I dropped farther behind. Lewis, reading the problem, sped ahead out of sight and disappeared. A couple of miles ahead, I saw Lewis re-enter the highway from a parking lot and follow the van. It was my turn to pass and repeat the maneuver.

I passed the van in the far left passing lane and sped ahead, nestled in a cluster of vehicles. When the van was out of sight behind me, as reported by Andrea, I detached from the cluster of fast vehicles and found a street to pull over. Thus we leap-frogged the surveillance on the van all the way into Baton Rouge rush-hour traffic, which seemed to always last for more hours than it should.

Once we were in Baton Rouge traffic, it became easier. A driver had to keep his eyes forward to react to traffic stopping and starting, and only had time to check his rear-view occasionally, as when changing lanes. A mile before the I-10/I-12 split, the van started working its way to the left lanes.

"He's going to the junkyard," Andrea said. It was the first time she had spoken in an hour.

"Looks like," I agreed. I called Lewis, who was ahead at the moment, three vehicles behind the van. We were in one of the middle lanes, which left us the option of going I-10 or I-12 if we had to.

"Yeah?"

"He's probably going to the junkyard on 190, outside Holden, so he'll likely take 12."

"Okay."

"You haven't been there, but you probably watched our movements on your surveillance."

He just laughed, but refused to confirm FBI methods.

"If he takes the Holden exit, he'll come in from the west. If he takes the Albany exit, he'll approach the junkyard from the east on 190."

"So, whoever is closest behind him at the time should take the other exit and let the other take the exit he takes. Sound okay?"

"Works for me." I could hear the tension in Lewis' voice, and I could feel it in my throat, as if it took more effort to speak.

"Then we can bracket him and spot which way they go, hopefully figure out what they're doing."

"Good. They can break out any number of directions once they hit the interstate."

"Yes, it's bad."

"We need more people."

"And we don't have them."

"Can you call Cossich, ask him to start heading this way?"

"Will do."

While we were talking, the van did take the I-12 at the split, headed east, toward Holden and the junkyard. Whatever they planned, it seemed to be imminent. I took my own advice and breathed some deep belly breaths.

I was in the front position when the van passed the Holden exit, so I pulled off and drove to 190, ignoring the small community's speed limits and drawing dirty looks from other drivers. I sped east on the two-lane, the old Hammond-Baton Rouge highway, paralleling the van and Lewis out of sight on the interstate, but behind them. I was trying to get to the junkyard before the van. The phone rang.

"He's taking the Albany exit. I passed him by and let him go instead."

"Okay, I'm close to the yard where I can get visual."

"I'm doubling back at the next exit ."

"Okay, head to the stoplight. If you take a left, you're close to the yard. You should probably hold at that corner with the little store and gas station. I'll bracket from the other side."

"Got it."

I pulled to the gravel shoulder of the road at a driveway a half-mile to the west of the junkyard. I was pretty sure the van had no reason to come this far or he would have taken the Holden exit to begin with. Then Andrea pointed, "There it is."

"Don't point, it's not polite, not to mention obvious."

She started to give me a dirty look, then laughed. I smiled.

"We're in the middle of nowhere, dumbass." And we both laughed louder and longer than was proportionate. It was nerves.

She was right, though. The van, a half-mile ahead, was turning into the yard. I called Lewis and told him.

"What next?" He wasn't asking for instruction, just coordinating.

"I'll take a peek."

"Be careful."

I told Andrea to drive, and as we switched places, passing each other in front of the truck, I took her hand for a moment. She squeezed back and let go. That little moment of regret and contact mixed with the soft engine sounds of my truck and the whishing of a passing car in the mostly quiet countryside.

She drove while I put my back against the passenger door, scrunched down a bit to hopefully keep me from being seen with the cell phone camera in one hand with video running and the binoculars in the other hand.

It was hard to monitor the video while looking through the binoculars, but I was hoping the video would catch something I might miss with the quick look through the binoculars as we passed.

We passed the junkyard at a slow but acceptable speed so as not to attract attention. Once we had passed, I said, "There's Lewis, on the left."

"Pull in?"

"Yes, pull in." He was backed into a parking space in front of the store so that he had visual of the highway. I hoped the men at the junkyard didn't have friends or relatives working at the store, or shopping. We were kind of hung out there.

We got out of the truck and got into Lewis' car. Andrea got in front, which I found assertive. I got in the back.

"And?" Lewis asked.

The video was not great, jumpy and cluttered with frames of the truck interior and window frame, and a shot of Andrea looking grim, but it did show a cluster of men at the vans parked at the back of the yard, and the one van parked at an angle to the others. I reported what I had observed through the binoculars.

"All these guys are wearing jumpsuits. Their heads and faces are white, too white, like they just cut off all their hair and beards."

"Shit."

"Yeah, that."

"So we wait and follow," Lewis said.

"And call in other police as soon as we can," I added.

We agreed, and we went back to my truck. I backed out of the parking space and drove back to the highway to turn right and find another, less obvious place to watch for the vans to leave the yard on whatever mission they were gathering for. There was a line of several cars and trucks stopped ahead of me, pointed west. I heard some car horns.

I opened my door and stood up on the running board to see over the line of vehicles. My heart thumped at the sight. A tow truck with a smashed red compact slung behind it was pulled across the highway, blocking both lanes. The driver was out of his vehicle, door open and holding both hands up as if he had no control of the situation. On the other side of his tow truck, a line of five vans was pulling out and heading west, away from us. I caught a glimpse of the magnetic signs on their driver side doors as they turned onto the highway.

XLII

We were on the wrong side of the tow truck from the convoy, and it was on the move. Whatever was going to happen was happening now. Other cars had pulled up behind us. I backed and tagged the bumper of the blue mid-size Nissan behind me, then U-turned into the oncoming lane which was empty thanks to the tow truck blocking everything from the other direction as well. I floored it as the driver of the blue car got out and started yelling. No time for the distraction. I flew past Lewis' position without stopping. That's what phones are for. I grabbed mine, punched redial and tossed the phone to Andrea.

"Tell him, tell him they're moving."

She picked the phone up from her lap and talked into it short of breath, "A tow truck blocked the highway and all the vans are leaving. They already left."

Evidently, Lewis was asking questions she didn't have the answers to, so she handed the phone to me. I snatched it.

"I figure they're headed west toward Baton Rouge, or they'd have come this way. The question is, do they take the interstate or keep on 190? I'm headed for the Holden access and I hope my timing is right. If they decide to head east after all, I'll see them on the other side of the highway and double back. Why don't you go parallel on 190 and chase them? You're going to have to use your flashers to get past all the backed up traffic, though."

"Right," was all he said.

"Leave the line open, okay?"

"Right," again.

I made it to I-12 and sped west, scanning the opposite lanes for a convoy of white vans. I was driving a lot faster than they would be on the two-lane 190. I was driving fast enough and changing

231

lanes so quickly that Andrea was hanging onto the hand grip above the door frame like she was standing on a runaway subway.

"Try not to kill us before we find out how this ends," she shouted. I laughed. My guts were better. The adrenaline had evidently shut off everything down there.

When I reached the Holden exit, I took it faster than I should have and almost joined some cows behind a fence in a nearby pasture, but corrected and braked with a less than professional fishtail as the lighter back end of the truck tried to come around. I found a gas station parking lot and we watched traffic coming up from 190 to the interstate. I picked up the phone.

"You there?"

Lewis' voice in a bucket quality indicated he was on speaker, "Yeah, nothing so far. I'm still running people off the road going and coming, but I don't see anything ahead. When I do, I'll kill the flashers."

"Okay, keep the line open."

"Okay, okay, got it."

I pulled my binoculars and scanned, interrupting my surveillance from time to time with a fingernail that needed chewing. Then, in the distance, a banner of white against the backdrop green of trees, the convoy. I jammed the binoculars so hard to my eyes I probably would have a black eye, or two.

A gray SUV was leading, then the five vans. I studied the cabs, saw two men in each van. In the third one, I saw the guy who had picked up the box at Robert's earlier. Was he the leader of the field operation, or just a courier? Being in the middle made sense for the leader, not as easy to pick out or pick off, but were they that sophisticated?

"Tell Lewis," I told Andrea. Her fingers brushed my crotch as she took the phone from between my legs and I responded involuntarily. Even at a time like this, I thought, and laughed. I couldn't see Andrea's reaction as I was stuck to the lenses in front of me.

The sudden banging on my window scared the crap out of me. I brought down the glasses and grabbed my Kimber from the console beside me, bringing it close to my chest, pointed outward. A fat guy with a comb over was standing there. I powered down the window with my binoculars hand.

"You're blocking the air machine," he yelled at me.

"I'll be out of here in a second," I said. He saw the pistol pointed at his gut, which would be an easy shot.

"I'm calling the police," he said, taking a step back as if a foot or two made a difference in his safety margin.

"I am the police, you fucking moron," I put the pistol back on the console. "While you're at it, let some air out of your fat ass."

I pulled out, found the first turnaround, and followed the convoy. There was an SUV at the back as well, security elements front and back.

"Did you talk to Lewis?" I asked Andrea. I had been distracted by Mister Air Machine.

"He was past Holden, he's turning around."

"Tell him he's good with his flashers all the way to the interstate. It'll get him here faster.

"Okay."

I could hear their conversation on speaker. I shouted over that I was in contact and that the convoy was headed for Baton Rouge. He came back with an okay.

The convoy proceeded at just under the speed limit. Just east of Denham Springs, I saw Lewis in my rear-view in the far left lane. He passed slower traffic in the middle lane and then pulled back to the left. When he caught up with us, he eased off, worked his way to the middle in front of us, and allowed us to drop back into the traffic clutter. Just a nice peaceful drive in the country, with radioactive weapons and crazy terrorists.

We transitioned from Interstate 12 to Interstate 10 at Baton Rouge, and still the convoy hung together. We speculated.

I had the phone back and asked Lewis, "What are you thinking?"

"I guess separate vehicles means separate targets. What do we do when they start to separate?"

"I'm thinking follow the middle van. That's the guy who picked the box up from Robert's. I'm hoping he's the commander. Maybe he'll give orders to the others. He's not driving, so maybe he's maintaining communication. If we stop him in the act, maybe we stop everything."

"And maybe not."

"Well, that, too."

"Alternative?"

"Let's see how they separate," I suggested. "Did you talk to Cossich?"

"He's waiting in La Place for further instruction."

"Hope we have some for him."

We drove on, past Sorrento and Gonzales, Gramercy, to La Place, where the rear-most van took the Belle Terre exit.

"Where's Cossich?" I asked.

"He's not at this exit. He's up by the spillway."

"Can we get a BOLO from St. John Sheriff's to do a routine traffic stop, with all caution, high-risk?"

"We can try." I heard him click off as he switched to call mode and put me on hold.

In a few minutes, as we convoyed onto the Bonnet Carre spillway span of the interstate, I saw a black Crown Vic in my rear-view as Cossich joined us. I called him.

"Bowie?"

"Yes, welcome to the party."

"Ha, yeah, what is the party?"

"We don't know yet, but we're going to spoil it."

"Good, I hate parties." We both laughed. I looked over at Andrea and could tell she didn't share the excitement. She was so tight I could have touched her arm and struck a note, a very high one.

She saw me looking at her and asked, "How can you joke at a time like this? I'm scared to death."

"That's why we're joking."

She shook her head. It looked like it made her dizzy. I hoped she didn't throw up in the truck. "If you have to be sick, roll down the window and hang out."

"That's disgusting."

"Disgusting is riding in a truck full of vomit."

"I'll hold it," she insisted, but a few seconds later, powered down the window and let fly.

In the rear-view, I could see Cossich's windshield washer squirting and the wiper blades smearing a mess.

"Could you give a guy some warning?" Cossich asked when he called back.

"Sorry. The lady's not used to this."

"Who is?"

I punched up Lewis and we were on three-way. Lewis was laughing when he picked up.

"Oh, man," was all he could manage.

"Give the lady a break," I said, trying not to laugh for her sake. She was huddled on her side of the truck, perishing from embarrassment.

"Laugh, it'll do you good," I suggested, but she was rummaging in her purse until she came up with breath mints. I handed her a fresh baby wipe to clean her chin.

"Oh my God, what?"

"You caught some blowback."

She scrubbed at her face, taking some of her makeup with it, and then lowered the visor to study her face in the mirror.

"Feel better?"

She thought for a moment, then said, "I do, actually."

"Then it's all good. Don't worry, I've seen tough policemen do the same thing at times like this."

"Lewis," I asked on the three-way, "did you get in touch with St. John Sheriff's?"

"Yeah, I got some dumb supervisor who thought I was crazy when I couldn't tell him why he should stop the van. I even gave him the plate number."

"Is he going to do it?"

"Maybe, and maybe he's going to call the New Orleans office to confirm me, and then there will be more shit."

"Christ, dumb country cops," Cossich said, and laughed, because he was a country cop. We laughed too. Even Andrea laughed, though I'm not sure she got the joke.

Vans one and two peeled off as we passed through New Orleans and the convoy tightened up again. This brought on another discussion.

"What do we do?" Cossich asked.

"Carl, can you call NOPD and ask them to BOLO and stop those vans?" I asked Lewis.

"You have the plates?"

"I don't have the exact numbers, but Andrea has the full list. They're consecutive."

"I'll have NOPD call you for the numbers once I contact them."

"Okay."

Lewis switched off to make the call. We were left with two vans and two SUVs. I felt better about sticking with the middle van, which was now the lead van, since the security element was staying with it, and the guy I took to be the commander.

We continued through New Orleans and then over one of the double bridges leading to the west bank of New Orleans and Jefferson Parish.

When the van at the rear took the Lafayette Street exit, Cossich said, "I'm going to have to take this one. They could be heading to Plaquemines, and I can't just let them go."

"Go," I said.

XLIII

I had wondered why the terrorists, as I was now sure they were, instead of garden-variety criminals, had not just chosen Baton Rouge for their operation. It was closer to their base, but maybe too close. It looked like they were trying to hit the largest metro area in the state, New Orleans and adjacent parishes.

Lewis, Andrea and I were on our own for the moment. I did not like the idea of having Andrea with me. If I had protected her only to put her in the middle of a shootout now, it made no sense. But we were still riding the tiger and couldn't get off.

The remaining van and the two SUVs exited the elevated West Bank Expressway and drove on the surface level. Then they turned in at the Sheriff's Office Headquarters Building. The two SUVs pulled into the visitor parking lot before the checkpoint's lowered barrier. I hung at the entrance, shielded by the high wall, so that the men in the SUVs could not see us. Lewis was behind me in the pullover lane. I should have called in reinforcements then, if not earlier, but things were happening too fast now.

I could see the van driver's arm as he reached out and showed a paper to the clerk manning the checkpoint. She looked at it without taking it to read and pushed the button to raise the security arm. The van pulled through. We followed, and the security arm came back down.

I waved my ID at the clerk and told her the car behind me was FBI. Seconds ticked off. Finally the security barrier went up. I shouted at the clerk.

"Call the building. Tell them to lock it down. That van you just let through has bad guys!"

She fumbled and the security barrier came down as she hit the button accidentally. I drove through it, knocking it askew. Lewis followed. We parked on the grass and ran for the door.

"Those guys in the SUVs are going to assault now that they've seen us. Hold them until backup comes," I yelled over to Lewis.

The door was locked. I held up my ID and begged the receptionist to open the door. She didn't. I kicked the glass in the door. It flexed but did not break, so I put two rounds in it from my Kimber, and the glass made a crazy pattern as it shattered, but was held together by the tint film. I kicked my way through. Andrea was still back in the truck. I waved at her to come, since I figured the security element guys were about to start shooting.

Inside the clerk, whose mouth was a big O, cowered behind her high desk.

"Where did those guys who just came in go?"

She just stared at my pistol.

"Where?" I shouted.

"Fifth floor," she managed. "They had a work order."

"Fake. Call for backup. I ran for the next glass door. It was locked."

"It's locked down," the receptionist said."

"I know, I called for it at the gate. Let ME through."

She fumbled for the release and the lock clicked. I ran for the elevators. They weren't responding and I could see they were locked at the fifth floor. The receptionist hadn't released them. I ran for the stairs.

As I ran up the stairs, my heart began to pound and I tried to push deep breaths in. It wouldn't help if I got to the top and keeled over. It seemed to take forever. On the way, I ran into an HQ officer in uniform at the third floor landing. He was nervous and pointed his weapon at me.

"Not me, the fifth floor. Go help the FBI agent on the first floor"

I passed him, leaving him to make up his mind, hoping he didn't decide to shoot me in the back. When I got to the fifth floor, I burst out of the stairwell and into the elevator foyer. The door to the reception area was locked. I held up my spare ID and the secretary to the Sheriff buzzed me in. She didn't look concerned. For some crazy reason, the word had not gotten this far. Far away, I heard pops as Lewis and the four gunmen from the SUVs engaged five floors below. He wasn't going to last, I realized with regret.

"The alarm guys, where are they?"

"They're installing a unit in the conference room. A new alarm."

"Didn't you get the lockdown word?"

"No, nobody called." She was looking at my pistol.

"Anyone else up here?"

"No, the Sheriff is at a meeting. It's just me."

"Get out of here. Take the stairs. Leave the door unlocked so backup can get in. Go now."

She grabbed her purse, of course, and hustled for the door.

"Call the districts, bring backup."

I was left alone on the fifth floor. With everybody gone, maybe I could declare myself Sheriff and un-suspend myself. And give myself a promotion too. The men inside the conference room behind the secretary's desk had to have heard the shots outside.

Instead of taking the door in front of me, I slipped into the door to the left, the Sheriff's own inner sanctum. Then I walked carefully to the other door leading to the conference room. I eased it open to take a peek.

Evidently, the two guys inside were trying to complete their mission despite the mayhem below. One was on a ladder, finishing the attachment to the ceiling. It was one of the fire alarms. The other was holding a ladder and looking at the other door leading to the secretary's work area.

The guy on the ladder pulled a strip of tape protruding through an opening in the plastic housing of the alarm. Then he said, "It's live. We need to go now."

He scrambled down the ladder, folded it, and they made for the door. I kicked open my door and ordered, "Stop!"

They froze for a moment underneath the device. They both stole a glance upward, apparently trying to see the gamma rays bathing them. The helper tossed the ladder at me and tried to draw at the same time. I shot him twice in the chest and missed with the third. The installer, the evident commander of the operation, reached inside his jumpsuit and I had to shoot him too. I didn't want to, I needed him alive for information, especially since he seemed to be in charge. I caught him low in the belly and he went down to a knee.

I ventured into the conference room, my skin crawling with unseen gamma rays. I dragged him into the Sheriff's office by the collar of his jumpsuit.

"Where are the others going?" I yelled at him. He was unresponsive, in shock. I dragged him back into the conference room and left him to glow in the dark. I took their weapons.

Then I ran back down the stairs to support Lewis, if he was still alive.

XLIV

From the sounds as I pounded down the stairs, a firefight was still going on. I emerged into the foyer which opened onto the elevators and the stairwell, away from the lobby, and saw Andrea and the receptionist huddled in a corner, as protected as they could be from rifle bullets. I mouthed *I'm sorry* as I rushed by her.

I found Lewis around the corner. He was no longer firing. He was bleeding in several places and talking on his phone.

"How bad are you?" I asked.

"Flying glass and bullet fragments mostly."

"Mostly?" I asked as I inspected him and found a through and through wound low on his left side. He winced as I looked at it.

"What happened?" He looked upward, toward the fifth floor where I'd been.

"They were installing the alarm device in the conference room. Apparently they were hoping to irradiate the Sheriff and whoever he was meeting with."

"What a bunch of morons. What did they hope to accomplish?"

"Hard to say. We'll have to ask Robert and Brent when we catch them up."

Lewis used the new information to mobilize responses in New Orleans, Saint John Parish, and Plaquemines.

A couple of officers from the building, including the one I had encountered on the stairs earlier, were maintaining positions as firing went on outside. One of them said, "Patrol is engaging them."

I sneaked a peek and saw fire coming from a number of marked and unmarked units and return fire from the SUVs. In a couple more minutes, it was over. The patrol response, with rifles and shotguns, had overwhelmed the four gunmen.

When things got quiet, I stepped out through the empty entrance door frame with my ID held high. Several rifles and shotguns pointed my way and then lowered. I walked carefully over to a sergeant who was controlling the scene. He turned out to be my son-in-law. He slung his rifle over his shoulder. We shook hands.

"Travis," he said, "put that ID away. You're not supposed to have that, remember. You're suspended."

"Oh, right."

"What's this about?"

I caught him up and told him the building needed to be evacuated and a team brought in to clear the fifth floor of the radioactive material.

"There are two bad guys down in the conference room. I don't know if they're 10-7 or not, but they've been getting a radiation bath. Extracting them and crime scene processing is going to be interesting. An FBI guy in the lobby needs medical now."

He got on the radio and went back to work. I went to check on Lewis and Andrea. I found Lewis weaker from blood loss, but still on the phone. He took a moment to talk to me.

"I called my SA and got him to move on the house in Saint Francisville and the junkyard in Holden. I also told him to tell the SAIC to kiss his sorry ass goodbye. When it comes out about Robert, no one is going to remember telling him anything about covering for Robert. He'll make a lovely scapegoat." He laughed, a little giddy.

"You may be enjoying your moment of revenge too much," I said.

"Justice, not revenge."

"You're a hard G-man, but I have medical coming anyway."

As we spoke, medical arrived and began tending to him, and deputies filed by, rifles, shotguns and pistols still ready. The two officers who had held the first floor lobby with Lewis went with them.

"Don't go in the conference room," I yelled at them. "It's hot with radiation."

"Shit," one replied. "How close can we get?"

"I have no clue, but I'd just sneak a peek to make sure the two bad guys are no danger and keep a perimeter."

"Got it. Thanks, Lou, my wife'll kill me if she has mutant babies." We both laughed.

I checked on Andrea. She was standing in a corner smoking a cigarette.

"No smoking allowed by local ordinance and state law," I said.

"Shooting yes, smoking no," she flipped a finger at me. I smiled.

"Let's get you out of here."

We passed Lewis still working the phone as the EMTs hooked him up to an IV and cleaned his wounds and loaded him on a gurney.

We waited while he yelled at someone. While we waited, Cossich called.

"Are you ok?"

"We're fine here. We never let them inside the building. I called ahead and we swarmed them as they arrived at Headquarters. Took them down without a shot. I managed to convince one of them to admit knowing that one of the gang had paid a visit to my stupid cousin because they were worried he was a loose end. You're clear."

"That's a relief. Now to get my job back."

"Any help you need, brother, you call."

"Thanks, it's still a mess here, but I'll fill you in later."

"Not so easy there?"

"Lots of shooting."

"Sorry I missed it."

"Don't be. Got to go."

Lewis was waving at me.

"Two local units cleared the house in Saint Francisville. It was empty. There was shooting in Saint John and New Orleans, but it's over now and Code Four."

"Brent and Robert are running."

The hunt was on.

XLV

There was no point in returning to Baton Rouge and Saint Francisville. Robert and Brent, either together or separately, were on the run, unless they had a Plan B which we didn't know about, but considering how their crazy plan had come crashing down, I didn't think it would fare any better than their flagship operation. What had been their goal? Their attempt to install radiation devices in law enforcement offices would not have likely resulted in immediate deaths. Maybe radiation sickness, maybe just long-term risk of cancer or genetic mutations to the offspring of those irradiated. Not much of an impact in the present. There was not much point in terrorism if there was no theater, no dramatic demonstration.

I pondered these questions as I drove Andrea to her mother's house in Westwego. Andrea wasn't welcome back at her apartment complex after the shootout there, and her apartment was trashed anyway.

There was a nagging lack of completion with Robert and Brent still not caught, but at least now full law enforcement resources were involved. Whether I was reinstated or fired was still an open question as well, and I worried about that.

I was confident that Lewis would take the steps necessary to make sure the charges against Andrea were dropped. Would she get her job back though, with her son having been involved in the theft of the isotopes and the subsequent chaos?

"What are you thinking?" I asked her.

"Probably the same as you, what now?"

"Yes," I thought I should say more, but didn't have anything. Not only did I not have anything to say, I didn't feel much either. My mission, such as it was, had been to protect Andrea and myself, and one thing had led to another, until we had arrived on the West Bank Expressway heading toward a future which did not include each other. I think I was beginning to be okay with that too. I had at least done what I set out to do, so that was something.

Andrea called her mother to break the tension, although she had just done so a few minutes before. She told her we were on our way over. Her mother said okay, I guess, and disconnected.

I found it a measure of how little our relationship had grown in the year we had been seeing each other that Andrea felt the need to direct me to her mother's house, even though I had been there several times before.

"Turn here," she said."

"I know the way," I said back.

"Oh, yeah, right. I forgot."

I took the turn onto the quiet street of post World War II baby-boom houses which had yet to experience any of the gentrification which was taking place in parts of New Orleans and Old Metairie. The neighborhood was still populated by the elderly for the most part, original residents who had worked in the shipyards and the nearby plant, or the seafood processing industry, and had grown old in place or died, leaving widows and widowers to tend flower gardens or while away their days with little dogs for company. I saw one of the typical residents, an old woman, walking on the sidewalk, pulling an uncooperative puppy along on a leash as we passed.

I pulled onto the narrow strip of grass between the sidewalk and the street. The gate to the driveway was closed as usual, with Andrea's mother's little green Hyundai parked beyond. I opened the back door of my truck and grabbed both of Andrea's bags, determined to be the gentleman to the last.

As I waited for Andrea to open the smaller gate, the puppy on the leash scampered past me. I started to put down the bags to catch the little thing and looked back at the old woman on the sidewalk. She had produced a sawed-off shotgun from under her housecoat and was pointing it at us. I saw the dark eyes of Robert under the wig.

I had broken one of my rules, which was to never carry anything in my gun hand, and here I was standing there holding Andrea's bags like a bellboy. Not that there was much chance of outdrawing a shotgun pointed at your gut anyway.

"Inside," he growled in his characteristic rumble of a voice.

Brent was waiting at the side door leading from the carport with a pistol. We made our way into the small kitchen. Brent relieved me of my pistol while Robert covered me. In the adjacent living room, Andrea's mother was sitting on the couch, clasping her hands together.

"Sit on the couch," Robert rumbled. Andrea sat next to her mother and took her hands in hers. I sat at the other end.

"You call this a getaway plan?" I asked.

"Shut up," Brent ordered.

I ignored him, addressing Robert, "What was the point of this whole exercise?"

"Revenge," he answered, as calmly as if he were discussing the weather.

"How was that supposed to work? Because it didn't, you know."

Andrea launched into Brent, "How could you do this, terrify your grandmother, set me up?"

Brent shrugged.

"Answer me!" She screamed at him, breaking the quiet tone that had menaced the scene.

"I never forgave you for leaving Dad," he shrugged again.

"That was twenty years ago!" Andrea said.

"Still…"

"Back to my question," I stared at Robert.

"Revenge," he repeated.

"Could you explain?"

"The police have harassed me all over this country. I've got cancer, again, and I blame the police for stalking me. I decided to give some of them cancer too."

"You're nuts."

He didn't like it, but then he smiled, "May be."

"And what makes you nuttier than squirrel turds?" I asked Brent.

"I'm fighting the police state this country is turning into."

"Jesus, and I'm guessing you got paid for this, too."

"Our arrangement is none of your business," Robert interrupted. "Let's say, though, that Brent and I are, uh, close."

Andrea processed this comment and I could tell she didn't like the implication.

"Well, you'd better hope you end up better than his wife and girlfriend," Andrea said. Well done, I thought.

"What now? Why us?"

"We saw you on television," Robert said. "That's when we figured you were to blame for our, uh, failure. So we thought you could at least help us escape. The last place they'd look for us is here."

"And how is that supposed to happen?" I asked.

"We have a shrimp boat standing by at the Westwego dock. Everybody's watching the airports and highways. Probably not shrimp boats."

I thought, it's not a bad plan, but asked, "What does that have to do with us?"

"You're coming with us."

"What, we're all going on vacation together?"

"Not exactly."

Andrea had been fumbling in her purse for tissues for her mother and herself as they leaked tears into their laps. It was a shock, therefore, when the shot crashed through the room. Andrea shot Brent in the gut as he sat across from her, and he doubled over and fell off the kitchen chair he had pulled into the living room.

The surprise caused Robert to swing the big shotgun barrel away from me and toward Andrea. I leapt forward and struck Robert in the throat with my forearm. It caused the shotgun barrel to lift up as it fired, blowing out a chunk of wallboard above Andrea's head and showering her with dust and debris.

Robert fell onto his back and his face turned red, then purple, as he tried to get air past his crushed larynx. He kicked and spasmed. I let him, as I kicked Brent in the face before taking his weapon.

Andrea sat there stunned, as if she didn't believe what she had just done. Finally, she looked up at me, still holding one of my guns from my go-bag, which she had evidently helped herself to at some time in the past week. I was stunned too, considering her professed hatred of firearms.

"I can never forgive you for turning me into you," she said.

I shrugged. So it was my fault.

FALLOUT

The Sheriff stared at me for a few hundred heartbeats, but mine were going pretty fast. I met his gaze, trying to strike a balance between insolent and submissive, and awaited my professional fate.

"You're an embarrassment," he finally decided.

"Yes, Sir." I said without really agreeing. Agreement wasn't required.

The bookends nodded in the background.

"To the public, you're a hero. Again."

"Yes, Sir." It was like a liturgical litany in the Church of the Sheriff's Office.

"Hence, our dilemma. Fire you, commend you, charge you?" He held his hands palms up as if inviting me to view his stigmata.

"Detective Cossich and Special Agent Lewis are being commended."

Oh, good, I hoped. It would look weird if I got fired or worse.

"It's undeniable you saved lives, including mine, and these guys' behind me." The bobbleheads bobbled.

"So we'll see you at the ceremony, Captain. Get out."

Captain? Oh. Well, thy will be done."

THE END